"They're building nukes."

"Yep," Jack DuBois agreed grimly. "The Cubans are buildin' the bomb."

"No, guys," Jenny said soberly. "It's worse than that."

Hunter Blake whispered, "Jeez, that nuclear plant leaking already?"

"No," Jenny said, "but the latest intel says there's a plot afoot by our old buddies to make it leak—big time . . ."

Hunter sighed. "We knew they'd be back, we just didn't know when."

Jenny snapped, "This is critical to the tenth power. If they blow up the plant reactors, we'll . . ."

Sarah Green stood, clearly agitated. "We'll have a nuclear disaster that will make Chernobyl look like fun for the whole family! Within four days a radioactive cloud will blanket the southeastern U.S. Possibly half a *million* deaths in the first year alone!"

"She's right," Jenny continued. "And that's if the winds are with us. If the plant blows during a major northeast airflow, the conservative estimate would be *twenty million* deaths within fifteen years."

Stan spat, "We've got a lousy forty-eight hours to fly eighteen hundred miles, drop into a hostile country, in the dark, and stop a group of flaming lunatics bent on cracking a nuke plant?"

"Precisely," Major Travis Barrett said in his slow, soft drawl, "and get back out with total discretion." Barrett stood. "So saddle up, kids. This one's gonna get dirty."

MELTDOWN

Cliff Garnett

A SIGNET BOOK

SIGNET
Published by New American Library, a division of
Penguin Putnam Inc., 375 Hudson Street,
New York, New York 10014, U.S.A.
Penguin Books Ltd, 27 Wrights Lane,
London W8 5TZ, England
Penguin Books Australia Ltd, Ringwood,
Victoria, Australia
Penguin Books Canada Ltd, 10 Alcorn Avenue,
Toronto, Ontario, Canada M4V 3B2
Penguin Books (N.Z.) Ltd, 182–190 Wairau Road,
Auckland 10, New Zealand

Penguin Books Ltd, Registered Offices:
Harmondsworth, Middlesex, England

First published by Signet, an imprint of New American Library,
a division of Penguin Putnam Inc.

First Printing, March 2000
10 9 8 7 6 5 4 3 2 1

PUBLISHER'S NOTE
This is a work of fiction. Names, characters, places, and incidents either are
the product of the author's imagination or are used fictitiously, and any resem-
blance to actual persons, living or dead, business establishments, events or
locales is entirely coincidental.

People sleep peacefully in their beds at night
only because rough men stand ready
to do violence on their behalf.

—George Orwell

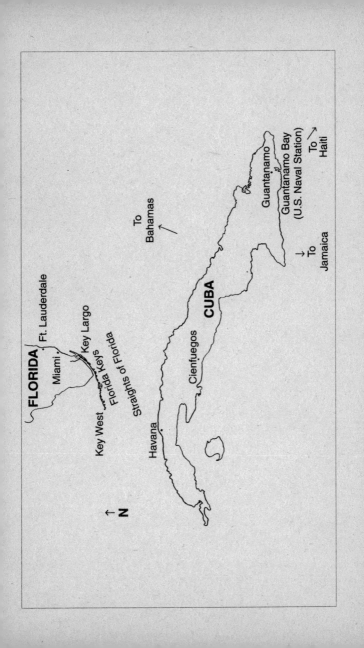

Prologue

There was no such thing as a nonemergency TALON
Action Directive, or TAD, in Sam's jargon. They were
all grimly urgent, but this one seemed unusually tense
to Sam Wong. Perhaps it was that this one hadn't come
over the computer zip line from the offices on the top
floor. In fact, it hadn't even come from Sam's boss, the
Joint Task Force Commander, Brigadier General Jack
Krauss. No. The *director* had *walked* this one down to
the dark communications cavern *himself*, Sam considered soberly, his heart thumping uncomfortably now. He
spun about in his chair to face the hulking bank of computer screens, switches, keyboards, and trac-ball devices.

But there was more, the young first-generation Chinese American thought, pushing his oval glasses up on
his nose and hurriedly perusing the director's handwrit-
ten notes. It was the look on Director Scofield's face
that had chilled Sam. It wasn't just that tired look he
always wore when there was a looming crisis and people
might die en masse. No, Sam thought as his fingers flew
on the keys, the look on the director's face just now
was . . . pale, like the director thought he *himself*, here,
near Washington, might be among the dying this time.

Who first? Sam pondered, struggling to keep worry
from clouding his concentration as he read Director Scofield's scrawl and typed simultaneously. He keyed the
buttons and a map of the United States appeared, showing small, red bird-claw symbols—TALONs—at six dif-

ferent places from east to west. Of course it was a differentiation of mere seconds, but who got the honors of first notification this time? *Jeeeesus,* Sam thought, reading the notes further.

First we zap the Boss. Then Big Jack. And fast.

1743 hours, Llano River Desert Plain, Western Texas

The three horses and their riders ascended the rocky ridge in the fading hour of sunset. At the top, the horses stood silhouetted against the sky, and the riders looked at the sunset.

Ten-year-old Randall Barrett stilled his restless pony expertly with a pressure of his knee. He removed his hat and held it to shade his eyes from the distantly setting sun. He desperately looked forward to the day when his Stetson acquired the character of weather and time that his dad's cool old Stetson had.

"Mom's new boyfriend sucks, Dad," Randall said after a moment.

"He does not!" Randall's twelve-year-old sister retorted hotly. "You just keep thinking Dad's going to come back! Fat chance."

"He cain't ride, he cain't rope, and he couldn't hit a Dumpster with a handgun if he was locked inside it," young Randall muttered.

"Like that's . . . like the ultimate standard for a man or something," Betty Sue groused sourly. "At least . . ." Betty Sue knew how the child-of-divorce shtick was played, but she also knew her dad didn't brook mind games. She decided to go for it anyway. "At least, Jeffery's here for us. He isn't *gone* all the time."

"*Jeffery* is a weiner!" Randall came back. "Dad's a Green Beret!"

"Jeffery is a . . . gentleman," Betty Sue sniffed. "A lawyer. He drives a new Lexus, not a raggedy Chevrolet pickup truck made the year he was *born.*" Betty Sue tried to display more disgust than she really felt. She just hurt. Dad's support checks were as regular as the presents he sent from all over the world, but his visits were whenever he could get here, and that wasn't often enough for Betty Sue Barrett. It hurt.

"Jeffery's a *dick*!" Randall snapped.

"Randall!" Betty Sue exclaimed. "You don't know what you're—"

"That's enough." Major Travis Beauregard Barrett had an almost gentle South Texas twang of a voice, always easy and slow, always relaxed. Yet it somehow conveyed the impression of a man of substance to anyone who listened, including Betty Sue.

"I'm a soldier, Betty Sue." Travis squinted at the huge orange ball of flame burning its way into Mexico, way beyond the Rio Grande. "It's what I do, darlin' girl. I don't apologize, but I don't blame you for not lovin' it."

Betty Sue sat on her mount silently, watching the sun.

Travis continued. "Randall, your momma's got enough to worry about raisin' y'all and runnin' the ranch and workin' at the bank. She needs your help, she don't need no grief over her choice of . . . companion."

"Yes sir," Randall said softly, without enthusiasm.

Travis Barrett jerked, feeling the coded pulses at his waist. Aw damn. Not now. Not this weekend. *Damn.* He concentrated on the decrypted morse.

b-o-s-s//t-a-d//s-m-e-l-l-s/b-a-d//c-h-o-p-s-t-i-c-k-s///

"Ah . . . damn." Travis sighed.

"What?" Betty Sue said, looking where her father gazed for what concerned him. She could never know that the TALON Force even existed, let alone that her father commanded one of the seven teams.

"We, ah, we ain't goin' shoppin' in Austin tomorrow after all, guys," Travis said. "I . . . I just remembered somethin' I gotta do."

"Aw . . . Daddy . . . not again," Betty Sue said wearily.

Randall hung his head, but said nothing.

Both gestures bore clear disappointment that broke the heart of a hardened combat veteran.

"You just figured that out?" Randall said, practically choking in his effort not to cry.

"Yes." God how he hated this part of the life.

"Yeah!" Betty Sue sneered, sniffing and wiping her cheeks. "Yeah! I *bet*, Dad! *Hyah*!" The girl spurred her pony; it squatted and charged away across the plain toward the ranch. The girl rode hard. When her hat blew off she didn't slow down or look back.

Travis gritted his teeth, though his lips drew back from them with the strain. When he looked at Randall, he saw the boy watching him, a tear running down one cheek. Travis reached to place a hand on his son's shoulder.

"I know . . . it don't make much sense right now, Randall, but . . . someday, son . . . I'll be able to explain some of this to you."

"When I'm a Green Beret?" Randall brightened.

Travis enjoyed a welcome if weak smile. "Yes, boy. Someday, when you're a soldier, too, if you care to be."

The boy beamed. "Race you to the house, Dad!"

"You're on, big guy. Say, look at that jackrabbit!"

"Where?" Randall said, looking away. Travis gigged his big Tennessee Walker and it lunged away down the trail.

"Daaad!" Randall yelled, spurring in hot pursuit. "No fair, Daaad! That's cheating!"

A hundred yards short of the ranch, Travis held ole Beau in check with just a touch of rein, enough that Randall and his hard-charging pony barely won the race home.

1743 hours, The Creole Cellar, New Orleans, LA

Big Jack was rocking, hence, so was everybody else in the smoky basement blues joint. The dancing couples were thrashing, pulling, pushing, spinning, singing. The wall-length mirror behind the bar quivered to the thundering bass drum, and both bartenders danced furiously as they poured, shook, and slid libations over the counter. The din was deafening, but it was *righteous*!

On the stage tunneled into the rear wall, Powderman McGhee looked like he was on the verge of a stroke, so hard was he blowing into the gleaming saxophone he waved in the foggy blue air. The veins stood out on his bald, black forehead. Skeens, the pianist, was aping a

Ray Charles white-toothed grin the size of the bumper on a '76 Eldorado, as his slender brown fingers danced over the keys. Go-Boy was making that axe *sing,* hanging the strings with a thumb pick like a man possessed. Dick Richeaud pulled a seismic electric bass that rattled every brain cell in the house.

But the driving force sat even to the rear of these musicians, at the pearlescent red drum set with its gleaming brass cymbals, though he was not exactly alone. Big Jacques Henri DuBois, captain, United States Marine Corps, slashed at the drums and cymbals with a frenzy only a six-foot-five-inch, 251-pound, rock-fit, sweating, grinning, squinting, howling black man could do. The sticks flew.

"Stagger Leeee!" The whole place roared. *"Went to the barroom . . . ! An' he step out onn dat floor! An' then heeeee up an' whup out . . . his long-barrellll . . . forty-fourrrrr! Yeeaaah, Stagger Leeeee . . ."*

Two tightly wrapped and splendid young black women flanked Jack DuBois as he played, oscillating their hips sensually in circles, careful as they drank not to spill anything down their sumptuous cleavage, and more careful still not to get in the arc of Big Jack's lethal drumsticks. Jackie boy, he loved it when you rubbed his love muscle while you talked between numbers, but girlfriend, when that man doin' the tunes, best stay out of his way.

Jack DuBois wasn't bald but he kept his hair cut so short as to shamefully waste a couple-hundred-thousand hair follicles. Jack DuBois was a jarhead and proud of it. Except for the tunes, of course, maybe some of the ladies, wadn't nothin' worth a shit but the Corps.

The entire joint careened into the fifth verse, wherein Stagger Lee he blast the fuck out of his two-timin' bitch and her jody-ass lover. It was Jack's favorite verse. He whaled the drums and cymbals with a fervor, consumed with the sweet justice of the musical murders. The scotch was *fine,* the hussies was finer, and the tunes was finest. This, Jack DuBois fervently felt, was why sperm cells and eggs ever got together in the first place.

"Stagger Leee . . ." Jack kicked a cannonlike thump on the bass drum with the pillow stuffed inside.

Then the signal arrived.

Powderman caught it first, a slight but unmistakable couple of nanoseconds off the beat. The fat man jerked a glance at Big Jack.

By now the huge drummer had stopped playing altogether. Absent its foundation, the number instantly fell apart. The musicians individually drifted to a halt, followed shortly by the collapse of the singing in the crowd. Everyone stared at the now motionless Jack DuBois who seemed to be in a trance.

"Hey Jack," one of the honeys by Jack purred, "is you all right, ba—"

Dropping the sticks to a rattling clatter on the floor, the big man heaved his bulk from the stool, vaulted off the stage, sprinted through a hastily parting crowd, and disappeared up the steps to the street.

"Well, I be gaddamn," one of the barroom hussies said.

As Jack ran down the street to his black Lincoln Navigator, he focused on the old-fashioned Morse code that came in the form of slight electric shocks from a very new-fashioned beeper worn between his belt and his waist.

b-i-g//t-a-d//s-o-u-n-d-s/b-a-d/t-h-i-s/t-i-m-e/b-u-d-d-y//
c-h-o-p-s-t-i-c-k-s///

Jack DuBois ran faster.

1743 hours, Echo Zulu Military Operational Airspace Zone, Southern Nevada, Advanced Flight Training Range Tango, Status: Active (USAF)

Tom Cruise with a Val Kilmer edge, that's what one young woman called Captain Hunter Evans Blake, III, U.S. Air Force. He was beautiful, smooth, likeable, but you never quite got over the suspicion that there were fangs somewhere behind that dentist's-wet-dream smile. Blake had grown up the son of a pedigreed Boston-socialite mother, but more significantly, an air force pilot father, and he'd started flying when he was ten, though he'd built hundreds of airplane models since he was five.

Crewmen who flew with Hunter Blake liked to say, "Captain Blake could fly the crate this aircraft came in."

At the moment, 6,000 feet up in the rear cockpit seat of the air force's ominous new "T-Rex" tilt-rotor gunship, Hunter Blake was bored. He was teaching select rookie air force pilots to fly the latest, largest, and most fearsome aerial gun platform since the dreaded Soviet Hind, but today the syllabus called for elementary airwork drills, grueling for the student pilot, but numbingly boring for instructors.

It didn't last. A galvanizing voice and the alarming red illumination of the master fire annunciator light cured Hunter's boredom fast.

"Fire warning on the master, sir!" the young woman Air Force lieutenant in the front cockpit said, a couple of octaves higher than necessary.

"I see it on my panel," Blake said calmly. Blake sat forward, the attention-demanding recorded voice calmly repeating *"master fire warning, master fire warning, mas—"* in the earphones of his oddly shaped visual-aiming helmet with the built in infrared and night-vision opticals. Captain Blake scanned his digital instrument display screen with a slight frown. He looked out to the tips of the stout wing at the big turbine-engine pods, tipped with massive, thick, whirling, four-bladed propellers, which swivel-converted from horizontal to vertical thrust when the tilt-rotor gunship landed.

"You have the controls, sir!" the lieutenant said urgently. Barely graduated from air force basic pilot training, she was anxious to relinquish this serious in-flight emergency to her instructor pilot. The heavy hybrid airplane/helicopter gunship wavered in flight with the student's frantic overcontrolling.

"Noooo, Lieutenant Herrera," Blake said casually over the intercom, "I don't have the controls. You do. I'm the instructor pilot; I'm just along for the ride. You are a qualified military pilot being transitioned into a new aircraft. So transition."

"But . . . sir! This . . . this is . . . *real*! I—you—we're on *fire*!"

"Looks like it," Blake said. "So you better get busy earning your flight pay, Lieutenant, and save the air force's thirty-million-dollar tilt/gun, not to mention our butts."

"B-but sir!" Herrera said with a note of panic. "I'm just—"

"Do dah expression, 'burned beyond recognition,' mean anythin' to yah, Herrera? Seconds count when the fire light comes on. You'd better do something fast."

"-ter fire warning, master fire warning, master fi—"
Herrera struggled to maintain her composure. "Yes . . . yes sir! I—we—"

"Think, Herrera. What's most urgent? Quick!"

"Control! Maintain control of the aircraft!"

"Excellent, aviator. Now stop sweeping the cockpit with those controls before you tear an engine off. What next?"

"warning, master fire warn—"

"Uh, landing area!"

"Correct, Herrera. We don't want to fly out of range of the only safe forced-landing area that may present. The only thing worse than a crash is a crash into water, trees, or a steep slope."

Herrera's head swiveled frantically, her own bulky helmet batting against the canopy. "Then, confirm the emergency!" she said, banking the big machine toward a distant open field.

"—re warning, master fire warning, master—"

"Excellent, Herrera, you're starting to resemble a United States Air Force pilot. Turn that vocal alert off so we can hear ourselves think, and then confirm your emergency." The maddeningly calm voice in their headsets stopped when Herrera pressed a panel button, though the large, red, fire-warning master still glowed on both front and rear instrument panels.

"Uh, no engine fire specific, uh, both turbine outlet temps are normal, sir." Herrera was getting a grip, Blake was pleased to see. "So are both engine oil temps, oil pressures normal. Transmission oil pressures and temperatures are . . . normal. Voltmeters . . . normal."

"See any fire, Lieutenant Herrera?"

"Uh, no . . . sir," Herrera said craning to look as far out both wings and aft as she could see from her nose-mounted seat over the twin-twenty-mil vulcan turret.

"Smell any smoke? Feel anything funny?"

"No sir," Herrera answered a little sheepishly now.

"So what are you going to do, aviator?"

"Ah, turn for base, descend to five hundred feet in case we really do have a fire, and fly from one forced-landing area to another until we get to the field."

"Well, damn, Lieutenant, you might just get to 'slip the surly bonds of earth, spin deliriously through endless halls of cloud, reach out your hand, and touch the face of God' after all."

"Yes sir," Herrera said, a slight smile cracking her chagrin.

"We evidently have a malfunctioning fire-warning master instead of a true fire, Lieutenant, but we'll make a precautionary landing just the same. You should alwa—" Blake cleaved his sentence in midword. He was feeling tiny electric shocks from the beeper against his waist, decrypted morse, he knew. Blake concentrated.

s-k-y-b-o-y/t-a-d//c-o-u-l-d/b-e/t-h-e/b-i-g/o-n-e//c-h-o-p-s-t-i-c-k-s///

"I have the controls," Blake said, instantly seizing the cyclic and collective. He pulled the collective to maximum short-duration emergency power and set the aircraft in a shallow dive for the distant airfield.

Now we do have an emergency, Blake said to himself.

1743 hours, Gymnasium, Officer's Club, Bethesda Naval Hospital, Bethesda, MD

The women in the class milled about heaving for breath, sweating profusely, staining their carefully mixed, expensive, and oh-so-trendy gym clothing: sports logo headbands; pink leotards over mauve panty hose, with pastel-colored, chicly non-matching socks bunched deliberately at the tops of overpriced, overengineered, athletic shoes.

Made in Burmese sweatshops fifteen hours a day by twelve-year-old slave children, I imagine, thought their instructor, naval Lieutenant Jennifer Margaret Olsen. Clearly fashions chosen to impress each other with, not to do vigorous stretching workouts in. Jen Olsen concealed her disgust as she watched the overweight, over-made-up, under-exercised navy wives gasp and wheeze. Christ, she thought to herself. There must be a better way to 'drop out of sight,' like General Krauss wanted, after she pulled down the Chinese spies at Los Alamos. She knew it was necessary to lower her profile in the world's tight intelligence community, but baby-sitting spoiled navy wives at a hospital base lost in a sea of suburbia was the pits. At least Krauss had promised it would last no longer than the next TALON Force action directive, and that couldn't happen too soon for Jennifer Olsen.

Commander Gavich's wife, Helene, president of the Bethesda Navy Wives Group, pulled her sweat-soaked leotard out to relieve that icky, perspiring feeling. Drat, she thought, my mascara's going to be a mess! Helene Gavich eyed Jen Olsen a bit sourly. Their instructor was obviously one of those disgustingly lucky, Scandinavian blonde beauties, a lesbian no doubt, oh Helene was certain of it. Just look at her. Five foot nine or so. *Maybe* 135 pounds, the lucky twit. A killer body of perfect muscle tone, yet without the grotesque look of women body-builders. And look at what she wore! Cut-off sweatpants, a U.S. NAVY sweatshirt cut into a sleeveless, bare-belly halter, and *bare* feet! On this dirty floor! I mean, *really*. It was so . . . gauche. Still panting, Helene spoke.

"Uh, Jenny, dear," Helene said. "I know I speak for all of us when I say how . . . thrilled we all are that you would donate your time to teach our women's self-defense class, but . . . is all this . . . bending and twisting really necessary?"

"Yes ma'am, Mrs. Gavich," Jen answered, her uncomfortable agate gaze drilling into Helene Gavich's eyes without blinking. What, you sanctimonious cow? Jen groaned to herself. I just made it all up so you'd get testy with me?

"Yeah!" One of the other wives echoed. "I mean I didn't come here to get an M.I. I just want to learn . . . you know . . . all those neat little karate tricks you see on Oprah. So I can just . . . *hi-yah*! Knock that mugger out."

There were several nods among the wives.

"I mean," Helene continued, "let's face it, we've seen how it's done in the movies. All you have to do if a rapist comes at you is kick him in the . . . testicles. Down he goes in agony. Problem solved."

The women nodded and murmured agreement, some giggling. Helene soaked in the approval.

One fat, three-chinned wife yelled, "Yeah, that's all there is to it! Just kick the bastard in the balls! When do we get a smoke break?"

The group laughed, though some tried not to appear approving of Sandy Dowick's crassness.

I've taken all of this I can stand, Jen Olsen thought.

"La-dees," Jen said, slowly padding about like a cat, spearing each woman with those piercing eyes, sobering their giggles. "If you are attacked by an adult male human, who will more likely have robbery on his mind than rape, most of you will freeze in fear, possibly even urinate down your panty hose."

Every smirk in the gym faded instantly.

Jen went on. "If you try to kick your assailant in the testicles, you'll probably fail. Even if you connect, you will almost certainly not accomplish any more than to enrage him such that he beats the living shit out of you."

Jen now had the undivided attention of the class.

"If all he does is split your lip, break out your teeth, flatten your nose, and fracture your jaw, you'll be fortunate."

The women looked ill and glanced nervously at the floor.

"Nature puts a lot of stock in a man's testicles, ladies." So do I, Jen restrained herself from adding. "She places them where they are very hard to kick effectively, and she programs men—who are also rather fond of testicles, especially their own—to defend them vigorously, and to reactively annihilate anyone who tries to damage them.

"I started Inshinru Karate when I was eight years old. I've earned a ninth-degree black belt in the Korean scoring system, I'm in very good condition, and I have been in winner-take-all fights with sixteen men in my lifetime—on two occasions three at a time. Two of them died of their injuries. I am what is known technically as one tough bitch. And I, ladies, would not try to kick an assailant in his testicles as a primary defense tactic. They're extremely difficult to hit when he's standing, harder still to hit hard enough to disable him, and there are better options. Remember, the goal in women's street defense is not to disable an attacker, ladies, it is to escape him. Now we'll take—"

Jen froze, to the amazement of her class. She jerked slightly to the mild shocks emanating from the tiny beeper clipped beneath the drawstring of her cutoffs.

"Excuse me, ladies," Jen said abruptly. "I just remembered I left something cooking on the stove."

Jen sprinted from the gymnasium, leaving behind a stunned assemblage, no less grateful to see her go.

w-o-n-d-e-r-w-o-m-a-n//t-a-d//n-o/d-r-i-l-l//c-h-o-p-s-t-i-c-k-s///

1743 hours, Officer's On-base Housing Unit 91, Norfolk Naval Base, Norfolk, VA

If male badgers were reincarnated as humans, they would look like Navy SEAL instructor Lieutenant Commander Stanislaus Michael Powczuk—low, wide, dark, heavy, and prone to killing things for the sheer sake of crankiness. Stan never let anyone call him Stanley—a nickname he despised—except for his diminutive and very Sicilian wife, Angela Luchia Elizabeth Maranello Powczuk. If female badgers were reincarnated as humans, *they* would look like Angela Luchia Elizabeth Maranello Powczuk.

"Stanley!" Angela yelled, stabbing a wagging finger at Stan Powczuk. "You lying, rotten, unfaithful, skirt-chasing, alcoholic *bum!*"

"Aw honey!" Stan whined, "Come on now, I don't drink that much." Squat, thick, Stan Powczuk pulled his prepacked go-bag from the top shelf and slid it across the bedroom floor where it stopped against the door. He hurriedly buttoned his uniform shirt.

"*Shut* up!" Angela snarled. "You're not fooling me, Stanley Powczuk, this is just another one of your sneaky *pussy* expeditions! You—what the hell are you doing!?"

Stan jumped and slapped furiously at his waist. "God-damn it! I'm gonna kill that little technoweeny when I see him! Ow! Goddamn, ow!"

"Stanley, what is the *matter* with—"

"Nothing," Stan said, grabbing his car keys from the dresser. "Honey, I swear to God, this is a legit callout! You know how Captain Ballestere likes to run these routine drills! I—"

"Bull*shit,* Stanley! That's what you said about the Balkan alert, then this little . . . Serbian *child* showed up on our doorstep with a *baby*! And she said—"

"Aw now honey, she was at least, uh seventeen . . . I think."

"Shut up! And then there was that Saudi *slut* who—"

"Aw now honey, she was actually part of the royal fam—"

"I don't give a damn if she was the *fucking* queen of Sheba! You had no business *marrying* her!"

"Aw honey, it was just a sort of, um, friendship ceremony, not a real—"

"Friendship your ass! You screwed her Persian tush to the ol' *magic carpet*!"

"Well now, I know that's what she said, but—"

"Liar!" Angela threw a book at Stan, which he reflexively batted away. Then she picked up the heavy, engraved, crystal eagle that SEAL Team Five had given him as a change-of-command gift.

"Not the eagle! Not the eagle!" Stan pleaded, which of course sealed the eagle's doom. Stan ducked as the eagle soared—tumbled ass over teakettle, actually—through the bathroom door and shattered in the tile shower.

"Awwww honey!"

"Don't you 'aw honey' me, you cheating Polack son-of-a—"

Stan leaped across the bed at Angela, and she took a fast couple of cuts at his face. He slapped them away, grabbed Angela, flung her on the bed, fell upon her and kissed her passionately. Angela *mmmfffd!* and fought for the appropriate time, then wrapped her arms around Stan's neck and sucked his tongue out.

In a moment they were squirming hard against each

other, kissing feverishly, tearing at one another's clothing.

Ten hard-driving minutes later, Stan pulled his bedraggled uniform about him and staggered, huffing, to the door.

"Stan!" Angela said, following him, nude, and throwing her arms about his neck. "I love you my precious baby, I love you! Please be careful! Don't let anything happen to my sweet little Stannibooboo! Please come back to me safe and—"

"I will, honey, I swear! I love you, baby! I love you!"

Stan backed through the front door, disengaging from the still naked and now crying Angela.

"I love you, Stanny!"

"You too, baby!" Stan shouted, slamming his car's trunk lid and swatting again at his beeper. "Ah! Ow! Goddamn it, Wong, you little fuck!" Stan snarled rhetorically, the car rocking under his entry. "If you don't get the voltage right on this fucking thing I'm going to tear it out and stuff it up your slanted Chinese *ass*!" Stan's Chevy Impala Super Sport blew a stream of gravel and squealed as the tires gained the pavement. "Ow! Ow! Jesus, Sam, I *got* it already! I'm *comin'* as fast as I can!" t-r-o-l-l//t-a-d//i-t-s/a/b-a-d/o-n-e//c-h-o-p-s-t-i-c-k-s///

1743 hours, Level-five Biocontainment Laboratory, Ft Detrick, MD

Five humans in blue bio-barrier suits stood around an elevated stainless steel table brightly lit from above by a hulking surgical lamp. White, hose/wire lines ran from the overhead to the helmet sections of each of the inflated plastic suits. Each person was wired with a small, light set of earphones and tiny microphones within their helmets over which they conversed, the hiss and whoosh of inhaled and exhaled sterile air always in the background. On the table was one rhesus monkey, on its back, split from throat to crotch and laid open, the chest walls and associated tissues held back by gleaming, stainless steel clamps.

One of these five suited figures was short like a gymnast, a woman named Sarah Greene, captain and physician, United States Army.

Dr. Greene spoke. "As you can see, doctors, this strain of Ebola lays waste to the interior viscera, and it does so in twelve to sixteen hours after onset, onset defined as a sudden three-degree rise in temperature accompanied by nasal and gingival bleeding."

One of the larger suited figures, also a woman, reached a gloved hand to probe the animal's liquified innards. Dr. Greene's gloved hand intercepted above the dead monkey. "I'm sorry, Dr. Washington, in a level-five hot op, we're all on a need-to-touch basis, so to speak. Ebola Motaba is the most virulent strain of the disease yet discovered. I regret to say it is even more destructive, faster, in humans. We're protected by our suits, of course, but protocol prohibits unmandated contact with a hot agent."

"Of course, Dr. Greene. Sorry. I was just interested in the consistency of the internal organs at this stage in the disease's progress. Can it be detected by external palpation?"

"Yes, but only after the deterioration has advanced beyond any chance of prophylactic treatment."

"In other words, Dr. Greene, by the time that I can detect the virus's effects by palpation, my patient—"

"Will be deader than lawyer ethics, Dr. Washington," Sarah said. The group of physicians chuckled.

One of the male physicians asked, "And, Dr. Greene, may I ask if Ebola in any form is being employed as a bio-weapon agent?"

She paused only a second. "Bio-weaponry isn't my field, Dr. Clark," lied Dr. Greene, one of the army's leading biological-weapon medical experts. "I'm afraid I don't know the answer to that. I would guess it to be unlikely, as Ebola is such a relatively volatile bio-agent." Sarah knew all too well that the American army was researching and experimenting with Ebola and other bio-agents; Sarah knew this because she herself secretly chaired three of the research panels. It was little comfort to her that many of the world's armies, including the so-called outlaw nations like Iraq and North Korea, were doing the same. In humans, Sarah mused, insanity drives insanity.

Sarah hated the big-brother aspect, but she made a mental note to forward Dr. Clark's name to security for having inquired into a sensitive matter unrelated to his field. Bio-weapons were too awesomely frightening to take the tiniest chance. A Walker or an Ames compromise in this field was beyond unacceptable. And if Dr. Clark was legitimate, he'd never even know he'd been checked out.

This, Sarah considered, must have been how Teller and Oppenheimer felt in 1945. How sobering, Sarah thought, staring sadly at the disease-devastated primate, to know your work can either become a boon to mankind . . . or its death knell.

In this frame of mind, Sarah almost welcomed the little electric charges suddenly emanating from the tiny beeper beneath her biosuit. Sarah knew the device well. Her little buddy, Sam Wong, had invented it.

Sarah shut out the other doctors' conversations and focused on the incoming decrypted morse. Her relief didn't last long.

e-a-r-t-h-m-o-t-h-e-r//t-a-d//v-e-r-y/s-e-r-i-o-u-s//c-h-o-p-s-t-i-c-k-s///

Sarah stepped unobtrusively but quickly to a panel of connections on a near wall. From a velcro pouch on her suit, she retrieved a small male adaptor on the end of a wire, plugged it into a female receptacle in the panel and pressed a button.

"Biosec," a voice said.

"This is Dr. Greene in conlab-five. I need expedited decon and exit, priority one."

"On the way, Dr. Greene."

Twenty minutes later, the guard at gate 4 saw the familiar yellow Volkswagen New Beetle approaching in the outbound release lane. Though the guard was in the uniform of a civilian security firm, he was in fact a highly cleared U.S. Army Airborne Ranger sergeant. The hard-faced soldier knew the black-haired woman was a captain and a physician, but more commanding of his respect, he knew she'd graduated in the same Airborne class he had, with the highest clearance. He would not, of course, salute Captain Greene in this scenario.

The little yellow VW stopped in the holding barrier, a single rose ensconced in its dashboard bud-vase. Dr. Greene looked directly at him, dressed in the same funky neo-punk Gen-X grunge clothes that she always wore with five silver rings in her left ear. He'd been required to memorize every detail of her face, and she made it easier by never wearing makeup. A face so naturally lovely needed no cosmetics, the burly soldier permitted himself to observe, the sort of thirty-five-year-old face that looked twenty-five.

While the plainclothes sergeant satisfied himself of Sarah's identity, other guards—also disguised soldiers—searched her car, albeit quickly, for they'd been informed that Dr. Greene was on a pri-1 exit.

Odd, the sergeant thought, watching Dr. Greene accelerate into traffic with vigor, the little car's engine straining. She *always* gives me that great Doc Greene smile, but . . . not today. Wonder if the doc's feelin' okay?

Chapter One

It was dark when the seven air force Falcon executive
jets arrived within two hours of each other, taxied in,
and deposited a single passenger each, so they were unlikely to be noticed by outsiders. No one paid much
attention to the C-130 Hercules, a yeoman, four-engined,
turbo-prop cargo plane that landed either, as the 167th
Airlift Wing was a C-130 unit. Not even the local guard
employees thought it odd that this typically gray C-130
bore the dull black lettering of the regular air force,
instead of the West Virginia Air National Guard.

The seven TALON Force members were zipped
quickly out on the flight line to the droning C-130 in a
dark-blue personnel van. All seven, wearing black BDUs
with no patches, rank, or other markings whatever, sat
quietly in the dimly lit rear of the van, full of questions
but asking none. They knew the drill. Briefings would
answer all in due time.

Stan Powczuk did mutter to no one in particular,
"Jesus, Mary, and Joseph. West goddamn Virginia. Why
the hell do we launch from so far back on the frontier
we could've come in on mules?"

Dr. Sarah Greene kept staring at the floor of the van,
but she answered rhetorically. "How many spies or wire-
service reporters do you suppose hang out up here?"

"Good point," Stan admitted. "But I'm still lucky
some inbred Deliverance goon didn't stick a root up
my toot."

Travis Barrett silently eyed Stan and Sarah as the van bounced over divides in the tarmac, and he smiled slightly. It was a welcome relief from the depression he'd felt since leaving his kids at the ranch.

The van screeched to a halt. The two M-16–armed air force military policemen in black berets, who had been their escort since their arrival, yanked open the rear doors, then trotted to warning stations before the ominously whirling propellers of the number 1 and 2 engines. They peered away, eyes always moving, like Secret Service agents on duty.

Travis was last to exit the van. When he stepped down he was surprised to see navy Lieutenant Jennifer Olsen waiting out of view behind the van, her short blonde hair whipping in the propeller turbulence.

"Anything wrong Je—" Travis began, before Jen grabbed him by the lapels of his black fatigue shirt, yanked him close to her, and kissed him hard, deep, and long. She parted with a smack and smiled. "God knows when I'll have a chance to do that again!" Jen shouted over the scream of the turbines. Then she ran around the van, across the tarmac, and leaped up the short stairway into the big transport.

Travis stood for a moment, still a little surprised. He wiped his mouth. "Good to see you too, Lieutenant Olsen," he mumbled. As he trotted to the airplane, he noted the big cammo-painted plastic hard cases that contained TALON Force Eagle Team's high-tech toys were being loaded through the lowered rear ramp of the C-130.

Travis jumped nimbly up the step, bore right around a bulkhead, and entered the cavernous cargo bay. Sam Wong's satellite commo equipment was tied down in the center front, leaving two aisles at either side where the six team members sat on web seating facing inward. Sarah, Jen, and the giant Jack sat against the far hull; Hunter, Sam, and Stan sat against the near side.

Aft of them, lashed to an aluminum pallet, itself locked to the bay floor, was a low, lumpy object about thirty feet long and four feet high, covered in a thin black shroud. The shroud had PROJECT HOPE stenciled in white letters in numerous places, along with MEDICAL

SUPPLIES stenciled in yellow lettering beneath. Beyond its odd shape, nothing else could be derived by looking at it.

Behind the object, lashed to pallets anchored to the now rising tail ramp, were the TALON gear pods. Travis spread his feet for balance against the rocking of the rapidly taxiing aircraft, its prop noise droning loudly through the hull. He made his way to a seat and strapped in. As they taxied, the air force load master shouted the usual "In the unlikely event of an in-flight emergency . . ." safety spiel, leaning for balance on the long, lumpy, shrouded PROJECT HOPE item.

There was no pause at the run-up zone. The load master strapped in as the big transport lumbered onto the runway without slowing. The engine/prop noise rose to a hellish howl, and still once again all aboard marveled at how anything that big could accelerate that fast. The nose whipped up, followed shortly by the high, loud whir and thump of the main gear trucks retracting.

In six minutes the plane leveled off. Hunter, ever the pilot, detected the throttles being pulled back from climb to cruise power. The load master threw off his belt, gave Travis a thumbs-up, and exited up the stairway to the cockpit deck, whipping a curtain shut behind him, leaving the TALONs alone. When Travis released his belt, the other six quickly threw off their own. The diminutive Sam Wong sprang instantly to the gear tied down before them and popped open a pod containing eight odd, drab-colored, lightweight helmets stored in racks. He rapidly pitched one to each TALON, then donned his own. He pressed buttons and flipped switches on a panel in the case beneath the helmet rack. Everyone hurriedly strapped the asymmetrically shaped lumpy helmets on and extended a sturdy, crablike, wing arm recessed in the side of the shells. The little arm stopped above the eye line.

Instantly, Stan's jagged grumble filled everyone's ears, causing them to squint from the audible pain and blink frantically into their eyepieces to turn down the helmet earphone volume.

"Goddamn it Sammy! If you don't fix the voltage in my beeper so I don't feel like I'm getting the big one at

Angola Penitentiary every time you transmit a TAD,
I'm going to qualify you for handicap tags!"

"Oooookay," Sam said, his soft-spoken voice also
seeming to fill the ears of each helmeted TALON as
though emanating from half an inch away, "so we have
audio and Stan's vocal. Jack?"

"Gotcha, little buddy," DuBois rumbled happily, with
a voice like a grizzly in a cave. It was not necessary for
the wearer of the light, cammo-painted helmet to speak
above the softest whisper to be heard clearly by the rest
of the team.

"Hunter?"

"Ten over ten, Sam."

"Sarah?"

"Good evening, everyone. Nice to see you all again."

"Jen?"

"Do Chinese guys really have sideways dicks,
Sammy?"

Sam choked off a grin. "Someday maybe you'll get to
find out, Aryan princess. Your helmet working, Boss?"

"Hello guys, looks like Uncle Sam's toys are clickin'."
Travis's easy drawl sounded as though his lips were at
each listener's ear.

Jen shivered.

"Eagle Team's toys always click, Boss," Sam said. "At
a hundred-eighty-six-thousand bucks a copy, they ought
to. We have one spare BSH helmet, guys; don't break
Uncle Sam's toys. And if you lose it, you better leave
your head inside it."

Travis wasted no time. "Listen up. Mission briefing
now begins. You've each had your departmental special-
ity segment briefings en route in the Falcons that
brought you to Martinsburg. Pay attention, people. This
one's ugly. Jen?"

Lieutenant Jennifer Olsen of Naval Intelligence sailed
a half-normal-sized floppy disc at Sam, who stuffed it
into an encrypt/decrypt-capable radio-computer contained in a small, black, cordura-bound waist pack he'd
retrieved. Its stubby antenna was barely visible. He
buckled the stoutly made pack about him, the pouch in
front, and fiddled with small buttons within.

Each TALON trooper raised their gazes toward the

small monoclelike device extended above their eye line. In so doing they were instantly in a virtual-reality visual theater created by a holographic image projected directly upon the retinae of their eyes. Small, red, digital lettering appeared at the top and bottom edges of the images they saw. To clear this image from their eyes, each had only to lower his or her gaze to normal angle. These graphite/kevlar composite, total-communication helmets weighed one-point-three pounds each.

In two seconds, 3-D images of photographs appeared in everyone's eyes, as vivid, clear, and detailed as high-resolution intelligence images should be.

"Got to hand it to General Krauss," Hunter said, looking up at the first photograph. "These things are awesome."

Jen spoke fast, but clearly. "Map of the Republic of Cuba, faded communist jewel of the Carribean. Look at the west central province of Cienfuegos, the heart of sugar country. Look now at the port city, also called Cienfuegos, located on the northwest edge of the large bay recessed in the southern coast. This is a major seaport, the largest sugar-shipping facility in the world. The old section of the city is very graceful, blessed with much lovely Spanish colonial architecture. That's the good news, people; it goes downhill from there, fast."

The holographic intraoptical images changed to a closer scale photo of the greater Cienfuegos Bay area.

Jen continued. "This is the latest satellite rendering, maybe twelve hours old; you see it in three parts, real-eye, infrared, and topographic. Note the industrial port section east of the old city—that's where you see most of the large, ocean-going ships docked—now move your gaze farther east along the coast; see those two rings, isolated?"

"Got 'em."

"Yep."

"Oh shit."

"Well said," Jen resumed. "Lady and gentlemen, behold the recently activated, Russian-built . . . Juragua Nuclear Electric Production Plant."

A new, ground-level photo image appeared showing

massive domed buildings rising above bulky substructure, all surrounded by tall, slender construction cranes.

"Still under construction in eighty-five," Jen said, identifying the photograph.

"They're building nukes," Stan whispered.

"Yep," Jack agreed grimly. "The Cubes are buildin' the bomb."

"No, guys," Jen said soberly. "They're not. Not yet, anyway. I'm afraid it's actually worse than that."

That remark won Jen narrow-eyed glances from everyone but Travis.

"These are twin Soviet-designed, V-three-eighteen nuclear reactors, the export derivatives of the Soviets' VVER-four-forty pressurized-water reactors. They aren't the junk that popped at Chernobyl in eighty-six, but by western nuclear safety standards, they're still junk. The Soviets started building these reactors in eighty-three, then mothballed the project, ninety-four percent complete, in September of ninety-two after the breakup of the Soviet Union. In ninety-seven, construction was resumed after Cuba raised three hundred million dollars from European investors and our old backstabbing, manipulative, Russian friends, who gave them eight hundred million. If you ever wondered where some of your hard-earned tax dollars went, it was foreign-aid money Clinton gave the Ivans. Anyway, three months ago . . . Juragua Nuclear went on line."

"I'm waiting for the other shoe," Hunter said.

"That plant has to be unsafe, even if all they're making is electricity," Sarah, in Greenpeace mode, said. "Cuba is one of the world's ecological outlaws. The Alemendares River that flows through Havana is *the* most contaminated river in the western hemisphere. It's completely dead from pollution, no animal life whatever. Cuba has the largest coral reefs in this hemisphere, yet over forty percent of them have been destroyed from Cuban industrial contamination. Since nineteen eighty, Castro has spent over a billion—billion with a 'b'!—dollars on the research, development, and manufacture of biotechnical and chemical agents. They've actually had to evacuate areas of Cuba due to leaks of these agents. And now we're supposed to believe they can handle nu-

clear waste, or run a nuclear reactor built by the same
great folks who brought you the Chernobyl disaster that
killed a hundred-and-twenty-five-*thousand* people!''

"Sarah's on the right tack, here," Jen said. "The Juragua reactors sit in an immensely corrosive seaside environment, and they're built on a known seismic fault, for
Christ's sake. But . . . that's not the worst of it."

"Oh Jesus," Hunter whispered. "It's leaking already."

"No," Jen said urgently, "but people . . . the hottest,
verified, state-of-the-art intelligence data says there's a
plot afoot to make it leak—big time—by a terrorist orga-
nization known as the Swords of Allah."

"Ah Christ," said Jack.

Jen spoke again. "This is—I can't find the right
word—critical—even that doesn't do it—this is *critical* to
the tenth *power*! If we can't stop the Swords from blowing up the Juragua reactors, we'll have—"

"What we'll *have*," Sarah said, standing, clearly agitated, "is a nuclear disaster that will make Chernobyl
look like Disney World. The average thousand-megawatt
nuclear reactor contains as much long-lived radioactive
material as would be created by a *thousand* Hiroshima
atomic blasts. What we'll have within four days of a
blowout at Juragua is a radioactive cloud that could
blanket the southeastern U.S. from Houston to Washington! Possibly half a *million* deaths from radiation within
a year."

"Christ in a teacup," Stan said softly.

"Indeed," Sarah continued, almost choking. "And this
is assuming winds in our favor. If Juragua blows during
a major northeast airmass flow, the Nuclear Regulatory
Commission estimates—conservatively—*twenty million*
deaths from short-term radiation poisoning and long-
term thyroid cancer and leukemia within fifteen years."

"When do we think the Swords plan to strike?" Sam
asked tersely.

Jen went on. "Some of you may be familiar with the
Swords of Allah. The world intelligence community
knows them as the most ruthless, out-of-control, Arab
terrorist cell in existence, composed of Muslim funda-
mentalist fanatics of the most brainwashed order.
They're men and women who have been told since they

were born that the U.S. is 'The Great Satan.' They were trained from diapers to hate Americans, they're major-league, hardcore, political alley fighters, any one of whom will gleefully immolate themselves if they think they can kill a half dozen Americans in the process.

"The Swords are Arab patriot zealots, the worst splinter psychopaths expelled from Hammas, Black September, the P.L.O., and other groups for being too unstable. They are utterly possessed by their devotion to their people and hatred of their enemies, and they've been highly trained as insurgent guerillas since they were children. We know they are well led, heavily financed, and excellently equipped. They've brought off six of the world's most 'successful'—read deadly—terrorist strikes in the last ten years. Now they've found their ultimate wet dream, a way to kill twenty million Americans. They're going after the Juragua reactors."

"*When,* Jen!?" Sam snapped. "How long do we have?"

"Sorry. The NSA, CIA, and Mossad have been onto this thing for about three weeks, Sam. Apparently one of the Swords' women in Amman needed an emergency caesarian section. A French medical resident was observing the operation when the woman started muttering under anesthesia. The French doctor knew enough about what he was hearing to become alarmed. Thinking the threat involved a nuclear detonation in Israel, he notified the French embassy, which notified Mossad. Mossad learned enough to determine that the threat had to do with Cuba and was to be a Swords operation. Just . . . about eleven o'clock zulu this morning, they learned that the Swords of Allah are going to hit the Juragua nuclear plant sometime within . . ." Jen looked anxiously at the zulu clock high on the forward bulkhead of the airplane ". . . fifty-one hours. Midnight, two nights from now."

"Shit!" Stan spat. "We've got a lousy fifty hours to fly eighteen hundred miles, drop into a hostile country in the dark, and stop a group of lunatic sand monkeys bent on cracking a nuclear plant? Which, incidentally, has more fucking security than our national gold reserves at Fort Knox!"

"And the plot thickens," Hunter hissed.

"Say," Jack interjected. "If this is so damn serious, why can't the JCS just go in there with all the toys and boys, and hit Cuba like Patton hit Sicily?"

"Hell, I can answer that and I've not been told a damn thing except how to be the combat technoweeny for this mission," Sam said. "We can't *invade* Cuba without explaining why to the American people. Can you fathom the panic that would take place if the public got the idea Cuba was going to melt into the Caribbean, but not before dusting the entire Confederate States of America with Black Pollen!? When those horrifying downwind kill numbers got out, anarchy would explode. You couldn't move a motorcycle on I-seventy-five, I-ten, or I-ninety-five. Airplanes couldn't land or takeoff in Florida, Alabama, Mississippi, or Louisiana without being swarmed by panicked, evacuating hordes, a là Tan Son Nhut in seventy-five. Every boat on the eastern seaboard would be swamped. Real estate values would fall below the radiation-contaminated water table. Wall Street would go into fatal seizures. Social services would be innundated."

"Precisely," Travis intoned. "Which is why we have to get in there to stop the Swords from trashing Juragua. And by the way, we don't even know how they intend to do it yet, but we have to stop them and get back out without creating a ripple that makes it into the news media."

Sam said acidly, "Just how *do* we get out?"

"Out is *my* job, people," Stan said, smiling. "We go out by boat to a submarine."

"How do we get *in*?" Sarah asked. "There were no HALO chutes on my equipment manifest, and I haven't seen any since we came aboard. Besides, even in the best high-altitude-low-opening scenario we couldn't pinpoint our landing at night with enough accuracy. We could come down in the middle of a prison yard or a military base."

"Tsk, tsk, tsk," Hunter clucked, rising and walking to the long, low object beneath the PROJECT HOPE–stenciled shroud. Exhibiting a slight smugness, Hunter began removing the velcro straps that secured the shroud. Even though he was twenty feet from his fellow TALONs, his voice still sounded close in everyone's Battle Sensor Helmet earphones. "All this talk of parachutes. Oh ye of little faith." Blake hopped quickly down the side of the pallet to its rear, where he began to draw the loosened shroud off rearward.

"Comrades, meet Night Phoenix, prototype one, the only composite/resin stealth glider in all the world."

Bracing against the gentle sway of the aircraft, all members of the team rose and gathered about the strange craft emerging from beneath the shroud. At first glance it looked like a large, long bobsled with a roof. It was a dark gray matte in color, rested on runners molded into its belly, and possessed two long, slender wings that were folded, rearward, tightly against its sides. The wing tips extended well beyond the tail. At the tail, what amounted to a sleek, V-shaped, rudder/horizontal stabilizer combination was hard mounted. The craft had one narrow windshield in the nose.

"Uh-oh," Sam mumbled, making his way aft, staring at the bizarre-looking glider. "I don't like the looks of this."

"Maaaann," Stan purred. "*Look* at this thing, will you?"

Jen ran her eyes over the glider. "Don't tell me, Sky King, you designed this thing?"

"I wish. The chemistry and math in this baby are way above my level, Air Force Academy aeronautical-engineering masters degree, notwithstanding. But I did all flight testing and provided a lot of input."

"The allied glider forces at Normandy took fifty percent casualties!" Sam said. "How much flight testing has been done on this thing?"

"The requisite silly military alphabet moniker for this thing is ZERAIS-PIG," Blake said, smiling.

"Zee-rice-*pig*!?" Jack groaned.

"Oh come on," Sarah said skeptically. "We're doing a night insertion into Cuba in something called a zee-rice-pig?"

Blake smiled weakly. "You know how our beloved military leaders are, my dear, they can't call anything what it is, they've got to have an acronym for it. In this case, 'Zero Radar/Infrared Signature, Powerless Insertion Glider,' I shit you not."

"How much flight testing?" Sam repeated.

"It's invisible, people," Hunter said, excitedly. "We can sail this baby right into a Cuban Defense Forces radar sight and they wouldn't know it until we ran over them on landing. Neither the Ivans nor anybody else can see it with a satellite at night. There's nothing metal on the airframe. The RIA paint dissipates the IR signature and radar receptions completely. It's the latest achievement in stealth engineering."

"How much flight testing have—"

Stan cut Sam off. "What? It's . . . parachute-extraction launched?"

"Hey!" Blake smiled again. "Polack SEALs one, other TALONs zero. Very good, Stan. You're dead right."

"Not the best choice of words," Sam said. "How much flight test—"

Hunter was becoming more animated with his presentation. "Check this out, it's great!" He twisted pop-in knobs recessed in the skin of the glider and lifted a twelve-foot section of the roof like a clamshell. He propped it open with plastic rods. Within were butt-shaped, molded ripples and foot rests in the floor, which constituted seats of a sort, and nothing else but for a set of elementary flight controls in the very front behind the small windshield. Hunter lifted and latched open another, smaller clamshell door aft of the seat tube. The compartment was bare within except for rubber tie-down rings in the floor.

"Gear storage," Hunter said, indicating the rear compartment. "Cabin," he pointed to the floor ripples, "and the cockpit. My seat, of course. We all sit spoon fashion, between the thighs of, and leaning back against, the person behind us. Jack, as the biggest, you're in the rear, over the wing root, for weight and balance reasons."

"Back of the bus, again. Why doesn't that surprise me?"

"Then it's Travis, Stan, Jen, Sam, Sarah, and me. The toys go in the back. We're launching from twenty-seven thousand feet after this plane makes its predictable turn southeast over the Yucatan Channel. To the Cuban radar guys and the Russian satellite monitors, it'll be just another American flight to the Soto Cano Air Force Base in Honduras, one more mercy flight to carry relief supplies to Central American hurricane victims. After we load at launch-minus-five minutes, our air force host will lower the tail ramp and deploy the snatch chute."

"Watch it." Jen suppressed a smile.

"The chute has all-absorbtive, plastic hard fittings and is designed to open gradually as it trails in the slipstream, but we're still going to feel like a rodeo calf being yanked short when it goes full open. Three-point-seven Gs, decel."

"Ooh." Sarah winced.

Hunter continued. "There are nylon seat belts with plastic friction buckles, and foot props at the outboard edges of the floor. Use 'em. The chute will pull us out the back in an instant. Once the PIG slows from launch speed—about three hundred knots—to deployment speed—sixty-two knots—we jettison the chute and deploy the wings to their extended position."

"We drop the parachute and *then* try to put the wings out?!" Sam cried.

"With the wings deployed, and from launch altitude, in the winds aloft I was briefed on, we can remain aloft about six hours, but we'll be on the ground in a little over two hours."

"If we don't get run over by another of the many aircraft using the narrow Yucatan vector between Mexico and the Cuban Air Defense Intercept Zone," Sarah groused.

"Hey," Hunter said, smiling and holding up his hands to Sarah, "these hands, my dear, have been blessed by the *gods*! Compared to me, Icarus was a *turtle*!"

"Icarus fell out of the sky! How much flight test—" Sam was choked off again.

"We won't be in that airway five minutes, Sarah," Hunter said. "We will 'boldly go where no man has gone before,' smack over the length of Cuba from the western Cape of San Antonio, over the Gulf of Batabano—you'll be able to see the lights of Havana to the north, from that altitude, if it isn't too hazy."

"Don't count on seeing those lights," Sarah said. "Cuba is an air-pollution outlaw."

"Only way I care to see Havana is through a laser smart-bomb sight," Stan muttered. "Preferably homing on the Great Bearded Bozo's stogie."

Hunter continued. "Then we'll descend into Cienfuegos province and land in . . . uh, land."

"I caught that!" Sam said. "Land where?"

"Um, a well, a sugarcane field."

"What!?"

Sarah said dryly, "I'm not a pilot, let alone an Icarus blessed by the gods, but I think that when airplanes come down in sugarcane fields, Hunter, the correct term is not 'landing.' It's 'crashing,' sweetie."

"Trust me! The cane field is flat, the cane will act as a decelerator, and it will conceal us after we land."

"Hey!" Sam fairly shouted. Everyone flinched and blinked their volume levels down. "Hunter, watch my lips! How many times have you flown this thing?"

All eyes turned to Hunter Blake.

"Well, um . . . once, but—"

"Once!?" five voices, excluding Travis's, demanded.

"Listen up," Travis's even voice commanded. Everyone looked at him, because he rarely intruded. "Anybody here don't want to go, now's the time to speak up." He looked levelly at each member of Eagle Team.

No one even thought about speaking.

"Then let's wrap this up. We're going to need sleep bad. Stan, you give the weapons briefing, Sam, you review us on commo. Then it's beddy-bye, everyone. I want the whole team to get a minimum four hours sleep. We'll have the crew wake us at launch minus twenty. Any questions?"

The team was fully suited and wedged into the uninspiringly named ZERAIS-PIG, with weapons, by launch minus five. It was a snug fit.

What is my black ass doin' here? Captain Jack DuBois thought. I better git to bag me some Cubes on this trip, is all I can say.

Travis Barrett, packed snugly against Jack's chest and

sitting between his thighs wondered what Randall and Betty Sue were doing right then.

Stan Powczuk, Lt. Commander, U.S. Navy, SEALs, thought, hail Mary, Mother of God, blessed art thou among women. Be with us now and at the hour of our . . .

Naval Intelligence Lieutenant Jennifer Olsen thought, Christ, I hope the intel was good on this one.

Sam Wong certainly couldn't feel much through the silky electrical illusion battle suits all the TALONs had donned after waking. Nonetheless, Sam oscillated between how nice it felt to be sitting between Jen Olsen's sumptuous thighs, leaning back against her bounteous breasts, and how terrified he was of living out the rest of his life in the basement cell of a Cuban dungeon. Or watching his flesh fall off from radiation poisoning.

One half-million in the first year, Army Dr. Sarah Greene thought. Twenty million over fifteen years.

Air Force Captain Hunter Blake put his feet on the rudder pedals and one god's-blessed hand on the uni-stick between his knees. With the other hand he jammed a fierce thumbs-up at the windshield. The gray flight-suited load master and crew chief, who stood squinting against the cold night air blowing in through the lowered tail door at twenty-seven thousand feet, nodded, saluted, and released the drag chute out the lowered tail door. They scrambled forward to clear the big glider on its slides.

The huge parachute fell back a hundred feet behind the droning C-130, then inflated. The stout kevlar connecting straps twanged taut. The TALON Force Eagle Team, to a person, grunted sharply and snapped forward in unison from the impact of the sudden and severe deceleration.

One 3.8-million-dollar composite/resin stealth glider and seven good souls were sucked out into the black night.

Chapter Two

Seat belts bit deep and helmets knocked together as
Eagle Team's stealth glider was snatched from the gaping maw of the C-130. There were several guttural grunts
and one mild cry of pain.

"Juh-EEE-zus!" squeezed from between Stan's
clenched teeth.

The intense deceleration from ejection to wing-
deployment airspeed lasted seven seconds, which seemed
a minute long to the members of the team hurled forward against their restraints and each other. In unison,
they rocked back in their cramped, reclining positions
when Hunter released the huge drogue chute as the aircraft slowed to 67 knots. Cold, high-altitude air began
seeping into the tight, sweat-smelling cabin.

But now the long, sleek glider dropped like a
greased anvil.

Sandwiched in darkness between Sarah and Jen, just
aft of the rudimentary cockpit, Sam frantically bobbed
his head from side to side to see around Sarah's helmet.
He hurriedly eyed the night-imaging readout in the helmet screen just above his eye line. Viewing the greenish,
infrared-enhanced light magnifier, Sam could see almost
as though the glider's interior were lit. As he observed
Hunter's busy form ahead, Sam's testicles began to retract and he was seized with a sick feeling. He did not
have to be a pilot to tell that Hunter was struggling
feverishly with an apparently malfunctioning control.
"What is it?" Sam said over the commo net, a faint color

of panic in his voice, his breathing audibly elevated. "What . . . what's . . . why are we . . . Hunter! What's wrong?"

"Easy, Sammy," Big Jack, in the rear, uttered calmly, his deep voice close but comforting in everyone's ears. "Let Hunter do his thing, man."

In the tiny cockpit, Hunter was doing his thing, but the 3.8-million-dollar, one-of-a-kind, radar/infrared invisible, composite stealth glider regrettably wasn't doing its thing. The long slender wings, folded back against the craft's sides at launch, were now supposed to extend to the sides, but when Hunter had yanked the extension lever nothing had happened. The torpedo-shaped glider, with wings folded longitudinally, now plummeted steeply at an accelerating rate of descent. Hunter knew that if a solution wasn't effected in seconds, the glider would accelerate past the maximum speed at which the wings would sustain deployment without breaking, thus converting the entire mission into a helplessly falling object, one that would hit the Yucatan Channel, twenty thousand feet below, at a collision speed that would instantly convert everyone aboard to red mush.

Come on, boy, Travis thought silently. He knew something was wrong, though he couldn't know what. He also knew there was nothing he could do but ride and hope. Come on, boy, Travis repeated to himself.

Jack sourly thought, if this white-boy's folly doesn't work, I'm going to kick me some serious ass.

Through his own night imager, Hunter grimly watched the elementary, analog airspeed-indicator needles spin toward terminal velocity, the airspeed above which the wings would fold even if he succeeded in deploying them. Twice, viciously, he recycled the deployment lever. Nothing.

Hunter instantly thumped an unmarked button the size of a golf ball in the cockpit wall near Jen's booted left foot. To his quantum relief, he heard the crack and hiss of the backup nitrogen blow-bottle firing. The bladders within the wings inflated with the force near that of automobile airbags. A glance out the tiny cockpit window by his eye confirmed the wings extending, as did the decelerative drag they created.

Slowly, to avoid exceeding the G-load limits of the long slender wings, Hunter drew back on the stick and the glider began to level and slow.

"Let's hear it for Icarus, people," Sarah said, releasing a deep breath.

"Icarus will generously absorb your adulation after he gets us on the ground alive," Hunter answered quickly, his labored breathing audible. "Right now, I need to get us down to eighteen thousand feet so we can have enough oxygen to breathe safely. World War One air aces occasionally used to dogfight at twenty thousand without supplemental oxygen. Men have climbed Everest to twenty-eight thousand feet with no supplemental oxygen, but it's not recommended, believe me."

"Hope that mammoth parachute doesn't come down on some Cuban patrol vessel," Jen, ever the intelligence agent, muttered.

"Oh ye of little faith, Jen me luv," Hunter said, his glibness again intact. "The whole drogue was permeated with something called Compound-Agate, a substance that converts to a fast-acting acid forty seconds after being exposed to oxygen. The chute's already vapor."

"Man," Jack grumbled, "it's darker than Watts during a blackout down there. How the hell do you know where we're going?"

"I don't, Jack," Hunter said. "But I know how to lock black boxes onto a satellite laser directional beam, and I promise you it will place us accurate to thirty-six feet."

"In the middle of a sugarcane field," Sarah said, softly.

"Doc," Hunter replied, "on the ground, you and I could lift this whole aircraft empty. One of the things we designed out to make it so light was landing gear and brakes. That sugarcane field is our brakes, Sugar."

Travis asked in his Texas twang, "Time to touch-down, Hunter?"

"We're riding a tailwind, boss. We're at T minus . . . two hours, seventeen minutes."

"Okay, listen up people. Here's your next time-block briefing. We're to be met when we get on the ground by an agent of the CIA—even I don't know his name or anything about him, yet. Only the recognition code. He won't know where we're coming down 'til he gets an encrypted radio message from NSA at T plus five. This guy—I'm guessing it's a guy—will guide us to a safe house we will use for an operational base. Sam will set up a sat-link and Jen'll get us an intel update. There's no telling what we're going to encounter here, people. General Krauss's folks had to put this one together in a kick-ass hurry. Let's everybody stay alert, but don't be shooting anybody that doesn't fire on us first, unless you get a green from me. Jack, that means you, buddy. Don't be cappin' our contact guy."

"Who, me?"

"Jen, don't chopsocky anybody to the hereafter unless you're attacked or I tell you to do him."

"Aye-aye, boss. I'll be a good little girl."

"Without this contact, our asses are hangin' out, people."

"Not to mention twenty million other derrieres, north of Miami," Sarah muttered.

"Stan," Travis said, "talk weapons."

"Set those XM-29s on three-burst, not on kill-'em-all-and-let-God-sort-'em-out unless we run into Mongol hordes. I want aimed three-bursts, not spray and pray. These new brassless cartridges allow us to pack in a hell of a lot of ammo, but if we do run dry, we ain't gonna be able to buy combustible smart-rifle ammo at the local sporting goods store. Keep the twenty-mil grenade tube loaded with all four rounds, but watch where you use them. Distance targets only, with the twenty-mikes, or we'll be eatin' our own shrapnel. We'll go in wearing the light-reactive battle suits, in case we land in the shit. Questions?"

After a pause Travis continued. "Sam, talk commo."

Sam was relieved for something to take his mind off riding a thin, unarmed, unarmored, composite glider through the Cuban Air Defense Intercept Zone into the heart of that hostile, communist nation. "Right, boss. Guys, it's BSHs at all times; nobody takes them off unless Travis commands. Remember, these voice-activated frequency selectors are very sensitive; you don't have to yell the function codes, even under fire. Especially under fire. Remember to use data-specific language. Say 'frequency, two-two-five', not 'two-twenty-five.' I'll do all the extra-squad commo, and I'll change your intrasquad links simultaneously myself so you don't have to worry about it. But if I'm . . . taken out . . . you can all access the encrypted chips that have the uplink data. Code in with your birth dates minus three. That's it, boss."

"Sarah?"

"Thank you, Travis. Lady and gentlemen, oh, and you too, Hunter . . ."

"Ooooh. Slam-dunked again." Hunter smiled slightly, sweeping the sky for airliners and other aircraft who would not be able to see the ZERAIS-PIG and would not be warned of it by Cuban Air Traffic Control because Cuban ATC could not see them on radar.

Sarah continued. "Your inoculations are up to date, including malaria of course, so you need fear no intraordinary Cuban bacteria or virus. I'm having a BSH briefing on nuclear plant radiation hazards prepared as we speak; we'll draw it off the satellite before we go into Juragua. Now, you know the development problems we've had with the shock/trauma response functions of these new battle suits. Stan, in the last op, you got staples clamped where you had no wound."

"Hurt like a bitch. Felt like I'd been bit by a pit bull."

"Yes. Well, we've done extensive new testing since the Saudi op and I believe we've eliminated that glitch. Just remember, if you take a hit that penetrates the kevlex armor fabric, the suit's inner fibers contacted by blood will bow-contract and attempt to seal the rupture to reduce blood loss. The suit will inject the appropriate antibiotic thru the suture staples themselves. You should not feel pain from the autosutures due to the pain of the wound itself."

Sam said, "Oh that's a comfort."

Sarah replied, "You can, of course, self-medicate morphine should the pain be disabling. You needn't fear overdose as the suit's regulator will govern the dosage and rate."

"I think I'll get high on dope," Sam said. "I'm even more fearless when I'm stoned."

Sarah smiled. "Wrong, genius. The regulator will not release morphine unless you bleed first. Questions, anyone?"

There was silence, but for the rush of air by the close sides of the glider fuselage and a slight hum from taut control cords.

"Anybody else?" Travis asked. "Jack?"

"Nope. Just don't get your cream-puff asses between me and the Cubes. Or the Swords of Poobah, if we lucky enough to make contact with 'em."

"Silence!" Hunter said suddenly. "Cuban ATC just cleared fighter jets into— Never mind. Disregard. Routine training flight. You can go back to sleep, they still have no idea we're here. *Man* this is neat! We still have a good tail wind, our ground speed's better than expected. We're going to arrive early with altitude and darkness to spare."

"Glad to hear it," Travis replied. "Jen, you got anything?"

"No. I haven't received anything new since we left West Virginia. I know NSA is tearing the world apart for more intel though. As soon as they know anything they'll transmit it to me by sat-link; I'll convert it to a BSH visual and brief you all."

"Okay. That's it for now. I know it's cold up here, guys; I'm feelin' it, too. Go easy on your LOC suit heat; it eats those power cells like candy. Everybody sleep if you can; meditate at least. I want—"

"Sleep!" Sam exclaimed. "You've got to be joking!"

Travis went on. "I want everybody as rested as possible before we make Cienfuegos. The next forty hours or so promise to be a cast-iron bitch. Hunter, alert us at landing minus ten, unless you see something we need to know sooner. Advise me of anything out of the ordinary, immediately."

"Wilco, boss. We're scanning all the Cuban military surveillance frequencies and I'm hearing nothing peculiar, not a goddamn thing. We're invisible, people. You guys try to rest, you're—what the hell is that vibration?"

"It is not the airplane," Travis drawled dryly. "That's Jack snoring right behind me. He's sacked already."

Deeee-deeee-deeee-deeee-deeee-deeee-deeee . . .

"Rise and shine sleepyheads," Hunter said, his voice

on each BSH headset seeming to its wearer to be a half inch away. "It's party time."

There was as much stirring as the cramped, spoon-stack seating would permit. The air within the glider had become warm and stuffy.

Sarah looked out the tiny Lucite window by her eyes. The slightest hint of dawn defined the distant eastern horizon. Below, Cuba was still black as coal but for the lights of the massive Cienfuegos harbor complex and city, miles to the southeast. Vehicle headlights could be seen slowly traversing the sparsely traveled roads.

"Forty-two hundred feet and descending, guys. Cinch up your seatbelts. Secure your weapons. Tray tables to the upright positions, please. We're on the downwind leg."

Sarah could feel Sam's elevated respirations. She patted his shoulder. He reached to pat her hand in thanks.

"You all know the drill," Travis reminded everyone. "The instant we stop, Stan, Sarah, Jen, and Hunter establish a perimeter to the left; Sam, Jack, and me to the right. Keep your BSHs on the correct encrypted freqs, and remember you don't have to speak above a whisper."

"Turning final," Hunter said, just a touch of terseness in his voice. "I've got a good NVG visual of the landing zone, right where the laser said it would be. Looks as advertised in my briefing. Slight upward slope. Thick, uniform, eight-foot sugarcane growth. No hot organisms in sight. Thirty seconds, people. Everybody lean forward and grip the person in front. Short final, flaps down, airbrake out. Here we gooooo . . . level . . . flare . . . speed dissipating . . . seventy knots . . . sixty . . . fifty. Brace for impact. We're almost—*Jeezus Christ!*"

Hunter hauled back hard on the stick and the big glider seemed to slam against a floor, then bound skyward. There was a loud crack and ripping sound. The glider careened up, then steeply down.

Chapter Three

"We hit something!" Hunter said tightly, yanking the glider violently to level it. Seven BSH helmets batted wildly against the interior. "An old, rusty god knows what! Hang on!"

There was suddenly a staccato clatter of sugarcane stalks striking the wings and belly. Everyone lurched forward. The clatter grew louder, then became deafening. The glider hit hard, eliciting concussive grunts from several TALONs. The heavy cane stalks slapping the wings and cockpit sounded like rapid-fire gunshots in the tight, confined cabin. The craft bounced, settled hard, bounced again, then ground to a rocking halt.

"Blow!" Hunter cried, and he yanked the canopy release. Everyone shoved hard, up and left. The light-weight composite canopy caught in a slight breeze and flipped away. Hot humid air flowed in like molasses. The team commanded stiff, sore muscles into action and bailed out. They scrambled over the splintered, horizontal cane stalks, then into the standing cane and cover. There they each lay, silent, the volumes on their BSHs boosted to the max, listening, scanning down endless rows of cane, searching the light green/dark green BSH NVG imagery for any sign of movement.

There was only the sound of crickets on the pre-dawn air.

In the dim moonlight, the team would've been invisible to any observing with the unaided eye. The amazing LOC suits and BSH helmet, with weapon cloaks, absorbed light from the surroundings, which was read by a tiny computer, which determined the color and wave composition of the incoming light and directed the flex-fiber-optic fabric to exude nearly identical colors and patterns on the opposite sides of the suit. The team's weapons were cloaked in a similar fabric powered off the suits. The result, even in daylight, was that anyone looking at the combatants in their flex-fiber-optic battle suits, as long as the TALONs were still, would only see an almost indiscernible wavy optical disturbance similar to rising heat distortions. If they moved, exposed metal gun parts and possibly the bottoms of their boots could be seen, but the images were so unhuman in appearance and hard to discern as to render the wearers nearly invisible, especially in poor light. The suits were on a secrecy level with the unspoken-of SR-1 Aurora spy plane, still seen only by select defense workers at Area 51.

After a long, tense minute, Travis's voice was the slightest whisper in everyone's ear. "Anyone see any movement?" Silence. "Power down the LOC suits unless we have contact; let's save those batteries. Jack, Stan, Jen, extend a three-point watch fifty meters. Hunter, Sarah, and Sam, meet me at the glider. Move."

"Some kind of metal stand or something, Trav," Hunter whispered as they converged on the wrecked glider. "It was ambient temp so I didn't see it until we were all over it. We almost hit it head on."

"Don't sweat it a second, partner. Any landing we all walk away from is a goddamn milestone of aviation achievement. Let's get the toy boxes out."

Sarah, Sam, Hunter, and Travis slung their XM-29s, gripped the handles on the three equipment pods, and heaved. Sam slid quickly about the pods surveying for damage. He shot Travis a fast thumbs-up. They dragged the pods twenty feet away.

"Everybody close," Travis whispered, facing outward. "Move." Jen, Stan, and Jack crunched in from their sentry positions, ever scanning the rows of cane.

"Windmill tower," Stan said on his arrival. "An old, rusty windmill tower without the fan."

"Jesus Christ," Hunter said.

"Hey Icarus," Stan grinned. "It was heavy gauge

angle-iron. If we'd hit that fucking thing head on we'd all be grated cheese. Nice work, buddy."

"Hands touched by God," Jen said, slapping Hunter on the butt as she passed.

"Destruct, Hunter," Travis ordered.

"What a shameful waste of a beautiful flying machine," Hunter said.

"Not to mention three-point-eight million bucks," Sam said.

"Well," Hunter said. "Here's one reason it cost so much." He removed the fist-sized power cell that had powered his radios and connected the terminals to two electrodes protruding from the emptied aircraft shell. Within seconds, the entire glider began to wrinkle, bubble, and sizzle. With startling speed, the acid reaction spread, discharging a slight smoky vapor. The craft hissed and converted to gases before astonished eyes. The consumptive chemical conversion ate its way rapidly out the wings.

"Now you see it—" Hunter said, staring at the dissolving aircraft.

"Now you don't," Jack said, staring, shaking his head.

Hunter charged the canopy with the battery. It began to sizzle and hiss.

"Olsen," Travis said.

When she faced him, he tossed her a collapsed Coca-Cola can retrieved from a leg pocket of his battle suit. She caught it, studied it with puzzlement, but knew that when Travis wanted to explain to her he would. She stuffed it in her own leg pocket.

"You're on point, Jen," Travis ordered, glancing up at a global-nav BSH projection. A slight compass rose overlay was readable. "Thataway. Move. Grab those pods, people. Let's boogie."

Jen hurried away carefully, her rifle at the ready. The team paired up on the three toy boxes and, in a fast single file, followed her down a cane row.

In two minutes, all that remained of the world's only ZERAIS-PIG was an odd, black stain in the dirt of a Cuban sugarcane field. Hunter had destroyed and buried the small, combination laser-guidance receiver and radio.

After ten minutes of difficult, hot, squeezing through

stout cane rows, Jen's tongue clicked twice in each BSH earphone. Instantly the team stopped, set the pods quietly down, knelt, and unslung their short, chunky, XM-29 smart rifles. Each faced a different outward azimuth.

"Got a dirt road, here, boss," Jen said over the BSH net in a soft whisper.

"Bingo. We wait, troops."

Twenty minutes later, as traces of dawn lightened the sky, Travis glanced up at his holographic projector and read the time in both zulu and local formats. "Heads up, Jen," he spoke softly.

"Headlights closing," she said shortly. "Slow, sounds like a truck."

"Green fog lights?" Travis asked from deep within the cane.

"Hey!" Jen whispered back. "How'd you know?"

"That's our contact. Battle alert, everybody. Stealth on. Let's hope our boy hasn't been compromised. Jen, toss that coke can into the road."

Jen complied, then backed away from the road and crouched with her shouldered rifle, not unlike a lioness on the African veldt. Jack and Stan moved quickly to parallel firing positions in the cane bordering the road and settled. Jen briefly watched them virtually evaporate as their LOC suits powered up the light-duplication systems. They seemed only barely detectable patterns of warm, wavy air. Amazing, she thought, and powered up her own.

Travis clicked off the safety on his twenty-mil grenade-tube trigger. "Jen, if this is our contact, he'll stop when he sees the can. He should get out and pick up the can. He should rap it four times with his knuckles, then toss it to his left."

"If he does?"

"Then you approach him and search him. Stan, Jack, Hunter, you cover her. Watch that damn truck for surprises."

At the road, the lone Mercedes truck ground slowly nearer, its overworked seventies-vintage engine groaning and blowing blue smoke from a rusty exhaust. When the crushed coke can came into headlight range, the truck's brakes squealed loudly and it lurched to a stop. The diesel engine rattled noisily at idle and dust flurried in the headlight beams. The truck was ostensibly an old four-horse van, with a right-side folding ramp and high-mounted, small, darked-out windows along its sides and rear. The cab door on the far side creaked, then thunked shut, then into the headlight sphere walked a refined-looking, handsome man in his late thirties, surprisingly well-dressed in expensive trousers and loafers with a pressed, white-linen shirt worn with the squared tail out, Cuban style. He had dark hair combed back to a short ponytail and a trimmed mustache. He looked worried. He stopped by the can and picked it up. He examined it briefly, tapped it four times with his fist, then flipped it off the far side of the road.

Jen rose instantly and padded silently across the dust, her rifle shouldered and aimed dead at the man's back. She stopped six feet from the man, who now looked up at the dawning sky. *"¿Habla Ingles, señor?"*

The man spun around as though stuck with a cattle prod. His mouth opened and his eyes widened, then squinted as he struggled to comprehend a pair of lovely eyes seemingly emerging from within an almost clear gassy cloud before him. He had no difficulty making out the steel muzzle and titanium foresight of her rifle, however. He recovered with a nervous smile. *"Sí! Sí, seño-rita!"* he blurted with a heavy Russian accent. "Yes. I speak English. I—"

"Then hear this. You put a hand where I can't see it, and I'll kill you where you stand. *¿Comprende?"*

"Yes! Of course! I only—good *Christos,* what are you wearing? How—"

Jen closed fast, seized the man by his expensive shirt, and swung him about her to place him between her and the idling truck. She stuck the stubby muzzle of her rifle in his crotch and watched his eyes carefully while she patted him down. She groped him hard in the groin, slid a hand under his shirt and about his waist, then she stepped back. "No toys, no wires, boss."

"Cover him," Travis commanded. "Search the truck, guys. Move."

Jack, Stan, and Hunter sprang from the cane, rifles aimed. Hunter peered carefully into the cab. Jack drew

a bead on the side doors as Stan hurled them open.
There was nothing within but two rows of seats. Quickly
they scanned the truck for hidden radio transmitters, explosives, or other unwanted accessories.

"Clean," Stan said.

"Jen covers. The rest of you get back here for the
toy boxes."

The men disappeared into the cane. In a moment they
reemerged, Travis at the lead. As the pods were shoved
into the truck, Travis walked to Jen and the stranger.
"It's hot in Cuba this time of year," Travis said, staring
the man in the eye.

"Indeed," the sophisticated man replied with his half
of the code exchange, risking another nervous smile.
"The heat is both blessing and curse."

At this correct response, Travis released a smile of his
own and extended his hand. "Stealth off, people. Major
Travis Barrett, sir. A pleasure to meet you."

"Yuri Nobakov! Yuri, please, Major," Dr. Yurevitch
Nobakov, Russian chief of nuclear medicine at Juragua
said, visibly relieved as Travis's LOC suit materialized
into common camouflage fabric before his incredulous
eyes. "My word, you people are thorough. And those,
those . . . *outfits* you are wearing! Astonishing! No wonder we lost the cold war."

"Let's get out of here," Travis said over the BSH net.
"Sarah, you up front. Everybody else in the back. Jen,
break out the civvies. People, shuck the LOC suits and
pack 'em. Move."

Eagle Team disrobed in the roadway and passed their
suits to Jen who exchanged them for loose-fitting, unre-
markable, standard Cuban civilian wear. Standing un-
concerned in cotton panties and athletic bra, Sarah
tossed her rifle and BSH helmet to Jen, then shrugged
into a baggy, colorful blouse and skirt. Boots were hurriedly traded for appropriately worn-appearing running
shoes. Everyone but Sarah and Yuri scrambled into the
box body of the van.

Sarah entered the truck's passenger side as Dr. Nobakov climbed back behind the wheel. Sarah palmed her
polymer-frame Baretta 9mm pistol beneath the loose tail
of her blouse, its muzzle pointed at her chauffeur.

Yuri Nobakov ground the old truck through its gears.

In the rear of the truck, after all the LOC suits were stowed, Jen and all the men but Sam busied themselves watching through darkly tinted high windows in the old horse van's sides, bracing themselves against its rocking. Sam broke open the commo pod and set up a satellite link for Jen to receive an intel update. The interior of the truck still bore a faint odor of manure, but was otherwise clean.

Up front, as the van swayed and lurched over the dirt cane field road, Yuri extended his right hand to Sarah. "I am Dr. Yurevitch Nobakov, Dr. Greene! Call me Yuri, please."

Sarah stared with surprise at the man's engaging smile of straight white teeth. Robert Redford, your replacement has arrived, she thought. Sarah shook Yuri's hand but only awkwardly, with her own left hand, keeping it above her potential line of fire. "How do you know my—"

"Dr. Greene, I am Russian nuclear physician. I am chief Russian medical officer at Juragua nuclear facility. I have read all your unclassified papers on Ebola Zaire, and some of your classified papers on anthrax as artillery-deliverable payload. I feel as though I already know you."

Nobakov's innate charm and warmth made Sarah uneasy. Chief medical officer for the Juragua hot plant. That explained a lot.

"That's interesting," Sarah answered, cursing herself for sounding so lame.

The truck rumbled out of the cane field and onto a poorly maintained public highway. Tall grass grew right up to its ragged edges. Its center stripe was so worn as to be barely evident, and it was spotted with a leprosy of asphalt patches. The road was just one of endless indications of the breakdown of the Cuban infrastructure that had commenced upon the cessation of Soviet foreign-aid billions when Cuba's adoptive big brother went broke. Communism in Cuba, as everywhere else, couldn't pay its bills. As the old horse transport van gained speed, the wind whipping through the cab relieved some of the sticky heat that was growing with the rising sun.

Sarah watched Cuba materialize as the sun rose. Open trucks of Cuban sugar field workers rolled by, the already tired-looking laborers holding onto their tattered straw hats. Big cane-transport semis lumbered past, spewing black diesel fumes. There were few cars, and they were almost all '50s-vintage American models, with the occasional Yugo or sputtering Russian Lada.

Bracing against the rock and sway of the truck in the rear, Jack stooped and peered out a small side window. "Lots of brothers and sisters down here," he grumbled.

"Cuba was a Spanish slave state before Alabama ever existed, big dude," Sam said, standing on tiptoes to see out the same window.

"Jesus," Stan observed, also gazing out at the passing scene. "Looks like a goddamn antique car show."

Jen smiled. "Down here, they get along on the cars that were here when Batista fell in fifty-nine and Castro took the country communist. The U.S. slapped an embargo on them then that's still in effect. They have a few newer, cheap European or Japanese cars, and the rich have some nice wheels, but the working guys gets by in his fifty-eight Impala. If he has a car at all."

The van passed some small, dirty, tile-roofed, adobe or clapboard homes near the highway, though on distant, lushly green rises in the plain were what looked to be an occasional palatial Spanish villa. As they left the oceans of cane fields and drew closer to Cienfuegos they passed rows of dreary apartment hives with drying laundry fluttering from lines in the windows or on tiny, shelflike balconies. Starved dogs roamed the roadside. Decaying auto bodies nested in clumps of tall grass. The businesses Sarah saw all looked shabby, hanging on month to month by a fraying fiscal thread. Everything she saw looked secondhand, rundown, like a movie filmed in 1950s black and white. Sarah did manage a smile for a group of joyful, waving children who pumped their arms at Yuri to blow the truck horn. He did, and they squealed with delight.

"I had wife," Yuri said oddly, as they passed the children. "She was also physician who worked with me at Juragua construction site from ninety to ninety-two."

Sarah looked at Yuri. His expression was an alarming mixture of pain and hate. She looked away, feeling a little guilty at the pistol she still held out of sight.

"When Rodina collapsed, there was much bitterness in Cuba. We were seen as abandoning little communist cousin to the great American ravager. Those of us who left when construction of the Juragua reactors was suspended were most hated as we were living symbols of Soviet 'betrayal.' Annatava was wife's name. She was pregnant when Castro's . . . pocket *nazis* interrogated, beat, then raped her. Six of them, including a *colonel* of *policia.*"

Sarah's gaze whipped back to Yuri. He drove on, staring straight ahead, a tear trickling down one cheek. "Annatava miscarried . . . a uterine infection from . . . *leather riding crop* the colonel . . . stuck into her. The same one with which he whipped his *horses*! There were not enough strong antibiotics needed to stop infection in time. She . . . miscarried at twenty-two weeks. She was very . . . emotionally traumatized. She never overcame it. Home, in Russia, I sought therapy for her, but whole country had fallen apart. Were few social services, private psychiatric hospitals were only for very rich. No one in working class had more than few rubles worth nothing. Annatava could not manage depression. In August of ninety-six, I found her naked in bathtub, in pool of own blood."

Sarah felt her jaw muscles flex.

Yuri looked quickly, fiercely, at Sarah, then back at the road, at Sarah again, back at the road and the thickening city traffic.

"So!" Yuri almost shouted, "I know you wonder . . . you wonder, why does this man, this Russian, physician, spy for the United States of America? Why does he work for CIA? Because I *hate* communists! I *hate* the communist state! For, even more than capitalism, communism does the very thing it claims to deplore about capitalism, it concentrates wealth in the ruling elite and leaves worker to scarcely subsist. Communism is merely dressed-up slavery."

Yuri seemed to realize he was unseemly. He sniffed, tightened his face, and concentrated on his driving. By now they were in the outskirts of Cienfuegos, weaving among heavy pedestrian traffic, bicyclists, and scooters. The air pollution was palpable. Palm-shrouded, stucco huts crowded to the edges of narrow streets. There were many people, mostly Negroid, walking, but few cars. And fewer trucks.

"I despise the Cubans," Yuri continued more calmly, "for what they did to Annatava. But my own countrymen are worse. We have become nuclear whores, Dr. Greene! We sell substandard nuclear technology to highest bidder with no concern for long-term nightmare we are creating worldwide. Nuclear weapons, plutonium. Bargain price—how you say—*flea market* nuclear reactors! The reactors at Juragua sat idle during the suspension of construction from ninety-two to ninety-seven, five *years* in salt-sea atmosphere! The site itself is seismic fault active as recently as late eighteen hundreds. It is madness, Dr. Greene! Nuclear insanity! We know blown reactor is like hundred nuclear bombs in downwind radiation death. But Russians so desperate for hard currency we sell this terrible technology to criminals and madmen."

Sarah studied Yuri. "Don't feel too guilty, Dr. Nobakov. Yuri. Russia isn't the only country peddling nuclear lunacy."

Yuri looked again at Sarah. This time an engagingly warm smile seemed to signal a temporary relief from the anger he obviously felt.

The groaning old horse van and its clandestine cargo passed through the poorer suburbs of Cienfuegos and moved onto a high plain where the houses became nicer and the lots slightly larger. Mowed lawns appeared by a few flower gardens. Then Yuri swung the truck into the short driveway of a three-story villa bordered by tall palms swaying in the salty sea breeze. The pleasant, Spanish-style home was recessed against a sandy slope; only the second and third floors rose above ground in the rear. A high electric garage door ahead of the truck hummed and rose. Yuri pulled the truck in, narrowly

clearing the overhead, and buzzed the door shut behind them.

Eagle Team instantly sprang from the old truck with
their short, high-capacity, oddly light, titanium XM-29
rifles, and moved to windows. Travis and Stan hurried
without preamble to the upper two floors. Ignoring the
well-appointed furnishings and the expensive Degas
works on the walls, they quickly studied the surrounding
terrain through windows, analyzing likely assault routes,
ascertaining the best defensive positions, and determin-
ing escape avenues. Jen hurried about, surveying the
premises for bugs and cameras with a handheld electronic scanner.

. Hurrying back to the basement, Travis and Stan
helped heave the toy boxes from the van. Stan opened
one and deployed a claymore mine to face the ground-
floor entry door. Yuri stared, somewhat overwhelmed.

"Hunter," Travis said easily. "You have the first
watch. There are two one-hundred-eighty-degree-plus
vantages in the bedrooms on the top floor. Sam, get the
intel updates sat-linked. Jen, find out what's happening
with General Krauss's people. We need fresh info on
the Swords of Allah bad. Where are they? How do they
plan to hit the reactors, and when? You know what we
need. Get it. Sarah, why don't you and Stan get three
hours sleep, in your LOC suits, with all helmet inputs
off except the GQ alarm. Keep your weapons in reach.
Do it."

The equipment pods were already being hauled up
the stairs.

"Major Barrett," Yuri said. "There is much good food
in my kitchen. Please indulge yourselves!"

"Thanks, Doc, but we brought our own."

Yuri was baffled.

Sarah walked by. "On ops, we consume freeze-dried
foods, Yuri. It helps ensure no one poisons us. No
offense."

"Dr. Nobakov," Travis began, "you—"

"Yuri, please, Major."

"Okay. No offense, sir, but you never leave our sight
unless I say. Clear?"

"Yes, of course."

"Yuri, I need you to turn this van around and back it in here. Leave the keys in the ignition all the time. Put the door down, but leave that door buzzer on the dash. How much gas in the truck?"

"It's nearly full, Major. I filled it before departing the city this morning."

"Excellent. What shape's the battery in?"

Yuri smiled. "Major Barrett, as you have no doubt observed, most every vehicle in Cuba is quite old. Down here, we take care of our cars and trucks."

"What about your neighbors?"

"This is a communist state, Major," Yuri answered bitterly. "Here, unless you are the Cuban police, you—how you say—'mind your own business.' My neighbors believe I am a powerful foreigner in the graces of Castro's hierarchy, an important figure in the operation of the Great Leader's pet project, the Juragua Nuclear Plant. My neighbors don't want to know any more about me, Major. They are terrified I might complain about them to the government."

Travis nodded and went up to assist Sam's setup of the sat-link equipment. Yuri went up to the second floor kitchen where he found Sarah filtering tap water through a titanium water purifier. She smiled at him. "What a lovely view, Yuri!" she exclaimed.

Yuri joined Sarah and looked out over shallow rolling hills to the great, lakelike Cienfuegos Harbor in the distance where scores of huge sugar freighters and other ships lay at anchor or secured to warehouse loading docks. Near the southern horizon, a thin, light blue line of Caribbean Sea could be seen. The air smelled like salt and rotting seaweed.

Yuri looked down on Sarah's smooth, clean, black hair. He could smell her heat. "We nuclear whores demand our luxuries, Dr. Greene."

"Call me Sarah, please. Clearly, Yuri, you're no nuclear whore."

"Sometimes I feel like I am, Sarah. I see where proliferation of nuclear technology is taking us. I do studies. I see safety shortcuts and failures. I treat irradiated workers. Nuclear power facilities, especially Russian bargain-brand types, are generating ultimate toxic wastes in deadly quantities, fuel rods and cooling water that will remain fatally radioactive for hundreds of thousands of years in some cases. One more Chernobyl-class accident could cause deaths that have to be measured in million-counts. Aaaah . . . You already know this, Dr.—Sarah.''

"Yes, I do."

"There is so little I can do. I must sit by while planet is poisoned, while they risk killing millions. The best I can do is treat the sick."

"And help us stop a horrible destruction at Juragua?"

"I certainly hope so, Sarah. The only thing worse than my country's nuclear pandering would be to allow terrorists to accelerate nuclear disaster. Can you people stop the Swords of Allah?"

After a pause and a sigh, Sarah answered. "We have to . . . somehow, Yuri." She looked up at Yuri's deep, green eyes. "The downwind fatality projection is five hundred thousand within thirty days. Twenty *million* in fifteen years! We *have* to stop them somehow."

Several seconds later, Yuri and Sarah were startled to find they'd been staring at each other. They awkwardly looked away.

From across the room, Travis watched them through squinted eyes.

0703 hours

Colonel Rafio Raimundo, commander of the Cuban Internal Security Cell, answerable only to Fidel Castro, was also squinting.

A tall, gaunt man with the eyes of a vulture, Raimundo's hard, pitiless face was tracked with two ugly scars, one sustained in a fencing match, and another he'd received as a thirteen-year-old revolutionary soldier repelling the Yankee invaders at the Bay of Pigs. He wore a crisp, coatless uniform like an old fashioned horse cavalryman, with tight, khaki riding pants, and polished, knee-high boots. He carried with him always a short, stiff riding crop of braided leather. It had become his trademark in interrogations.

Colonel Raimundo bent beneath whirling rotor blades and squinted against the swirling dust of the dirt cane field road. When he cleared the screaming, French-made, Aerospatiale Dauphin helicopter painted Cuban Army tan, he strode briskly to the Russian-made field car, the door to which was hurriedly held open for his entrance. The green, knobby-tired utility vehicle roared away.

Next to Raimundo in the back seat, the local state police commander sweated nervously and spoke. "We thought little of the incident, Colonel. Just an old man on a burro hallucinating, perhaps from the mescal. But when our officer reported what he found, I . . . I thought you should know."

"Reported? Reported what?" Raimundo demanded harshly.

"With respect, sir," the other policeman said, "perhaps it is best you see."

The driver suddenly turned off the narrow road and plunged down an even narrower avenue of flattened sugarcane. In a rough, bouncing moment, the vehicle lurched to a stop and the two officers stood out.

Before them was another, larger avenue of destroyed sugarcane. A path began in the distance with only the tops of the stalks cut, but it graduated as it drew nearer to a wide swath of cane cut off near the ground. At its end, the ground was blackened with what appeared to be a thin stain that had soaked into the soil. As they stepped about examining, a policeman called from a hundred meters away. They looked to see him waving. When they reached him in the field car, they found that he stood by a tall, rusty tower that had once borne a windmill propeller for pumping water to the fields. Another policeman was on the tower extracting from an intersection of angle-iron struts a torn, hand-sized, gray piece of . . . plastic? He tossed it down to his commander.

Colonel Raimundo and the state police commandante examined the odd, incredibly light scrap of some sort of fiberglass, perhaps. There was a thin layer of dust and cane anthers on the item.

Raimundo squinted at the tower, at the stain on the ground, then north, at the sky. *"Americanos!"* he hissed.

Chapter Four

Stan awoke and took command, while Sam, Jack, and
Hunter grabbed some Zs on the floor. Travis lay down
in Yuri's bedroom and was nearly instantly asleep.

An hour later, Yuri walked into the kitchen shaking
his head. "Bloody Cuban telephone systems," he muttered in his Russian accented English. Sarah elected not
to tell Yuri that Travis had ordered Sam to temporarily
disable the phone system in Yuri's home.

When it became Sarah's hour on watch, she ascended
to the third floor, hung gyro-stabilized binoculars about
her neck, and paced slowly between the two bedrooms
that presented panoramic views of the approaches to
Yuri's neighborhood. Yuri joined her.

"You have cut my phone lines, haven't you?" he
asked, with a slight smile. "Am I . . . free to come and
go, Sarah, or am I prisoner?" He didn't seem upset, just
amused and curious.

Sarah studied him as they moved to the balcony.
"Don't take offense, Yuri. Outside the team, we trust
no one, by operational policy. It isn't personal. We're
grateful for your help."

"Oh, no offense taken!" Yuri said, laughing lightly. "I
have been aware that someone has been watching me
constantly since we got here. I am only glad that I was
allowed to go alone into bathroom! Is very . . . professional, very wise of you. And regardless . . . if I am to
be prisoner, I can think of no one whom I would rather
have as captor." Yuri leaned slowly toward Sarah, who

was astonished to find herself unmotivated to draw back. He tilted his head, his eyes still on hers, and kissed her lightly on the lips. They parted, but Yuri's lips remained an inch from Sarah's. They stared at each other, both breathing at an elevated level.

"Hooooo!" Jen suddenly said from the doorway, with a grin. Both Yuri and Sarah jumped, embarrassed. "I sure hope the whole Cuban army didn't slip up the hill while that kiss was going on. My watch, kids. Sarah, you mind staying for a minute 'til I draw down the next briefing?" Jen nodded at the sat-link apparatus in the corner.

"Of course not," Sarah said softly, turning deliberately away from Yuri and raising the binoculars.

Yuri coughed nervously and walked for the door. "If you'll excuse me," he murmured to Jen.

Jen booted up the sat-link system while Sarah walked to the other bedroom and back. "Wow," Jen said wryly, "I know Travis said keep this guy quiet and contained, but you're sure going the extra mile!"

"Not funny!" Sarah snapped, chagrined. Then she softened. "I'm sorry, Jen. It was only for a second, but you're quite right; it was unforgiv—"

"Whoa, whoa, Sarah. We've been through too much together to be apologizing to each other. I've been on how many ops with you now? You don't need to defend your actions to me, sister woman. Say . . . how was he?"

Sarah smiled in spite of herself and resumed her lookout. "Pretty damn fine, since you ask."

Jen came off watch and went to wake Travis, but of course he was already awake. His internal alarm clock was legend on the team.

"Hey girl," Travis drawled. "Tell me you got us some kick-ass info on the Swords."

"I downlinked some kick-ass info on the Swords, boss."

"Hot damn."

"I'm ready to brief on your order. Say . . . Travis?"

"Uh-oh. I get worried when it starts off 'Travis.' " He smiled. "What's up?"

"You . . . ah . . . you know how, well, how lonely Sarah's been lately?"

"Hell, Jen, we're the loneliest seven folks on the goddamn planet."

"I mean since her shit-for-a-heart boyfriend left her because he couldn't hack her career."

"You're gonna tell me she's getting hung on the good doc, right?"

"Damn, Travis! You're no fun to gossip with. You noticed too? Sarah's a stone pro at what we do. We all know that. But . . . she's real vulnerable right now."

"Yeah. Thanks for the tip though, darling. I know Sarah's hurting these days, but she's a sharp troop. She'll handle it." Travis sighed and picked up his rifle. "Let's keep our eyes open anyhow."

Sarah picked out rehydrated beef stew, reinflated pound cake with malaria inoculin, and cups of orange flavored analax booster. The team, all in LOC suits with BSHs, retrieved their titanium trays and cups. Sam and Hunter went to the lookout stations. Yuri was asked to wait on the living room balcony, in view.

Everyone glanced up at their holographic BSH projectors while eating. Jen initiated her briefing, her amplified voice seeming a scant half-inch from each TALON's ear, though one could not have heard it standing three feet from her, absent the BSH system.

"General Krauss had been kicking ass and taking names all over the world intelligence community," Jen began. "He's made two calls to the president to have him shake up anybody who was slow giving up data we need. The prez threatened to cut Israel off at the pocketbook if Mossad didn't get with the effort. They did, pronto. Here's what we know to time, guys.

"Mossad knows the Swords are in-country Cuba. Their Cuba people say they're in a safe house in the Arab enclave of Havana. Unfortunately, they don't have a hard address yet, but they do have this."

A holographic image of a short, hollow-eyed, dark man with a mean face appeared on each trooper's retinas.

"Al-Sahd, you son-of-a-bitch," Stan said acidly. "You

shot at me from six hundred yards away in Riyahd and hit me in the ass. I owe you, you shithead, and I'm coming for you."

"That was a tribute to the LOC suit's autosuture feature if ever there was one," Sarah said. "Without ballistic armor to soak up most of the impact, and autosuture to close the wound, you'd have bled to death in thirty minutes."

Jen continued. "Madras Al-Sahd, the Indian-Arab fanatic thought to be the sniper for the Swords. Our—"

"'Thought,' my ass," Stan retorted. The team chuckled.

"Our boy Al-Sahd can drop a running man at six hundred yards in neutral winds with a scoped Draganov seven-point-six-two mm, but like all you studs, he's got a weakness for the ladies."

"That's it," Jack said. "Sexual harassment in the military. My lawyers'll be on your ripe, round, succulent ass in twenty-four hours, Olsen."

Jenny grinned, ignoring Jack and moving on. "Ol' Madras likes to tip a few and consort with the ladies of the evening."

"He's an alcoholic whoremonger," Stan simplified.

"Exactly," Jenny said. "He's been disciplined twice by the Swords for drinking and whoring on ops. So there's a damn good chance that if we find the Arab district brothel or watering hole, we'll find Madras Al-Sahd. Mossad's evidently got a good source in Cuba. He or she seems to have a good tag on the Swords. Still, they don't know when or how the Swords will hit Juragua. To say they're working on it is a masterpiece of understatement, trust me."

"Okay," Travis said on the BSH. "Havana is one hundred thirty-five miles from here, or about three hours by stone-age horse van. Airplanes are out 'cause even if we could steal one, the Cubans monitor air traffic too closely. Allowing time to outfit, we should get there by early evening, or about dark, which is good. We'll plan and brief en route. BSHs and LOC suits en route, in case we get into trouble, but Jen, we'll need Cuban civvies in Havana."

"Wait 'til you see the sexy outfit I got for you," Jen said to Travis.

"So what am I?" Jack grunted. "Chopped liver? What did you get me—some sugar picker's getup?"

"You don't *pick* sugar, bonehead," Sam laughed. "You harvest it."

"Heeeeeyyyy!" Hunter said suddenly, from his post on the third floor. Instantly everyone seized weapons and slid quickly to windows. "I got two marked cop cars coming this way! About twenty points east of north. Mile and a half."

Travis bounded up the stairs three at a time and slid in by Hunter by the east bedroom balcony. Hunter was studying the cops through the gyro-stabilized binoculars.

"Cienfuegos town clowns, boss. Looks like routine patrol, except there's two cars together."

"Good eyes, Hunter."

Travis and Hunter tracked the two patrol cars until one turned away from the other, and both moved in directions away from the hill on which Yuri's villa sat.

"Stand down, people," Travis said. "Looks harmless."

In an hour, a handsome young Russian physician drove an old horse van northwest toward Havana. Who could know it carried seven of the most advanced equipped, trained, and motivated shock troops in existence?

1515 hours, Policia Headquarters, Cienfuegos, Cuba

Colonel Raimundo didn't know yet, but he was trying damned hard to find out. He slammed his braided-leather riding crop down hard on the local police commander's desk. Into the phone he roared in Spanish: "I know goddamn well it's a long shot, General Torejos! But who else has the technology to make an entire airplane go up in vapors?"

A pause.

"No, I didn't *see* any airplane! I . . . No, of course I don't know how they could incinerate an entire airplane, General; if I did I'd be a fat, overpaid American scientist, not our Great Leader's most trusted internal policeman!"

This last remark must not have been lost on the general.

"So!" Raimundo snapped. "I want all the CADIZ radar records from sunset last night. Anything those Russian pigs will give us in the way of satellite reconnaissance in the greater Cienfuegos area. Now! *Muy pronto!*" He slammed the phone down.

2044 hours, Cienfuegos-Havana Highway, Cuba

The team attempted to rest in shifts on the long haul to Havana, but, as they were all recently rested, trying to sleep on the hardwood floor of a lightly loaded horse van traversing a Cuban maintained highway at a noisy 65 miles per hour was ludicrous.

Endless sugarcane fields dissolved into the descending darkness. In two hours, everyone was disgusted with the bouncy old truck. Travis conducted a briefing on the BSH net while Jack watched the rear through a window and Sarah watched through the front window into the cab where Yuri drove, fast, but not fast enough to get unwanted attention.

Travis spoke. "All right, guys, Jen says CIA's Cuban sources in Havana tell them there are brothels all over Havana, of course, but—"

"Havanaaa, Havanaaa," Hunter sang a lá Sinatra's *Chicago,* "it's myyyyy kind of townnnn!" Jen thumped Hunter hard on the shoulder. Hunter winced. Jen could do 300 straight-back push-ups.

"White boys can't jump," Jack groused. "White boys can't sing. What the hell are y'all good for?"

"Oh, I can tell you a few things about that," Jen said promptly. The team, including Sarah, snickered.

"But," Travis continued, "CIA feels Al-Sahd at his horniest would never stray far from his buddies and his Draganov on an op in a hostile foreign country. Whatever else can be said about him, he's a totally dedicated wet worker. So they think he's going to be in one of two shag shacks near the Arab enclave."

"Right," Jen picked up. "The Arabs are notoriously

hypocritical about sex; they'll frequent brothels, but in their Islamic piety they won't permit one in their zone, so General Krauss's people think Madras Al-Sahd will be in one of the two . . . dives . . . bordering the Arab enclave. A place called Fietra's, or one called Casa Del Sol Madrugada, otherwise known as—"

Travis was groaning. "Oh please, not 'House of the Rising Sun.' "

Jen smirked. "I knew you'd love that little touch of quaint local folklore."

Stan wasn't in a humorous mood. "Don't suppose we got any floor plans, or any inside recon on these flophouses. Security? Local cops or military? Little incidentals like that?"

"No," Jen answered. "Just addresses."

"Shoot the fuck in. Shoot the fuck out. There's your plan," Jack grumbled.

"Thank you, General DuBois!" Sam said, suppressing a laugh. "Now you're gonna tell us your favorite author, Sun Tzu, wrote that too."

"Sun Tzu never hit a Cuban cathouse, I bet," Hunter said.

"I don't want a shot fired," Travis said sternly, getting everyone back on the problem. "We go in or out shooting and we'll have the whole damn Cuban Defense Force, and everything with a badge and a gun, all over us. You want to go high-speed evading through Cuba in a twenty-four-year-old horse truck?"

"Good point, boss," Hunter said.

"We boys'll go in one at a time in civvies, armed only with concealed OHWS forty-fives with suppressors and subsonic ammo, and grenades taped to our ankles. If all shit breaks loose, that ought to get us back to the truck. Jack, you'll hang outside at the door and cover any entering gendarmes and our hasty retreat. You're too big and attention-getting to go in. Sarah, Jen, you girls will stand out even more than Jack, so you'll guard the truck and our gear, and watch the doc."

Jen said, "Damn. You guys get all the fun."

"What kind of *fun* would *you* want in a whorehouse?" Sam asked.

"Will we have time to get Chopsticks laid?" Jack asked pleasantly. "The lad's too old to be a virgin."

"Bend over and I'll virgin *you* up the old cosmic black hole, precious."

"Hoooooooo," everybody but Travis and Sam said in unison. Jack's Cadillac-bumper grin glowed. He held out his mammoth hand and Sam high-fived him. From long experience, Travis Barrett knew such banter went a long way toward relaxing tense nerves before an op.

"Okay," Travis went on when the laughter subsided. "Me and Hunter and Stan and Sam will go in. We've all seen Madras Al-Sahd's photo a hundred times, but none of us have seen him up close and personal."

"He saw Stan real personally," Sarah quipped, "through a scoped sight."

"Yeah," Stan said with an edge. "Gonna be the most expensive shot that fuck ever made."

"As far as we know," Travis continued, "nobody on the outside has any knowledge of TALON Force, let alone photos of us, but we can't be sure. We were in LOC suits with the face shields the day Al-Sahd shot Stan, so he doesn't know our faces, but let's keep a low profile, anyway. Circulate around, but nobody go out of sight without clearing with me. If the glue melts while we're on this op, we'll have to carry our asses in a hurry. If we find Al-Sahd, we'll try to isolate him and take him with us, if possible. If not, we try to interrogate him on-scene. Worse case is we can't interrogate him, or he doesn't talk, and we'll—"

Stan butted in. "Oh he's gonna talk."

"Have to run," Travis continued. "Just be sure somebody caps him. I don't want to be in his crosshairs at Juragua. Might get shot in the ass."

"If he's there," Stan said, "his search for trouble is over."

"Remember, people." Travis made eye contact with each TALON trooper. "The primary objective tonight is to get a location on the whole Swords cell. Killing Al-Sahd is the secondary. Stan?"

"I got you, boss. First he talks. Then he dies."

1704 hours, Policia Headquarters, Cienfuegos, Cuba

"Colonel Raimundo?"

"Sí, General Torejos. What do you have for me?"

"The CADIZ radar tapes do not show a single unaccounted-for target, Colonel. Nor, I regret to say, could the Russians be of help with their satellites."

"There's a shock," Raimundo said with undisguised sarcasm.

"They say there was no local cloud cover last night, and there were absolutely no aircraft over the western Cienfuegos Province cane fields in the time span specified."

"Russians could not find their own asses with both hands and a five-battery flashlight, General."

"Yes. Well. Be that as it may, Colonel, they did have some interesting information for you."

Raimundo sat up and grabbed a pen off the desk. "Yes?"

"Our Russian friends do at least one thing very well, Colonel. They intercept radio communications and break codes. They believe a certain Arab splinter group is now in Cuba." General Torejos pronounced his country's name as virtually all locals did—Cooba. "Some gang of Islamic thugs who call themselves the Swords of Allah. They—"

"The Swords of Allah are in Cuba?!" Raimundo exclaimed.

"Sí. Just another group—"

"No. No, General, I assure you the Swords are not 'just another group.' Where are they?"

"They are thought to be in Havana, Colonel." *Habahnha.*

"General, there are two-point-two million people in Havana! Where—"

"They do not know, Colonel!" The old general had had enough of the lower ranking Raimundo's insolence, Castro's confidant or not! "Perhaps," he added snidely, "they expect our chief of Internal Security to know where to find them!"

Raimundo choked down a raging urge to tell Torejos

his mother was a troop whore. "Did they say anything else, General? What is the objective of this Swords group?"

"This, too, they know not, Colonel. They had nothing more to offer. Neither . . . do I."

Raimundo slammed the phone down without another word.

What were the Swords of Allah doing in Havana? Were they after the Great One? Why? The Cubans were one with the Arabs in their hatred of *Norte-Americanos*. Castro had provided sanctuary and training for numerous Arab patriot cells over the decades. Why would they wish to kill him? What did this have to do with the mysterious goings-on in the Cienfuegos cane fields?

One thing Raimundo knew in his black heart. Americans hated the Swords of Allah for the Chicago day school bombing, the Washington subway ammonia attack, and the kidnapping and murder of the secretary of state. There was no way such a clear indication of American military infiltration as the cane field mystery could just coincidentally occur at the same time the Swords of Allah were touring Cuba for whatever reason.

If the Swords were in Havana, they could only be in the Arab section, otherwise the gang of heavily armed Middle-Eastern fanatics would raise alarm all over the city.

Raimundo's mouth smiled, if not his eyes. Yes. Find the Swords of Allah, who were almost certainly somewhere in Havana Arab Town, and Raimundo was willing to bet he'd find the Americans also!

"Start the helicopter!" Raimundo yelled, springing from his chair.

Chapter Five

The streets of Old Havana teemed just after sundown when the old horse van rolled through the narrow streets bordered by rundown, paint-peeling, Spanish colonial buildings. The team stood watching through the small, high windows.

Here, dark-skinned Cubans played cards and smoked. There, in an alley, a cockfight raged, feathers flew, men shouted angrily, and money changed hands. Two sultry, black beauties in pink and red spandex pants and halter tops strolled with great style along the cracked sidewalk. From some nearby establishment, a fast, vibrant Cuban brass band played and a woman sang in animated Spanish.

"Heeeeeyy, sistahs," Jack said to no one as he watched the girls in skintight, shiny attire undulate away, "y'all ever seen the inside of a real horse van?"

"Hotel Ambos Mundos," Hunter mused out loud. "That's where Hemingway lived."

"And drank," Sarah added.

"Cops!" Hunter said, from his lookout in the rear of the van. Everyone gripped their weapons. Travis stepped to the rear and looked.

"Single cop," Travis said. "He's not watching us and he isn't using his radio. There he goes." The police vehicle turned away, and the team loosened slightly.

"We are almost there!" Yuri called from the cab. "If this address and my map are correct, we are three blocks away from—"

"Pull up at the end of the block," Travis ordered,

scrambling forward and peering through the little cab window. "Over there, between those two buildings."

Yuri steered the truck into a paved, temporarily deserted parking area between two large commercial offices that appeared to be closed for the night.

Jen was already throwing colorful local clothing to the men, who were shrugging out of the silky, camouflage-patterned LOC suits.

"Turn the truck around, Yuri," Travis called. "Jen, you and Sarah stay in LOC suits in case you have to cut off anybody chasing us back here. Both these two joints are nearby. If we come from this Fietro's place, we'll be coming from over there." Travis pointed. "If we come from this Casa Del Sol Madrugada joint, we'll approach from there. Guys, leave your XM-twenty-nines; bring your forty-fives under your shirts. Two loaded extra mags in your pockets."

The OHWS was the new .45 caliber pistol specifically created for special operations forces. Manufactured by Heckler & Koch and Colt, the OHWS consisted of three components: a .45 caliber semi-automatic pistol, a laser aiming module (LAM), and a removable sound and flash supressor attached to the barrel. It held a seven-round clip and was effective up to fifty meters. With a 2.5-inch maximum extreme spread in a five-round shot group at twenty-five meters, the OHWS was not your father's .45.

Sarah pitched Hunter a roll of duct tape. He began taping grenades—one incendiary, one frag—to the inside of one ankle. He passed the tape on.

Stan rifled through his gear until he found a small medicine bottle of deep red liquid. This he dropped into his pocket.

Travis, Hunter, Sam, and Jack exited the van one at a time, at intervals, and proceeded separately down both sides of the street. Yuri nervously raised the hood of the old truck and pretended to be examining the engine. Jen and Sarah readied weaponry and then watched out both sides of the truck.

Sam was excited. He was scared witless, which he considered merely a sign of intelligence, but more, it was the vitality of Havana's nightlife. Music, both recorded and live, emanated from several sources as they walked the crowded streets, no one in Havana's multiracial, rainbow-colored populace paying them the slightest special heed. There were the smells of perfume, cooking meat, rum, and fine cigars in the air. Laughter spilled out from the restaurants and bars they passed. Most women were clearly not dressed for church. Several graced Jack and Hunter with alluring smiles as they passed.

A few very old Chevys and Fords and even Studebakers rolled by, but mostly people flowed along the crowded sidewalks, their arms draped about each other. Many carried bottles.

"Hoooo, momma," Jack said, looking at a passing woman dressed in a flowing yellow skirt and yellow-ruffled strapless halter, her hair wrapped in a turquoise headband. He glanced quickly back toward Travis who was on the other side of the street. If commands came now, they would be silent hand and head signals from the boss.

In two blocks, Travis stopped. At separate intervals, the other three also stopped, though all appeared to have done so without connection, and all appeared to be watching girls or looking into merchant's windows. Subtly, Travis inclined his head. When the other men looked unobtrusively, they saw, several doors down, a raucous sounding bar with a blue neon sign hanging crooked in one window that said: *El Circulo De Fietra.*

Fietra's was smoky and loud when Travis, Hunter, and Stan entered at different times. Sam entered last. Jack watched the street.

A long bar lined the wall to the left. High-backed booths lined the other three walls, encompassing a broad area containing a half-dozen busy pool tables and a small dance floor. The whole place quivered from the concussive bass of the sound system.

At two slightly elevated stages in corners, dancing girls writhed to the music. They could have been called strippers, except that they were already nude but for spike-heeled shoes.

Several men sat in the booths drinking with over-painted, tightly wrapped ladies who would never be confused with nuns. Some men and short-skirted girls played at the pool tables. In the rear of the room a single door draped with a beaded string curtain led away to the rear, where the real commodity of the establishment was traded in small rooms that smelled of sweat, perfume, and semen.

Outside, Jack leaned against a column fronting the neighboring building, where he would have both cover and a fire-pattern in three directions if needed. He appeared to be slightly drunk and leering at the passing girls, though he was actually alert for cops, soldiers, or other trouble.

The beefy, moustached, thick-armed doorman at Fietra's eyed Jack menacingly, but when Jack met his gaze, he looked quickly away.

Inside, Travis ordered a *Cuba Libre* and struck up a conversation in Spanish with one of the bartenders.

"Buenas noches, señor. Cuba Libre, por favor." When the bartender slid the drink to him, Travis handed him a highly coveted U.S. twenty dollar bill, which was six times what the drink cost and worth three times its U.S. value in Cuba. He waved off the bartender's offer to make change and produced another twenty, which got the small man's attention and an obsequious smile fast.

"I'm looking for my friend," Travis went on in Spanish. He sipped the drink laced with powerful, 151-proof Cuban rum. It was like drinking from the high-octane pump at a Texaco station. "Perhaps you have seen him tonight. He, ah, he favors the ladies." Hunter exchanged knowing smirks with the Cuban.

"Policia?" the bartender inquired with false pleasantness.

Travis looked offended and drew back the second twenty, which distressed the bartender visibly. "I look like some filthy *policia* pig?" Travis groused.

"No! No señor! It is just that, well, one never knows . . ."

Travis knew that in Cuba, especially in Havana, Castro's *policia con ganancia,* pocket police, made everyone paranoid.

"No, my friend," Travis continued in his well-accented Cuban-Spanish. "This man, he has, ah, how do I tell you, my friend? He has . . . left my sister with his child." Travis hung his head in shame.

"No!"

"Sí, amigo. She is only fifteen."

"Fifteen!" the man exclaimed, his whorehouse-bartender's sensibilities outraged. "Who is this son of a dog, señor?"

"Ah, my friend, he is an ugly man, but he has a . . . a charm with the young ladies, you know? We men, well, you know, my friend, we do what we must, but this man, he leaves my sister with no money, he discards her like a cigarette butt, you know?"

"Son of a dog!"

"He is a foreigner. He is about thirty-four, and—"

"Thirty-four!" the bartender retorted indignantly, as though his own boss didn't sell fifteen-year-old girls to men twice that age.

"Sí. And he is part Arab and part Indian. He—"

"Ah! Sí, sí!" The bartender lit up, feeling the second twenty already in his grasp. "Sí! I know this man! Ugly as the wart hog! Has a nose that hooks out and down, like this!" He curled his index finger and moved it to the tip of his nose.

"Sí!" Travis let the second twenty ease forward.

"This son of dog has been here, but no more!" The bartender gave a sweep of his hand, as though his establishment were much too good for the son of a dog foreigner. "He lets the rum rule him. He wishes to fight everyone. He wishes to beat the girls. Of course he is not the only one, but he does not know play from harm. He injures the girls and they cannot work, so we throw him out two weeks ago!"

"Ah."

"He says he is part of some terrible Arab gang, and he will come back and kill us all, but we have not seen him since."

"Do you know where he lives?"

"No, señor. But the word on the street is he favors Casa del Sol Madrugada."

"Ah."

The Cuban security policeman at the main gate of Internal Security's headquarters in Havana was nervous. The sleek, French-built helicopter had flown in from

Cienfuegos and landed nearly an hour before, and the
feared Colonel Raimundo had been in fierce briefings
with his officers ever since. Now the big, hard-faced,
grimly serious men were carrying their rifles to three
Mercedes sedans. Raimundo was waving his riding crop
and snarling commands, and the twelve select henchmen
with him, all veterans of the Cuban Army's Angolan
involvement, scurried with vigor. Raimundo was out for
blood. They'd seen him like this before, and it was a
very bad time to incur his wrath. Moreover, it was ru-
mored that some sort of American spies were in Old
Havana, in Arab Town, for God knew what reason!

The three heavily loaded Mercedes spun gravel and
disappeared toward the city. The guard snapped a text-
book salute as they roared past.

Casa del Sol Madrugada turned out to be a somewhat
more lavish affair than Fietra's had been. It was in a
nicer section of Old Havana, was a classier establishment, and clearly catered to a higher level of clientele.
The building had the appearance of a good supper club,
and the patrons the team observed moving in and out
were slightly better dressed than the Fietra crowd. There
were some expensive, newer Mercedes and Japanese lux-
ury cars parked outside, even a couple of smuggled-past-
the-embargo late-model Cadillacs. Two cars bore diplo-
mat license plates.

Travis and Hunter went in together. Sam and Stan
followed, each alone. Jack again hung back outside.

Inside, the decor was also superior to Fietra's. There
were two separate bars, the requisite pool tables, many
smaller cocktail tables, and a small stage to one side on
which a five-piece band played. A runway extended from
the other side of the room, upon which three dancers
stripped their way down to nothing but a smile. A few
patrons, virtually all Cuban or European business types
by appearance, danced with the working girls who themselves were a cut above Fietra's stable.

Immediately on their entry, Hunter and Travis were
approached by two stunning young Cuban lovelies in
tight, short cocktail dresses. They smiled and took the

mens' arms as though they were old and revered customers.

Mmm, Travis thought, looking around casually. This place has some sound leadership.

Stan pulled sweet perfume into the core of his soul, curled an arm about his hostess, and furiously tried to figure some way to work in a quick fire-fuck, even if he had to take it standing with her in a men's room stall. Grimly, he realized there was no way, José. Not tonight. Besides, as tasty as a quickie seemed right now, he was still much more motivated to find the camel-kissing back-sniping slimeball who'd shot him in the ass in Riyahd three years earlier. There were dues owed, and Stan Powczuk had come to collect. Pussy could wait. For now.

Sam was also instantly captured by a smooth and polished hostess with a diving neckline that flustered Sam and had him stammering for words and adjusting his glasses. She smiled, leaned close to him, and drew him to a nearby table.

All four men had no sooner hit their chairs than waitresses appeared, inquiring as to what they wished to drink and would they care to buy the young señoritas drinks as well? They would, of course.

Hunter and Travis pretended to be American tourists who'd bypassed the embargo by flying first to Mexico. Such tourists were welcomed by the Cuban economy for their dollars. Both men pretended not to understand Spanish, though Travis was fluent. The girls all spoke English, for no one wanted to miss out on a *Norte Americano* big spender.

"Aaaah! Americans!" one girl gushed to Hunter in English. "We *lof* Americans!"

To her companion, and still smiling, the girl said quickly, *"Estos Yanqui son bastardos arrogantes . . ."* Hunter and Travis smiled and nodded as though the insult in Spanish was a compliment to them.

"Sí!" The other girl said, leaning on Travis and giving him a close view of her cleavage. "We lof Americans!"

Stan lost no time establishing a bawdy rapport with his escort. Soon she was letting her hand rest on his thigh near his hardening plunger. Damn, Stan thought.

Maybe just for, like ten min—no, no. Travis would kick my ass all the way back to the states.

At Sam's table, the girl breathed into his ear before whispering: "Would you like to give me a bath? You would have to rub soap all . . . over me . . . like, *every*where."

Sam thought he would blow a fuse if something didn't happen soon.

It happened about twenty-five minutes later. The two girls with Hunter and Travis were trying to move the discussion to whether the men would prefer a hot tub, a massage, or a nude workout in the gym.

On an unobtrusive, routine scan, Travis caught Stan staring as though he were trying to weld something with his eyes. He was.

Madras Al-Sahd stood near the entryway looking meanly down his long, hooked nose. He surveyed the room as though he despised everyone and everything in it. He wore faded jeans, expensive leather loafers with no socks, a silk T-shirt, and a tan linen sport coat. His hair was a curly black rat's nest, and he bore a full, trimmed beard. His most striking feature was the superior disdain that seemed permanently molded to his face.

Suddenly the young woman with Travis looked up at the entry and stared with contempt of her own. In Spanish she muttered quickly to her fellow working girl. "Aiiee! It is him again. The Arab pig. The rough one. Thank God we are not up."

"Sí," the other girl said guardedly.

"What?" Hunter asked pleasantly, but watching Al-Sahd from the corner of his eye.

"Oh no-thing, babee. Jus' is someone we know, baht . . . we don' like heem ver' much. He ees a ver' mean man."

Sam turned to look. Jesus Christ, it's him! he thought. It's the guy! It's Madras Al-Sahd in the flesh!

Hunter recognized their target and thought, Bingo.

Travis noticed a tiny little point in the fabric of his jacket about four inches up from his waist. Big automatic nine-mil, probably a Baretta, he thought, tucked in the small of his back.

Stan grinned to himself. Hellllooooo baaaaby. Shot anybody in the ass, lately?

A man appearing to be a manager approached Al-Sahd and evidently lectured him on behavior, for there was much shaking of heads and cold staring between the two men. Finally Al-Sahd nodded grudgingly, whereupon the manager walked away with an expression of disgust. He eyed one of the idle girls by the bar and snapped his head at Al-Sahd. The girl rolled her eyes and got off her barstool. Al-Sahd walked to the girl, surveyed her up and down slowly, then nodded with a smirk, like she would do nicely. He took the girl by her waist and yanked her just slightly as they walked toward a hall leading to the rear from the main lounge. They disappeared.

Travis saw Stan was watching him. He cut his eyes toward the back.

Stan said, "Okay, baby. You talked me into it. Let's you and me take a little trip down the ol' back hall there."

The girl with Stan forced a smile and rose quickly. The hairy, barrel-chested American would probably pay premium, but there was something scary about him she couldn't quite define, and it worried her.

The hallway amounted to a long, carpeted motel corridor lined with rooms on both sides. Stan and his escort entered the hall just in time for Stan to see what room Madras Al-Sahd and his hostess disappeared into. Second from the end, on the left. As Stan and his girl proceeded down the hall, she produced a key to one of the rooms from her small purse, and Stan surveyed the hall for security cameras. None.

As they reached the room his girl intended to use, Stan looked both ways. No one else in sight. He clapped one hand over the girl's mouth and gripped her head tightly to his chest. He briskly carried her to Al-Sahd's door dangling by her head. Though she was totally panicked and she thrashed and flailed frantically, it was like her head was locked in a train coupling.

Stan turned the unlocked door knob.

"What?" the girl inside suddenly asked in Spanish, as she wasn't expecting company. Stan could hear fast thumping and he knew Al-Sahd must be trying to reach his weapon. Stan drew his H&K .45 with its bulbous suppressor from beneath his shirt and shouldered the door. It flew back. Naked and hairy, Al-Sahd was diving for his pants and the Beretta automatic pistol laying on them. The suppressor-equipped .45 emitted a concussive *PWEETchik!* noise as the silenced round fired and the pistol's metal slide cycled. The hollow-point slug hit Madras Al-Sahd smack in his left buttock. He grunted sharply, but he was not a world-class terrorist for nothing. He paused only a split second when the bullet hit, then desperately tried to claw his way to his weapon. As he reached for it, Stan's .45 spat viciously again—*PWEETchik!*—and Al-Sahd's gun hand was suddenly missing the forefinger and ring finger, little jets of blood shooting from where the knuckles once were. Al-Sahd curled into a ball, more concerned with his shattered hand than with the rhythmically squirting wound in his butt. He gaped in shock and fury at Stan.

Al-Sahd's girl was also nude. She was paralyzed with fear on the bed, unable to breathe, let alone scream. Stan hurled his own girl to the bed beside her. He stabbed the weapon at them.

"No, no, no, no!" one pleaded, waving her hands before her face.

"Shut up! You keep quiet, you live. You make a fucking sound and you're dead. *¿Comprende?*"

"*Sí! Sí!*"

A voice came from the hall. "Stan!"

Covering Al-Sahd, Stan backed to the door and opened it. Travis spilled in, holding his equally terrified girl by her head and mouth as well. He flung her near the others, withdrew a quarter-sized roll of duct tape from his pocket, and began to tape the girls' mouths and wrists. With the women secured, he turned to Stan.

"Has he—"

"Not yet. But he will."

"Better get busy, Stan. Looks like you got an artery with that butt shot. He doesn't have long."

Stan said to Al-Sahd: "We know you graduated from

college in England, hot stuff, so don't even try the no-speakee-Englee routine. The butt shot's payback, Al-Sahd. I'm the son of a bitch you popped in the ass three years ago in Riyahd, remember?"

Al-Sahd stammered, "A-American?"

"Hardcore. Now I'm gonna level with you. You gonna bleed out in about twenty minutes, be deader than Bill Clinton's credibility. But before you go you're gonna tell us where your little buddies are holed up. Sound off, boy. Give me an address."

Al-Sahd stared, baffled, the few seconds it took for him to comprehend this sudden and horrifying turn of events. But then the old hate, the trademark contempt, crept back into place.

"Go to your Christian hell, American pig!" Al-Sahd croaked, breathing heavily, clutching his destroyed hand with his remaining good one. "I will meet you there and finish this! Who do you think you are talking to? I am Madras Al-Sahd! Of the house of Mammir Muhammed Al-Sahd! I have killed *hundreds* of you infidels! I have shot your children for target practice! I have raped your women for amusement! I have blown up your holy sites! Shoot me again! Cut me! Castrate me! I am a Sword of Allah! I will tell you nothing! *Nothing!*"

Stan produced the small medicine bottle of red liquid from his pocket. "Let's cut the fucking hero shit, dick-head. What we have here is five ounces of the blood of a purebred Yorkshire sow. Pig-blood, Sword boy. Swine. How you gonna explain showin' up at Allah's front door with a mouth full of pig blood? Hmmm?"

Al-Sahd's fierce hatred faded almost instantly, replaced by the only kind of terror such a man, and a devout Muslim to boot, could know.

Travis alternated his attention from the women to Al-Sahd. He knew that Hunter had secured his woman in a nearby room and was watching the hall. Sam was in the safety in the lounge. Jack, outside, was the sentry.

"Sw-swine?" Al-Sahd said, sickly.

"You got it, tough guy. Blood of the ugliest, fattest, dirtiest old sow in Pennsylvania. You got two seconds to give me the address of your chummys, or you're gonna meet Allah choking on pig blood. I hear Allah don't allow no porky dudes in Muslim heaven. That so?"

Al-Sahd stared in horror at the vile object in the American's hand. It was his worst nightmare. It was the ruination of a life of serving Allah. He would be unclean, damned for all eternity.

"Infidel!" Al-Sahd charged, grimacing from the growing pain of his wounds. "How . . . how do I know you will not . . . defile me if I . . . tell you what you wish?"

"Look Al-Sahd, I'm a pro at what I do, just like you are. This is business, it isn't personal anymore, now that we've swapped butt shots. I don't hate you. I know you're a servant of the faith, and you do what you think Allah wants you to do. That's between you and Allah. I just want an address. I give you my word as a fellow warrior that if you tell me the truth, I will allow you to pass to the hereafter clean and whole. You don't tell me—right now—or I even think you're lyin', and I pour the blood of the pig down your throat while you're still alive, and then I swear I'll take a shit in your face. Time's a wastin', son. Speak up."

Al-Sahd clenched with his increasing pain and grunted. "You are an *evil* man!"

"Thanks, asshole, that's a helluva compliment coming from you. You aren't saying what I want to hear, my friend. And time is running out. Ticktock, ticktock."

Stan removed the top from the medicine bottle and held the contents near Al-Sahd's face.

"Wanna smell?"

Despite the loss of blood, and with shock now setting in, Al-Sahd recoiled as though the substance were acid.

"My brothers and sisters will kill you regardless!" Al-Sahd whispered, heaving. "The sooner you meet them the sooner they will kill you. Go to them, infidels! Eight-one-seven Avenue of the Flowers. Second floor. Go to them. Go to them now and die. But keep your word!"

Stan studied Al-Sahd briefly, before considering the depth of Al-Sahd's faith and deciding he'd been told the truth. He saluted Al-Sahd slowly with his left hand, rose, and walked to the bathroom. There he poured the blood down the sink in Al-Sahd's view.

"You got balls, son. And you were a hell of a shot. Too bad your head's been fucked up from childhood by all that Muslim-fanatic bullshit, or you'd've made a good soldier. I keep my word. So long, Stick. Hope you make it to where you want to go."

The terrified women on the bed flinched and squeaked through their noses when Stan shot Madras Al-Sahd through the mouth, blowing his brain stem onto the carpet and killing him instantly.

PWEETchik!

Chapter Six

Avenida de las Floras was on Yuri's Havana tourist map, high in the Arab enclave of the old city. Yuri nervously snaked the old truck through the streets. Jen watched him, and Sam looked out to the rear. All wore BSHs with the one-way face shields down. Everyone battle checked the LOC suit trauma-react systems and tested each other's light-pattern regeneration.

Sam watched as Jack activated the power to his LOC suit. In a matter of about six seconds, Jack's mass dissolved into a slightly wobbly but otherwise invisible shimmer as his LOC suit sensors absorbed the surrounding light patterns and caused the suit's fibre-optic fabric to regenerate nearly identical patterns on the opposite sides of the suit. Even in daylight, visual target signatures were reduced to virtually nothing. At night, the LOC suit rendered its wearer effectively invisible to all but the infrared observation capability of the BSH face shields. The TALONs could see each other, but were virtually invisible to unaided eyes.

"Check!" Sam said.

Jack powered down his LOC suit. Sam heard that pop/crackle you hear when you turn a TV off, and slowly Jack's hulking mass reappeared, clothed in silky camouflage, his face covered by the one-way cammo face shield.

"Listen up, people," Travis said over the BSH net. "Let's get in, get 'em, and get out, pronto. Somebody'll be finding the girls at the cathouse and Al-Sahd's body any time. It'll take cops ten minutes to get there at least, another ten or fifteen for them to get those women calmed down and interrogated. They won't learn much. Just three white guys with guns who waxed an Arab. Worst case is the girls might remember the address. It'll take another fifteen minutes or so for them to get to Avenida de las Floras."

"You left witnesses alive?" Jen asked sourly.

Travis wasn't in the habit of explaining his actions to subordinates, nor were they in the habit of questioning them, but he knew Jen's question was a fair one, under the circumstances. "The Havana cops aren't gonna be all that motivated over an Arab gettin' smacked in a whorehouse by foreigners, Jen, especially as he was despised by the locals. But we murder three helpless Cuban girls—whores or otherwise—and they'll tear this town apart, in force, looking for us."

Still watching forward through the cab, Jen snapped a quick nod. Suddenly she jumped.

"Cops! Three fucking carloads of 'em just went by! Uniformed guys with rifles in three, black, unmarked Mercedes!"

"I see 'em, I see 'em!" Sam said watching the cars disappear behind them. "They're still going away."

Colonel Raimundo grasped the hang strap as his driver slowed and swerved to miss some bulky old horse truck coming the other way on the narrow street.

"Pronto!" Raimundo snarled, cracking his cell phone into its cradle and waving his leather riding crop ahead. "Make haste, damn you! Havana *Policia* headquarters says some Americans just killed a man at Casa del Sol Madrugada! Rapido! Move, move, move!" The three heavily laden Mercedes sat low on their springs as they rocketed along the streets of Old Havana.

Sarah wanted to object to being left with Yuri to guard the truck, but she knew better than to whine, let alone on a critical op. Grim-faced, she busied herself checking the LOC suits and gear of the other TALONs for visible problems.

Travis knew Sarah well, though. "We don't need our doctor shot, darling," he said as he brushed by her.

Sarah and Yuri watched the remainder of the team disappear around the deserted office of a defunct shipping broker onto Avenida de las Floras, in Havana's Arab Town. She glanced around. Fortunately, at nearly midnight, there was no activity in the sleepy residential neighborhood of two- and three-story tile-roofed homes and businesses. Yet.

A lone dog barked from where the team had headed.

"Where're you going?" Sarah hissed at Yuri, who was plainly terrified, but bearing it well.

"Lenin's bloody ghost, Sarah!" Yuri answered in exasperation as he stepped around the corner of an alleyway. "May I *please* urinate in *privacy* for two seconds?"

"Of course." Sarah smiled. "Sorry."

Sarah busied herself, checking the condition of the old truck. Parked nose out. Leaking no fluids. Tires good. Keys in the ignition. Ready to go in a hurry. As much of a hurry as a twenty-four-year-old horse van can go in, she mused grimly. She jumped inside to confirm that the equipment cases were open and the special weapons were loaded, primed, and readily available.

Jen marveled at how lightly all 250 pounds of Black Jack DuBois moved in the tight confines of the old stucco apartment building. Up the cut-back stairs to the second floor. Pause and look.

"One door, end of the hall," Jen whispered into her BSH mic from the top of the stairway, peering down the hall over Jack, who knelt, his rifle trained on the door. The LOC suits were powered up, but the team could still see each other through the night-vision/infrared-capable face shields.

"Hold," Travis answered while he, Sam, Hunter, and Stan crept up the stairs. When the team made the landing, Travis spoke calmly. "Stan gives 'em an NLG dose at the door just before Jack goes through as entry man. Jen, Stan, and Hunter cover entry and do room sweeps. I watch the door, Sam watches the approaches. If it turns to shit, Sam and me are the reserve element. Let's stay sharp here, people. We all know these Swords assholes.

They're bad boys and girls and they ain't afraid to die. So let's let them do all the dyin'. Any questions? No? Let's do it."

Colonel Raimundo hurried by the uniformed Havana policemen standing by their old marked Plymouths with slowly rotating red lights. The tall, bony Raimundo hopped up the steps and entered the fancy brothel, his executive officer in hot pursuit. Inside, the music and gaiety had disappeared along with the customers when the body had been found, leaving only two scowling bouncers, a sober-faced proprietor, and several frightened working girls huddled about the bar. Raimundo shoved past them and strode down the hall to where the other policemen stood. They made way for the notorious commander of the Great One's Internal Security Cell, wondering what interest he could have in a whorehouse shooting.

Inside the room there was an unpleasant smell of perfume, blood, and the feces of the late Madras Al-Sahd. Al-Sahd's naked and devastated body lay in a pool of blood near his clothes. A plainclothes Havana police officer held Al-Sahd's pistol with a ballpoint pen inserted behind the trigger. Raimundo's nose wrinkled at the scene.

On the other side of the room, upon a rumpled bed, sat three young, attractive prostitutes, one wrapped in a sheet, shivering and crying, being comforted by the other two. Balls of gray duct tape lay wadded on the turquoise shag carpet.

"Who is he?" Raimundo snapped in Spanish at the Havana cop.

"No one knows," the tired old Cuban homicide detective sighed. "Some Middle Easterner with a yen for beating up the girls. He carries no identification, but he carries this." The policeman held up the black Baretta. "The serial numbers have been ground off, of course. You may wish to examine the deceased's fingertips, Colonel Raimundo."

Raimundo knelt and lifted Al-Sahd's intact hand to note with surprise that the fingertips were absolutely smooth where there would normally have been the curls, whorls, and lines of fingerprints. He dropped the hand.

"Acid scouring," the old cop said. "I have seen it once before, but only on an American mafia killer."

Or international-level career terrorists, Raimundo thought silently. This pile of Arab shit had to be one of the Swords of Allah.

Raimundo whirled on the three women seated at the bed. His furious, vulture's gaze wilted them. The girl in the sheet began to weep again.

"How do you know the men who did this were Americans?" he demanded.

The girl in the sheet sobbed uncontrollably. One of the dressed girls answered. "They said they were American *tourista, señor*. And they sounded *Norte Americano* like my cousin's husband in Miami!"

"What did they say? *Answer* me, girl!"

"That they would kill us if we—"

"Never mind that! How many were there?"

"*Dos, señor!*"

"Where are they, now? Where were they going? Speak up!"

"We do not know, señor! We only—"

"Think, *puta*!" Raimundo raised his crop. The girls cowered and drew back. "They must have said something!"

"Avenida de las Floras!" the weeping girl in the sheet cried. "They asked this . . . man where his *compadres* were, and he told them . . . somewhere on the Avenida de las Floras! I do not remember where, I swear it!"

Raimundo and his executive officer stormed from the room.

Stan crept down the hall carrying a cammo-colored canister about the size of a large hatbox. The team covered from the staircase. Stan set the Non-Lethal Generator before the door, inserted a flat, three-inch-wide wiring band beneath the edge of the door, and turned to the team. Travis nodded. Stan uncovered a safety-covered switch and flipped it briefly. There was an audible hum like standing too close to a power transformer.

Anyone inside would have suffered a nauseating micro-
wave scrambling of their bodily fluids.

Travis slapped Jack on the shoulder. The big marine
traversed the length of the hall in four strides, followed
by Hunter, Jen, and Travis on the run. Jack hurled himself into the apartment door, which blew back in splinters. Jack rolled to the floor and immediately aimed his
XM-29 at his assigned pie wedge of the first room. Jen
leaped through the door and covered her sector. Hunter
was a half-second behind. "One, clear!" he said over the
BSH net, suppressing his surprise.

The living room was empty, as was the kitchen, separated only by a breakfast bar. There was a strong odor
of warm food. Stan barreled past, rifle shouldered, from
the hallway to the bedrooms. The others moved quickly
to covering positions.

Stan peered around the door to the bathroom as Jen
scrambled past him. "Two, clear," Stan said, puzzled.

"Three, clear!" Jen spat angrily from the first bedroom door. "Damn!" Hunter and Jack bumped roughly
by her to the other bedrooms.

Hunter shouted, "Four, clear, boss!"

Jack yelled, "Fuck! Five, clear! The fuckin' place is
empty!"

Travis spoke calmly. "The place is empty, Sam, Sarah.
But there's fresh cooked food still cooking on the stove.
Heads up out there; we've been made!"

Stan crashed back into the room. He pressed a button
on his right sleeve and began aiming the High Energy
Radio Frequency generator on his wrist about the room.
Travis and Jen searched through the contents of the
room, quickly rifling papers, clothing, cardboard boxes,
and cupboards. Hunter and Jack covered the hall, observing at least ten bedrolls spread on the bedroom
floors. Prayer mats lay rolled in a corner.

Jen ripped open a box containing smaller boxes of
nine-millimeter parabelum ammunition. "Hellllo!" she
said.

The wristband HERF gun Stan was scanning with
emitted a squeal when aimed at the soiled old sofa in
the living room. He leaped to it, slid his hand gingerly

beneath the cushions feeling for trip wires, then snatched the cushions away.

Stan grunted as though struck in the stomach. In a hollow beneath the cushion was the bottom half of a small, cheap, blue-plastic toolbox. In it was a baseball-sized lump of gray clay from which protruded a probe connected by a red wire to a six-volt lantern battery and an old-fashioned wind-up alarm clock.

Ticking.

Rafio Raimundo, now driving the lead Mercedes, led the other two German sedans down Avenida de las Floras, which was many blocks longer than Raimundo had remembered, he was irked to note. Without a building number, any search for American or Arab terrorists could be a dicey, all-night affair.

In the passenger seat next to Raimundo, Major Arejo Nuñez snapped a thirty-round curved magazine of ammunition into his AK-74 assault rifle. "How many invaders are we dealing with, sir?"

Raimundo looked carefully at both sides of the dark street as the cars rolled slowly along. "We know there are at least two Americans, Major. Probably they employed at least one lookout. Figure there are as many as five. As to these . . . Arabs . . . there are probably at least as many." Raimundo glanced at an old horse van backed into the empty courtyard of an apparently abandoned shipping brokerage firm.

Ten, Major Nuñez pondered. Against our thirteen. Twelve Cuban Army combat veterans, all handpicked for their size, combat skills, and ruthlessness. And one colonel who had fought with the Russians in Afghanistan, against the tribes in Angola, and against the abundant domestic enemies of Castro. A man who'd personally murdered countless political prisoners and had ordered the executions of many more. A man whose revered father had been killed by American-backed insurgents at the great victory of the Bay of Pigs, where Raimundo, as a thirteen-year-old soldier of the Revolution, was himself terribly injured attempting to save his wounded father. Thus, Nuñez knew, was born the legend of Colonel Rafio Raimundo, who hated Americans more than the arrogant Russians, more even than death. Yes, Major Nuñez thought, glancing at his gaunt-faced commander whose bulging, buzzard's eyes still scanned the dark night. We will surely prevail.

Mmmm, Raimundo suddenly thought. Two similar horse transport trucks, in Old Havana, twice, in this same late hour?

The brake lights on the lead Mercedes brightened.

Damn! Sarah thought, seeing the brake lights of the three black Mercedes glow. She watched the cars all back up, weaving slowly through the street toward her. She couldn't simply activate her LOC suit and flee, for the team's arsenal, equipment, and escape—its survival basically—were in the old truck. And of course, there was Yuri, who was plainly out of his element.

"Yuri!" she whispered fiercely. He hurried into view, zipping up his pants, a worried look on his face. "Big trouble! Into the truck, quick! I'll stay out here. If they start to poke around the truck, I'll ambush them, and we'll run for the team. Quick! Into the truck and pretend you're asleep! If they ask, tell them you're sleeping 'til you make a transport in the morning. They may be satisfied. If they try to look into the truck, I'll take down as many as I can. You crank the truck and roll for the Swords' place. Don't worry about me! Got it?"

"Ye-yes . . . yes, I think so, Sarah!"

"Don't worry, Yuri. You won't see me, but I'll have you covered."

Sarah powered up her LOC suit and eased across the street to a vantage point where she could lay down maximum assault fire with minimum risk to Yuri. Vocally, she selected the team-wide, encrypted BSH channel. "Travis? Sarah," she whispered. "We have company at the truck. Those three carloads of cops we saw on the way over here. Looks to be about twelve of them, all with AKs. They've made the truck, but nothing's happened yet. Maybe Yuri can talk them off. I'll advise."

"Okay," was all Travis said. Sarah would make sound decisions, he knew, and the rest of the team was critically busy.

*   *   *

The driver of the nearest backing car twisted about to look back through the rear window, and narrowed his eyes. He could've sworn he saw something . . . quiver . . . wiggle, in the roadway. But as he looked more carefully, he saw nothing but the hot, dry cobblestones. Heat. That was it, the driver thought. Rising heat waves.

Yuri closed the truck door and tried to calm his thundering heart.

The three Mercedes sedans stopped in the street before him, and Yuri was more than alarmed to see that all within—four men to each car, but for the five in the lead car—held weapons with the distinctive banana clips of AK-74s.

But Yuri's biggest shock was yet to come, for out of the lead sedan stepped a tall, razor-faced man in knee-high boots, carrying a leather riding crop. The same crop that had been inserted into his beloved Annatava seven years earlier, after her rape by six Cuban officers. Yuri knew it was the same crop his late wife had described so many nights in his arms after she'd awakened from the sweaty nightmares that haunted her, because it was carried by the man Yuri hated more than communism itself, more even than the nuclear banditry of his people. The crop was the signature talisman of the commanding officer of Internal Security, the head of Castro's secret police force, the dreaded Colonel Rafio Raimundo. Murderer. Torturer. Rapist. Yuri almost smiled as his fingers closed around the silenced .45 automatic Sarah had left him.

Good, Sarah mused from the doorway across the street, the very slight hum of her powered-up LOC suit barely audible. Only two are getting out of the cars. Pop the two standers, fire two 20mm det grenades each into the cars before the remaining eleven men can clear the vehicles. Shrapnel, burning gasoline, and her gunfire should get most of them, and gravely occupy those who escape. She thumbed the safety off on her XM-29 and moved the armament selector to "both."

Yuri fought the rage within that screamed at him to shoot this bastard, kill this defiler of his beloved Annatava, slayer of his fetal baby! In only a moment the troll of a man would be standing by the door, an easy shot into his arrogant, cruel face. *Yes!*

Keep cool, Yuri, Sarah thought, unaware of who Raimundo was. Talk them away. She raised her rifle and sighted. The three cars idled noisily in the quiet night.

Yuri's gun hand trembled. Soon.

Raimundo was disgusted. This peon truck driver squinting into his flashlight beam was obviously a pig-faced Russian, not American or Arab. Just another underpaid Russian worker infesting Cuba these days, probably moonlighting to make ends meet. Still, twice in one night? Raimundo stopped. "You!" he demanded. "Get out and come here, this instant! *Pronto!*"

Across the street, Sarah tensed. I dare not wait until Yuri is in the line of fire. It has to be now. I hate to blow the lid off this op, but it has to be now or we could lose the equipment, and fail the mission. And that simply isn't an option. A lime-green laser-dot, visible only through Sarah's infrared/laser scope sight, jittered between Rafio Raimundo's shoulder blades.

So, Yuri thought, his heart about to blow blood out his ears. So this is how it all ends for me. They will kill me. Even Sarah, with her amazing American techno-weapons, won't be able to get them all. So be it. At least I will have shot the infamous Colonel Raimundo, the beast of Annatava's nightmares, as many times as I can pull the trigger—beginning with one squarely in his cold vulture's *face*—before the others take me down. Annatava, my love. I come.

Yuri opened the truck door and turned to slide down, the concealed .45 slippery in his sweaty grip.

Sarah took a shallow breath and began to let it out slowly, squeezing gradually, concentrating on the dancing yellow-green dot.

* * *

The jarring explosion shook the ground and broke glass up and down the street. Sarah, Yuri, Raimundo, and his twelve disciples all flinched and snapped looks down Avenida de las Floras, at the 800 block, where flame, smoke, glass, and debris gushed from the windows of the second floor.

"Shit!" Stan exclaimed looking at the old-fashioned but no less treacherous homemade bomb in the sofa base. "Bomb on a timer, Travis! Abandon ship!"

"Evac!" Travis said immediately. "Priority one! *Move!*" He swatted Jen on the butt as she scampered by. Stan snatched up the NLG cannister in passing. Hunter was shoved ahead by Jack. Travis was last to bolt down the hallway.

Jen, Stan, and Hunter had dropped down the staircase, but Travis and Jack were hurled down it by the blast. They landed in a heap at the cut-back landing and were immediately seized by their three teammates and dragged down the remaining flight of stairs to the street level foyer. Muffled screams and shouts were heard from the suddenly awakened population both within the building and in neighboring structures. Falling glass rang in the street like the Notre Dame Cathedral on Easter morning. Fire spread likc fleeing rats in the century-old wooden apartment building built long before the advent of sprinkler systems, drywall, or fire containment doors.

"Travis!" Sarah called on the intrasquad BSH net.

"We're okay, Sarah! They missed."

"Good god. The cops are coming, Travis. They all have AKs. Shoot for the heads and legs; they're wearing kevlex vests!"

Ibrahim Shanaan loved the sound of bombs. Bombs were lovely. Bombs were justice for his people. Bombs were his life, and his father's life before him. Ibrahim loved all bombs, no matter the agent. TNT, dynamite, cylonite, semtex, C-4, even smoky old black powder, and treacherous gasoline. Ibrahim Shanaan had blown up people and property all over the world using all these explosives and others.

Squatting by the trunk of a large palm tree in the dark, walled-off courtyard of a building across the street from the safe house, Ibrahim cradled his Heckler & Koch 9mm rifle like a baby.

Shanaan reflected that it wasn't just the exquisite, almost sexual beauty of eviscerated Israeli children hanging out of burning bus windows, or a derailed American Amtrak train plunging into a gorge, or passengers leaping into oil-inflamed waters from a sinking British cruise ship. These things were immensely satisfying, of course, but the real satisfaction came from outwitting the enemy so brilliantly.

These arrogant American infidels, for example. They thought they were so clever with their HERF guns that could addle the computer brains of the most complex time-delay detonators, and their Non-Lethal Generator devices to make every human in the down-field cone nauseous. Ibrahim grudgingly had to hand it to those infernal infidels, they *were* clever. It had taken him several humiliating failures to determine how they'd frustrated his works of art. They would just do that beam-directed, electro-magnetic hyper-pulse trick and fry the circuitry of every microchip within the band cone for . . . Ibrahim was suddenly agitated because he'd remembered that he still didn't know what the range of the new American device was.

No matter. He was far more intelligent than the swine-eating American infidels. They could never outsmart him for long. And the solution was so beautifully simple! Simply use a detonator-timer that had no radio, computer, or other microchip, as in the old days when his father blew up British barracks in the Sinai. A common, peasant, wind-up, mechanical clock made by the millions in Taiwan or Burma. Solder the contacts to the face and sweep-arm tip. Tick, tick, tick, boom! It would function through a nuclear hyper-pulse, discounting the blast effect of course.

So it was with great pleasure that Ibrahim Shanaan heard the fist-sized semtex blob beneath the couch cushion in the old safe house detonate. Poof. No more American shock-troop squad. The courtyard in which he and his brothers of the Swords hid was suddenly aglow with orange light from the fires. But then, the beauty of it was ruined. Something had gone so wrong!

Rashan, the beautiful freedom fighter, had stood and clapped her hands in triumph when the Americans were destroyed by his elegant couch bomb, but . . .

Sam felt like he was going to wet his pants when the bomb went off. In the street, hidden in a doorway despite his powered-up LOC suit, Sam pressed back to avoid flying glass and debris that snowed into the street. He was weak with relief to hear Travis say the team was all right. How all right they would remain was subject to question, Sam reflected, watching huge billowing columns of fire blowing from all the upper floor windows of the building.

Then some girl stood in the doorway across the street and clapped. Clapped! Who on Earth would be so pleased to see a bomb go off, here, now, but a Sword of Allah? Sure enough, as Sam saw on his infrared read-out, she had a folding-stock AK-47, the old Soviet paratroop model, slung at her shoulder!

Sam placed the laser lime-dot on the gleaming white-toothed smile of the armed and delighted woman, adjusted left two inches to offset the angle of her gaze, and squeezed his trigger. A three-burst of brutally fast, 4000-foot-per-second bullets fired from the new combustible composite hulls and sprayed her head all over the courtyard behind her.

Clap *that,* Sam thought, more uncharitably than he actually felt. In truth, he was feeling nauseated and his heart thumped wildly. He'd just killed a human being. A woman. What the hell was he doing here? But now, Jesus Christ, Sam thought, looking up the street to his left, the Cuban *cops* were somehow wrapped up in this Chinese fire drill!

When Ibrahim Shaan's brilliantly primitive bomb went off, Colonel Raimundo nearly suffered a stroke. This he had not expected. Who was blowing up whom!?

Without orders, Raimundo's deputies poured from their cars. Simultaneously, electrically released trunk lids rose. Three men frantically clawed in the trunks, and tossed kevlex battle vests to the others. From each car, a man withdrew an excellent, American-made, M-60-T squad machine gun. Another Cuban pulled green cans of ammo belts out as well. Still another hastily tossed fragmentation grenades to his comrades.

"Cover and advance!" Raimundo shouted, tucking his riding crop in his belt and catching a thrown AK-74 rifle as he ran. "Cover and advance!" The policemen rushed en masse to the irregular, recessed doorways of both sides of Avenida de las Floras.

From her doorway, Sarah debated whether to open up on the Cuban police, but she elected to wait. She was outnumbered and outgunned, Yuri could get killed, and a fight here, near the old truck, could cut off the team's escape and access to the special weapons. Breathing heavily, using the infrared/laser scope on her rifle, Sarah surveyed the cops as they moved away along the building fronts toward the growing conflagration in the next block.

Yuri was stunned by the sudden and violent blast only a few hundred meters away. By the time he'd recovered, the hated Colonel Raimundo was running past his car, shouting orders and donning a bullet-proof vest. Lenin's bloody ghost! Yuri cursed himself for his inaction.

Then a burst of rifle fire sparked from down the street. But where was the shooter? *Who* was the shooter?

Raimundo swore he would later shoot the policeman who fired without orders, but for now he threw himself into the meager cover of a doorway as one of his younger officers, startled by the rifle fire near the blazing apartment, opened up with one of the M-60 machine guns. Raimundo railed furiously, unheard, as vicious, glowing red rounds of machine-gun tracer fire zipped past and sailed down the street. Immediately, every other cop assumed they had somehow missed Raimundo's order to return fire and they all opened up, though there were not yet any identifiable targets. The deafening staccato muzzle blasts glittered and echoed between the buildings.

What in the name of Allah was happening? Despite his decades in the terror trade, Swords of Allah commander Nassir Al-Husseini was uncharacteristically dumbfounded. The bomb was to have cured all their problems. When it exploded, he'd actually relaxed, but then Rashan stood! She'd actually stood up and applauded! Only the young could be so stupid! Nassir had grabbed at Rashan, of course, but too late. A red mist filled with small chunks of meat and bone blew back. Lovely Rashan Amir, Nassir Al-Husseini's lover, such a passionate warrior for the cause, collapsed in a faceless heap.

Now there was heavy machine-gun fire chipping stucco over their heads, from still another source! Who? The other eleven members of the Swords of Allah, enraged by the cold-blooded "murder" of Rashan, their youngest, and startled by the sudden rapid boom of a squad machine gun from farther up the street, now broke cover in the courtyard and returned fire furiously.

Sarah allowed herself a slight, grim smile. How odd that Sam, sweet, gentle, scared little Sammy, should draw first blood. But now he was trapped between the advancing Cuban cops and the cornered Swords of Allah. Sarah keyed her laser sight, swung the glowing, yellow-green dot onto the back of the head of the nearer Cuban in a doorway across from her. She acquired the target and squeezed. Her XM-29 bucked and spat a rapid three-burst and the targeted head snapped forward. A thin stream of light smoke was discharged from the rifle, the incineration of the combustible cartridge hulls. The policeman heaped face down, lifeless in the din. His AK-74 clattered on the cobbles.

Sarah drew a breath, eased it out slowly, and moved the little death dot to the greasily oiled head of another wildly firing Cuban. Squeeeeeeeeeeeeeze.

Tatatat!

And then there were but ten little Indians.

Ho-leeee *shit*! Sam swore to himself as he cringed hard back into his doorway. From his left, the Cuban police had opened fire, and from his right and across the street, the Swords—believing the Cubans had shot their woman, Sam assumed, since they couldn't have seen

him—were now pouring return fire back at them. The
street glittered with muzzle flashes, thundered with gunshots, and was horrifyingly laced with tracer bullets zipping by in both directions. What the *fuck* am I *doing*
here!? Sam thought.

Carefully, heaving for breath, Sam selected "grenade"
on his XM-29, gripped the weapon tightly, knowing its
draconian recoil in the grenade mode, aimed, and fired.

The weapon gave off with a concussive *Ploonk*! A
20mm, self-propelled, light-antipersonnel grenade sailed
across the street and over the wall of the courtyard.

It was not evolving to be a good night for Colonel
Raimundo. Huddled in a shallow doorway recess, he
struggled to see enough to base an intelligent command
on. All he could see were sparkling muzzle blasts and
streaking tracers slicing the hot, black hair. Looking
back toward the cars—Fool! Why did you leave no one
to guard the cars?—Raimundo was shocked to see two
of his men already down. Oddly, they were farthest from
the firing.

But as he looked, still a third of his handpicked policemen pitched forward and dropped like a rag doll. From
the corner of his eye, Raimundo caught a muzzle flash
in the darkness way back across the street from the cars.
Then there was another from the same source, and—
Madre!—a fourth Cuban policeman simply went down
like he'd been turned off with a switch!

"Mother of God!" Raimundo swore. We are surrounded! They're cutting us down like cattle at a slaugh-
terhouse! Suddenly, a spray of rifle fire from the Swords
courtyard stitched along the sidewalk past the door
where Raimundo had sought refuge, peppering him with
stone chips. "Mother of God!" Raimundo repeated,
pressing back in the doorway.

Nassir Al-Husseini screamed commands, trying to re-
order and direct his people effectively, but with little
success. Confusion reigned, and with it fear, and with
the fear a savage, if poorly directed counterassault.

Al-Husseini himself was confused. Who was shooting
from up the street? The Americans? But they'd been

told the Americans were hitting the safe house. Did the bomb get them, or did they escape? How did they get that far back up the street unobserved? How many were there? Where were they? Brass hulls pinged the stones like broken glass and painful muzzle blasts stung Al-Husseini's ears.

At that moment, Sam's grenade round struck a palm tree behind Al-Husseini and exploded with a vicious *Crack*! Hassan dropped his rifle, clutched his face, staggered backward, and fell. The upper third of the large palm tree, having absorbed much of the shrapnel, slowly toppled into the courtyard with a crash and shower of huge palm leaves.

Flames were now consuming the blasted safe-house building with alarming speed. Travis, Stan, Hunter, and Jack looked away from windows at the stairway, down which the raging fires now roared like a freight train. They'd been following Travis's order to let both enemy groups shoot each other up without interfering, for the time being. Travis raced back down the first floor hallway and slid in by Stan and Jen. He keyed the squad-wide BSH net.

"Listen up, people! Looks like we got the Swords across from us in that courtyard; I can't tell if it's all twelve of 'em or not; watch your backs! Cuban cops between us and the truck. We're gonna have half the Cuban army and all the cops in Havana here in about five minutes, not to mention every fire truck in the city. And that's if this firetrap doesn't bury us first. We got to hustle.

"Sarah! Get back to the truck with Yuri and leave the way we came in. Circle out, go two blocks south and one block east of Avenida de las Floras, and wait for us. Move!"

"I'm gone, Travis," Sarah answered, her voice oddly peaceful, absent the background roar of fire and gunshots on Travis's end.

"Remember, our primary mission is the Swords! On my signal, we hit 'em with everything we've got, run 'em down and kill 'em for three full minutes, then we split. Whether we got 'em all or not. We cannot be captured, people! Three minutes of hell on earth, then we're outta here! Got that, Jack?"

"One block east, two blocks south, in three, boss."

"Sammy! Where are you?"

"In a doorway on your side, about three doors up, boss! I count seven of these cops left. They're pinned down but two of 'em have squad machine guns and they're tearing the street up! One of 'em—the leader I think, I can't get a shot at him—keeps yelling commands in Spanish. Sounds like he's getting them ready to break out!"

"Sam, can you get a grenade round on those machine guns?"

"One for sure, boss. Maybe on the other one. He's on my side."

"Do it, now. Jack, you help Sam with the cops. Hunter, Jen, Stan, and me focus on the Swords. Everybody got it?"

The distinctive *Ploonk*! of Sam's grenade shot could be heard through heavy machine-gun firing. Then there came another very loud *Crack*!, and one machine gun stopped instantly.

"Hit 'em!" Travis commanded.

Colonel Raimundo had just shouted commands to his remaining men. The two surviving machine gunners were to cover with a heavy stream of fire, while Raimundo and the others retreated for the cars. At the cars, they would cover the retreat of the two machine gunners. "Fire and withdraw!" Raimundo bellowed in Spanish. Both M-60s churned tracer down the street. Raimundo and six of his men sprang from their cover positions and scampered back toward the Mercedes, hugging close to the buildings.

Raimundo felt weak at the sound of the grenade that smothered one of his machine guns. Instantly the street was filled with bullets that weren't his. The Swords were blazing at an increased rate and, from somewhere near the flaming building, there suddenly erupted a scathing volume of additional gunfire that spit off the building walls near him like hailstones in a hurricane. Then, as though things were not already horrifying enough, that son-of-dog Russian truck driver was now shooting at him with a handgun! Raimundo dived into a small alcove, way short of his cars, just as Major Arejo Nuñez and another of Raimundo's lieutenants called out in shock and pain, skidded to the street, and lay still.

Nassir Al-Husseini saw the Cuban police break for their cars. In the chaos of the moment, he was convinced that these were the Americans who had somehow escaped his bomb trap, and he ordered all his assets to bear fire upon the fleeing men. He screamed commands and pointed, and the eleven surviving Swords, including Al-Husseini, rose and poured everything they had up the narrow street, including the Swords' Kalisnikov squad machine gun. The air was filled with richocheting slugs and chips of stone, stucco, concrete, and glass. Al-Husseini was gratified to see some of the running men collapse as they ran and crash to the cobblestones.

But even as they broke cover to shoot, they were shocked to find themselves scythed by the withering fire of very fast automatic weapons and some grenades from inside the burning safe-house building! Now the stone chips and bullets swarmed into the Swords. Who . . . wha . . . how many were . . . ? The Swords machine gunner went down with a thud of man and weapon. Another near the gate suddenly screamed and clutched his own throat with both hands, his AK-47 clattering to the stones.

Al-Husseini dropped behind the courtyard wall, stunned. This was it. Al-Husseini now knew that if the Swords remained they would be overrun imminently. This was, of course, unacceptable, as they had not come to kill an American goon squad, let alone be killed by one. The Swords of Allah had come to blow up a pair of nuclear reactors, which would spread a deadly cloud of radiation over the Great Satan, killing millions of the infidels. The mission!

"Baaaack," Al-Husseini roared in Arabic over the gunfire and exploding grenade rounds at his people. He unpinned and lobbed a grenade over the wall. "Escaaaaape! Through the building! Go! Go! Go! Go!"

The Swords' big bomb expert, Ibrahim Shanaan,

didn't have to be told twice. He seized his Heckler & Koch and crashed into the doorway leading within the commercial building from the courtyard, which had now become a killing ground. The remaining Swords scrambled behind him dragging canvas bags of ordnance and equipment.

Nassir Al-Husseini chucked one more grenade hard over the wall, then he seized Rashan's body and dragged it behind him into the building.

"Grenade!" Jen shouted a second time, but this one was closer and thrown higher. Instead of dropping down a storm drain and exploding harmlessly like the first, this one came right at the window. She dropped and balled up.

Travis and Hunter drew back and turned. Jack was two doors up, helping Sam with the Cubans. Stan slipped on debris.

The second grenade detonated at window level, blowing shrapnel fragments downward into it.

Stan bellowed, clutched his left thigh, and went down in a cloud of plaster dust.

"Yaaaah! Fuck! Right in the ass again! Aaah, *shit*!"

Everyone but Stan immediately stood and resumed fierce firing across the street at the Swords' courtyard, leaving Stan to his own devices, but he did not resent this. It was the business of combat. Mission first, men second.

Stan grabbed his XM-29, dragged himself to his feet, and, using a baluster from the shattered stair railing as a cane, stumbled to the window and resumed his own firing. In seconds Stan felt the LOC suit contracting at the site of his wound, which meant the frags had penetrated and drawn blood. Damn! The LOC suit's trauma-react function was kicking in to close the wound and slow blood flow to the affected leg. The built-in tourniquet bladders filled with air, tightening around Stan's thigh. His leg burned when the suture fibers detached from the shell fabric and curled inward, seizing his wounded flesh like a claw. It hurt, but Stan had been here before. Soon the suit would automatically inject a limited pain reliever. If that wasn't adequate, Stan knew, he could self-administer stronger doses by vocal command.

Damn! Stan cursed again as he stuffed another "magazineless-magazine," a forty-round cluster of bonded-together XM-29 rounds, into his rifle, aimed through the infrared/laser scope, and tore panels out of the door through which the Swords now seemed to be retreating. With satisfaction, he noted one of the fleeing Swords arch his back, drop his weapon and bag, and hit the floor. He could barely make out the man's scream of agony over the din.

Not much had ever scared Colonel Raimundo, but now he was scared witless.

The *bastardo* Russian had finally stopped shooting at him, probably only because he was out of bullets for the pistol. Raimundo had hugged the shallow depression of the alcove in which he'd taken cover. Leaning out to shoot back was out of the question, as murderous automatic-weapons fire and some grenades still spewed from the other direction on Avenida de las Floras. Raimundo's men were going down like the rubber boats in which the peasants fled to Florida.

Raimundo heard the old horse truck's engine groan to life, and he did lean out enough to see it bounce into the street and roar away to the north.

This, however was not the scary part.

Raimundo turned to look toward the now engulfed burning building and opposite courtyard. He could tell from the flashes and explosions that the Swords were exchanging fire with the Americans still on the lower floor of the fast burning building.

Even in the darkness, Raimundo could see by the firelight of the engulfed building eight bodies laying in the street, all his men. To his horror, one of these, Arejo Nuñez, his old companion from the revolution days, raised his head and was looking toward Raimundo, his hand raised as though pleading for help.

Raimundo cried out and drew back as, seemingly from nowhere, from out of the air near the far edge of the street, a very fast three-burst of automatic rifle fire sparked and crackled, and Arejo slumped to the cobblestones. Then, instantly, two sparking bursts of gunfire appeared from out of thin air, sustained this time, pouring into the doorway where José, the one surviving machine gunner, had been shooting until there was nothing left to shoot at. José had stopped and leaned out of the doorway, holding the smoking machine gun, to look at the old courtyard. Two rifle bursts had cut José down from only twenty feet away! He died with a look of shocked puzzlement, because *there was no one there!*

Raimundo was an educated man who was free of religious or other supernatural beliefs. He knew what it was. Somehow those rich, devious American bastards had devised an ingenious means of . . . of invisibility! Which meant they could be right next to him at this very moment and he would not know it until their rifles flashed!

Colonel Rafio Raimundo, chief of the Cuban Internal Security Cell, felt terror for possibly the only time in his life. Panicked completely, he spun madly and pounded the door behind him with the butt of his rifle, shattering the composite stock. Blind with fear, Raimundo slammed his body into the door until the frame cracked, and then he slammed harder, emitting little cries each time he hit the wood.

Jack thought he heard something, a human sound of some sort, down the street on the left. With his night-vision drop-shield, he could see clearly in a sort of green-and-white TV picture, but he saw no one. He turned to Sam who was advancing slowly alongside and several feet away, his XM-29 shouldered.

"Hearin' somethin' down there on the left, Sammy," Jack said over the BSH net.

Wired to his earlobes, Sam jerked his rifle to the left, but saw nothing on his own shield screen either.

Jack craned his head, and turned up the volume on his BSH external audio by blinking his left eye. There it was again, the maniacal pounding punctuated with whimpers. From about the fifth doorway on the left. He raised his rifle and stepped forward cautiously.

Colonel Raimundo felt warm urine trickling down his leg, soiling his riding pants. He hammered the old wooden door with both fists and his shoulders, knees, and butt. Now his whimpers were almost screams.

Jack broke into a trot. Sam did the same. Both heard it now.

Travis led Hunter and Jen out of the flaming building even as burning pieces of it began to fall into the street like comets. Stan hobbled behind, using the staircase baluster as a cane again.

"Jack! Sam!" Travis yelled on the run. "Let them go! Let's get the Swords!" Jack and Sam jammed to a stop. Sam ran back immediately, but Jack paused.

Raimundo split the door at last. On the verge of screaming hysterically, he kicked the split panels in and dived between them. Sharp splinters of wood dug into him and tore his shirt, but he did not slow a nanosecond. He clawed and crabbed his way frantically through the fractured door. He ran blindly into the dark building, tripped over a chair and fell hard, splitting his forehead on a desk. Without a pause he lurched to his feet and commanded aching legs and knees to propel him, crashing off furniture, smashing into walls, groping for doorways.

Just as he began to think he'd cheated death at last, there was another burst of that terrifyingly fast battle rifle the Americans used! The muzzle fire sporadically lit the room Raimundo thrashed his way through. He whirled, gasping a cry of fear. In the doorway there was . . . something . . . wavy . . . formless . . . but alive! Raimundo tried to scream but could only croak. The bullets tore pieces from the wall by his head. One seared the skin of his upper left arm. Another hit his belt, cutting his riding crop like a bolt-cutter and severing the thin leather belt that held up his riding trousers. Raimundo's pants dropped quickly to his knees, hobbling him, and he fell, crying like a baby.

"Jack!" Sam called over the BSH. "Get back here, man! Stan's hit!"

That was it, Jack thought. One of our own is hurt.

That Cube is probably deader than O.J.'s Visa card, any-how. Couldn't see that blubberin', fucking sugar-nigger for all that shit in that office, but I give him half a mag, heard him scream, and saw him go down. Fuck that Cube. Jack bolted down the street.

Progress was slow through the courtyard and the building into which the Swords had fled. Travis reasoned they'd almost certainly transited the building and were now fleeing down back streets, but . . . if they'd left behind just one wounded guy with another bomb . . .

By the time each blind passage and room had been cleared and the team exited the rear of the building, all that remained of the Swords of Allah were blood drop-pings and a huge blood smear from a body being dragged. They'd probably had a contingency vehicle out here, Travis thought. I would have.

Stan hobbled through the old fire door last. Growing louder and nearer, the team could hear the wailing and whooping sirens of the Havana City *Policia,* and the hee-haw Euro sirens of a flotilla of fire trucks and ambulances.

"Round one's a draw, Eagle Team. Let's carry our asses. Jack, you and Hunter give Stan a hand. Sam, watch our back; Jen you're on point. Go, go, go."

Sarah's idea was brilliant, everyone admitted, awe-some actually, if, as it turned out, a bit counter to the Hippocratic Oath.

As Travis pointed out, the horse truck had almost cer-tainly been made by the Cuban cops and God knows who else. Remaining in it for more than a half hour or so was an unacceptable liability. Predictably, after the small war that had just gone down, not to mention the major fire that was still burning, police would soon be mobilized from the entire city. Fire and rescue equip-ment from all over Havana would stream in, including several large, boxy Mercedes and Volvo ambulance trucks. Hospitals would be put on standby. The police would, of course, soon cordon off the city with road-blocks, in search of the terrible bandits.

And Stan needed medical care.

The team doubled back in the horse van to actually ride in on the tail of the armada of public service vehicles responding to the massive fire and "drug-gang shootout" that was alleged to have erupted in the Arab section of Old Havana. Bodies were said to be strewn in the streets, including some police. Injuries were likely for the battalion of firefighters that would be put to the task of controlling the fires that now raged, not to mention the potential for civilian casualties. The team frequently pulled the old van over to allow passage of screaming police cars, fire trucks, and ambulances.

Finding an ambulance parked off by itself, awaiting call, if required, wasn't difficult. The drivers were snatched from the cab by hands clamped over their mouths, tied up, drugged by Sarah, and left in the woods.

The ambulance, its siren wailing and red lights flashing, was waved right past police roadblocks by helpful Cuban provincial police officers. The entire TALON team huddled within, their rifles at the ready, along with millions of dollars in classified technology, and one very shaken Russian doctor.

They made Cienfuegos by dawn.

Chapter Seven

On the highway from Havana to Cienfuegos, Jack rode
in front with Hunter. Sarah and Yuri worked on Stan.

Yuri was astonished as he watched Sarah treat Stan.
She plugged a small wire bundle from a titanium-cased
laptop computer into a tiny receptacle on the belt of
Stan's LOC suit. Instantly, a comprehensive system readout appeared. All of the patient's vital signs were displayed in a corner of the screen. Sarah selected "working
injuries, penetration," and she trac-balled a glowing feature labeled "autosuture release."

Before Yuri's wondrous eyes, the portion of battle suit
that covered the wicked shrapnel hit in Stan's upper
thigh began to move as though something beneath it
was alive. Shortly, the readout on Sarah's laptop flashed
"autosuture separation," and the fabric over the wound
stopped undulating.

Yuri picked a clothing shear from the ambulance's
equipment box.

"Forget it," Sarah said. "You can't cut an LOC suit
with anything but a ten thousand psi water knife. Or a
direct, close bullet or shrapnel hit. If it wasn't so tough,
the fragment laceration and penetration here would have
been much worse." Sarah pointed to several marks on
the fabric near the penetration. "See the slight melting?
That's from the impact of white-hot shards of shrapnel
deflected by the suit's kevlex center fabric. Without the
suit, Stan would probably have lost this leg. As it is, if
we can ascertain the internal damage of the piece that

did penetrate, and if it hasn't gotten an artery, he might be walking unassisted by midday."

"Lenin's bloody ghost," Yuri whispered, stunned. "But . . . Sarah, if an artery had been severed, would Stan not have already bled to death?"

"No. The LOC suit's inner layer is composed of something called electro-designated contraction fibers. The sensors in the suit relay to the belt-mounted LOC suit computer that there is blood loss, where it is, and what the cc-per-minute rate of flow is. The computer makes a determination of the wound pattern and depth, then orders the affected fibers to separate from the inner fabric and curl into the flesh, effectively suturing it in place. It also pumps air to the suit bladders like an aviator's G-suit, restricting blood flow to the affected limb."

"But . . . what . . . isn't that suture function like being bitten by a large dog, and held? Isn't it excruciating?"

"It would be, of course, but the suit also has the capacity to transmit local anesthetic to neutralize pain in the affect zone. If it becomes more than that function can manage, the wearer may voice-direct other options."

Yuri slumped back, staring at Stan, who was now resting under a sedative. "And it . . . the suit makes you invisible as well! My word. How long have you had this?"

"Long enough," Travis interrupted with some force, causing Sarah to jerk a glance at him. "If you want, Sarah, I'll have Jen obtain a sat-link fax of the entire manual of composition for the Brilliance-Class Battle Suit and all its systems, and you can give it to Dr. Nobakov for his birthday. I'd say the technology is worth about a billion dollars on the world black market. How does a twelve-million-man Chinese infantry equipped with light-convertible, trauma-react battle suits sound to you, Sarah?"

"Are you through?" Sarah demanded, incensed. "Are you completely finished?"

"Sarah . . ." Travis said.

"Give us all a break, will you Travis?" Sarah said bitterly. "Excuse me, *Major Barrett! Sir!* I'm only relating to a colleague how the trauma-react functions of the LOC suit work! I'm not telling him how to build it, because I don't know! And don't you think that Yuri, who has risked his *life* just by becoming involved with us, who has *fought* and been *shot at* right along with the rest of us tonight, might *not* be a fucking spy?" Sarah glowered at Travis. "The man is on our side, Travis! What does it take to convince you? Does Yuri have to get killed before you lighten up on him?"

Jen suddenly sat up from her slump in a rear corner of the ambulance. "Hey, hey, hey, Sarah. Come on now. Relax. This isn't a medical conference in Cannes. The keystone of security is need-to-know. The LOC suit is one of the most classified technologies in existence. Yuri is *not* in the need-to-know loop! And you know that."

A pregnant pause hung in the rocking ambulance.

"Please," Yuri said, obviously distressed. "Please, I did not mean to become the focus of a dispute."

"There's no dispute," Sarah said, sighing. "Travis is right. Case closed. I just didn't think . . . Yuri . . ."

Travis's soft, deep drawl was gentle now. "What she's trying to say, Dr. Nobakov, is you're not a threat to our mission, but a vital key to its success. She's right. We're all—especially me—aware that you're here at great risk and out of conviction that what we're here to accomplish is important. And we appreciate it."

Before the big ambulance rolled out of the predawn darkness, secure from view in the basement garage of Yuri's villa, Sarah had run a field sonogram imagery on Stan's wound, and she had located the jagged thumbnail-sized piece of metal about 25mm deep in the muscle. She commanded the LOC suit to relax the suture strands, then disconnected the suit wiring and removed its trousers. Yuri and Sarah carefully picked out the now flaccid sutures, explored the wound, and retracted the shrapnel with a magnetic probe. Sarah stapled the sub-dural tissues and applied a short length of bio-absorbable suture tape to close the wound. Finally, she injected Stan with antibiotics.

Tired, sore, and groggy, Stan insisted on walking off the ambulance in Yuri's basement, albeit with the assistance of his makeshift cane.

"Astonishing technology," Yuri uttered, watching Stan hobble away.

"Nothing a little Yankee ingenuity can't accomplish,"

Sam said, walking by wearily, "if you throw in a few billion bucks."

September 25, 0717 hours, Nobakov villa, Cienfuegos, Cuba

Jen pulled the first guard shift, then slammed down for four hours. She awoke feeling rested but very stiff and sore. She climbed to the third-floor east bedroom where Stan was now walking with a limp from one room to the other, peering out over the shallow balconies with their wrought-iron railings. Occasionally, Stan would eye something through the gyro-stabilized, day-night binoculars, but nothing merited mention.

At a Mediterranean-style desk in the corner by a large plant, Sam had booted up the master communications pod and spread its small flowering dish antenna. Instantly the little dish gimbaled on its own until it optimized reception on the prevailing satellite. Jen sat down and Sam flexed the fiber-optic camera tube so that it played on her face.

Travis walked into the room, yawning, and stood behind Jen, his hands on her shoulders. She briefly patted one of his hands, a gesture not missed by Sam.

Travis and his intelligence officer were both of the same mind, and Travis knew it. The question they both pondered was how did the Swords so magically vacate their safe house before the hit.

The screen flashed ENCRYPT ENABLED—SECURE. Jen typed furiously and paused. The flat-monitor screen picture materialized quickly, and Travis and Jen were now looking at the drawn and tired-looking face of their boss, Brigadier General Jack Krauss. He was a lean-faced combat veteran with very short, gray hair. As always, when a TALON Force team was on an operation, General Krauss slept on a cot in his office, if he slept at all. Jack Krauss was the TALON Force's mother hen. He now spared no time on civilities.

"Travis. Jen. How's Stan?"

"He's sore and limping, but swears he's okay. Sarah

says he's operational, General. Salutes to the LOC suit engineers on that one."

"Good to hear. I've read your after-action report and discussed it with everybody in EVAL. You say Dr. Nobakov was monitored?"

"Of course. He never got near a phone or a radio, sir," Jen said. "He was watched by one of us all the time. Besides, why would—"

"CIA assures us Dr. Nobakov is a class-six risk. They say he's completely dependable. They've used him for years for some very delicate stuff. Since he was monitored by you guys in the pre-op phase, then the leak—if there was one—that tipped the Swords to your assault had to have come from somewhere on this end. In concert with CIA, we have instituted a system-wide silent dragnet, scanning for security anomalies. We'll advise as soon as we know anything."

"General," Travis said. "Sir, as I said in my report, I don't think it happened, but I can't rule out the possibility that we were seen by a Swords sentry. But they'd have had to be real alert, real fast, and real lucky to have seen us coming in powered-up LOC suits. They still had hot food and hot coffee on the stove."

General Krauss sighed and rubbed his eyes. "They say Nassir Al-Husseini is the Desert Eagle, that he never sleeps, that he has eyes that see through walls. I don't believe any of that shit, I think he's just a dedicated Arab patriot, but I do believe he's also a hard-case, professional soldier with years of field experience. You observed no sentries on your way in, but Al-Husseini would have had at least two out. Also, there's a high probability the Swords had electronic or infrared motion detectors and magnetic anomaly alarms in place at a minimum."

"Agreed," Travis said.

"Moving on," Krauss said, glancing at his notes. "We have been running ongoing scans of Cuban television, police bands, and military channels, with the best decoding assets in the net working on the encrypted stuff. You guys evidently really blew a shit storm down there. The fires in Old Havana are still burning, but the firemen have finally got it contained. Cuban TV is calling it a drug-gang shootout with brave Cuban Internal Security Cell police who took fatalities in their selfless quest to keep the Cuban people free of the drug menace. They're interviewing some Internal Security honcho named Colonel Rafio Raimundo, who effectively says he and his guys brilliantly ran the Estavez cartel to ground and 'dealt them a crippling blow.' Says he personally had a shootout with the drug-gang leader in which he sustained a minor injury, and he is sure he killed the drug lord. He doesn't explain why the Havana cops reported that all the dead bodies they found were Raimundo's hatchet guys, and, of course, if you're a Cuban TV reporter who wants to stay on TV and not in a cell, you don't ask embarrassing questions of Fidel's Internal Security commander."

"Dr. Nobakov knows that cop, General," Jen reported. "Raimundo's the thug who participated in a six-cop gang rape of his wife in ninety-two when the Cubans were so pissed at the Ivans for shutting down construction on the Juragua project without refunding their millions. Yu—Dr. Nobakov says Raimundo's a world-class asshole, shoots and tortures dissidents, rapes anything in panties, maybe even a few things that aren't. Dr. Nobakov unloaded fifteen rounds at him on the run when the balloon went up, but evidently he didn't hit him."

"Mmmm. Don't guess they taught Nobakov to shoot in med school. Anyway, while the official cover story is this heroic drug-gang shootout, and the cops are canvassing for Salvadoran powder peddlers, the military is on full alert with orders to find Arab terrorists and American spies. The good news is the search is concentrated in Havana, which they think they've effectively sealed off since the blowout. Also, they know the Arabs are the Swords of Allah, but they evidently don't have the first clue who you are. The bad news is, we're on high confidence that neither the Cuban cops nor the army have a clue where the Swords are or what they're up to. There's been no mention of anything further on them. Sam?"

"Si-sir?" Sam said, surprised. He pushed his glasses up on his nose and leaned into camera pan.

"You have electrical power for your power-cell chargers, right?"

"Yes sir."

"Good. Keep a live BSH sat-link up until further notice. If we hear anything indicating the police or the army are on to you, we'll need to chat in a hurry."

"Depend on it, General."

"Okay. Our people have been networking with every free-world intelligence agency that might be of use on this op and we've got a couple of breakthroughs for you from a source in the old Rodina itself. There's no word on how they did it, but the Swords are thought to have made it out of Havana. So much for Cuban roadblocks. The word is they're now on a ship in Cienfuegos Harbor. That's the good news. The bad news is there're at least fifty oceangoing ships in that port, not counting hundreds of small craft, and no one knows which vessel they're on. Further, the analysts feel the highest probability is that the Swords will fire some sort of guided missile from the ship they're on at the Juragua reactor containment domes. Depending on what they hit the domes with, they may get anything from a chipped dome to a breach and destruction of the fuel cores and cooling water systems, which will result in meltdown that'll make Cuba glow for years and kill Americans as far north as . . . here in D.C."

"When?" Travis asked, tersely.

"There's no information that counters the last low-confidence indication we got that they will move at midnight tonight. There's no way to know . . . no way we've found yet, to know if your encounter with the Swords will delay or eliminate their strike on Juragua."

"Or move it up," Travis said grimly.

"Or move it up," Krauss agreed. "If we hear anything, Travis, you'll be the next one who hears it, and you'll hear it quick, I guarantee you. POTUS has the entire miltary going to DEFCON 2, and they're calling it a drill. Obviously we can't start warning or evacking anybody, or we'd set off a national panic that can't even be imagined. Besides, where're all those people in the thirteen southern states going to go anyway?"

*   *   *

After the team meal, Sarah went topside with Yuri to stand guard. As everyone except Yuri had a BSH on, a secure briefing was begun by Travis. He brought Sarah, Jack, Hunter, and Stan up to speed on General Krauss's briefing.

Stan harumphed. "I ain't no nuclear engineer, guys, but I've seen the plans for the VVER-440 Russian export reactor like the rest of us. I *am* an ordnance engineer with lots of experience blowing the shit out of lots of things all over the world. Those domes are designed to withstand airplane crashes from the outside, and hellacious internal explosions, and still contain the radioactivity. They're not big eggshells. In my humble opinion, nobody's gonna penetrate those containment domes with some crappy little shoulder fired antitank rocket, or truck-fired antipersonnel rockets up to two hundred forty mm, or even antiaircraft missiles. All those are designed to cut up people, comparatively thin tank armor and aluminum-skinned airplanes, not to destroy steel-lined, steel-reinforced-concrete, nuclear containment domes, let alone do the major internal damage necessary to trigger a meltdown."

"So," Hunter picked up, sensing where Stan was headed. "You're saying smart bombs, or even dumb bombs?"

"Possible, Hunter. A big smart bomb like our people took out Iraqi bunker-hangars with might do it, but even that's marginal for internal destruction. And besides, how they gonna get 'em there? You told us there's a no-fly zone for five miles around the plant up to thirty-five thousand feet."

"Right," Hunter agreed. "And it's enforced by Cuban fighters that are in the air all the time, as part of Cuba's effort to keep the South American drug traffickers from operating in or over Cuba without paying the appropriate duty to the appropriate fat cats. All air traffic over and near Cuba is rigidly monitored; you don't just go for a Sunday afternoon sight-see in your Piper Cub. Down here the government signs off on every flight plan before anybody takes off."

"What about a renegade Cube pilot on the Swords payroll?" Jack asked.

"Possible," Hunter answered. "But real unlikely in a communist scenario."

"So," Stan said, "that leaves big missiles. If you're shooting with an ICBM, you don't need the Swords in-country. Now we're down to—"

"Cruise missiles," Jen said softly.

"Bingo," Hunter said. "Big, dam-buster class, cruise-monsters."

"Which you don't fire from small boats," Jen said.

"They're too heavy to carry, let alone launch from anything less than, say, a two-hundred-foot boat, a one-hundred-tonner or so, and even that's pushing the engineering."

Travis spoke. "Which still leaves a hell of a lot of boats and ships from a hundred tons on up to sixty or seventy-thousand-ton freighters. There are hundreds of vessels in that huge harbor."

"Except," Sarah piped in from the observation floor, "you don't cross oceans in hundred-ton boats."

"Sarah's right," Stan said. "Oh, you can cross oceans in boats that size in decent weather; they did for centuries. But if you're carrying an ungodly expensive and mission-critical cruise missile and all the fueling, launch, and guidance systems, and all the attendant personnel, *and* you want to be able to hide the whole schmuzoli en route and on station, you—"

"Haul it in a ship," Sam chimed in. "A big ship."

"Thirty-thousand tonner, five-hundred-feet long, minimum, would be a good guess," Stan concluded.

"So," Sam said, "as usual, Sam Wong the wonder weenie saves the day."

"How, oh Weenie One?" Jack said, the bags under his eyes drooping.

"We get down to the harbor with binoculars and scope everything down there that's big enough. They'll all have names painted on them."

"That's still gonna be a shit load of boats," Jack grumbled.

"Then I lock into NSA and up-task them to track all those ships, their ports of departure, and their cargo manifests. It's all computerized somewhere, which means we can almost certainly access it."

Jen sniffed. "Come on Sam. What? We're just going to look under 'big-assed cruise missile' on their manifests?"

"It's a start, Wonder Woman," Sam retorted with a grin. "You got a better idea?"

"You got me there, Weenie."

"Yeah, but . . ." Jack mused, and all heads turned his way. "If you're going to shoot off a cruise missile from a ship, how come you need the Swords in-country?"

Everyone in the room looked at each other.

Stan had an answer. "A diversion, to throw off counteractions."

Jen just guessed. "A recon in force?"

Hunter said, "Maybe they go in after the missile hits to ensure the necessary breach of the reactor itself."

"No chance," Jen countered. "They'd never know that the missile wouldn't breach the reactors and if that happened, they'd glow in the dark until they died within hours. Our best intel coming in was the Swords intend to live through this. They're planning an escape by ship. Maybe they're here as a defense. To keep anybody like us from finding and stopping the launch."

Jack said, "Or maybe they ain't using no missile. Maybe, they're gonna hit the reactors on the ground."

"With what?" Travis chimed in. "It'll take a lot of bang to crack those reactors open bad enough to get the kill-scope they want. And even if they get that much explosive past Cuban customs and overland to the plant, how do they get past the battalion of security that protects the place? I'm still betting on the cruise missile idea."

The team pondered in silence.

"Hunter, Jen, Sarah," Travis said after a moment. "Y'all can look local enough. Thank Christ there're so many racial types down here. Jack you go along as the reserve man. Stay away from the group, but back 'em if they run into trouble. H&K forty-fives and ankle grenades under civvies. Questions?"

"Travis?" Sarah said over the BSH net from upstairs. "Shouldn't we take Yuri with us? He knows the city, he can save us a lot of time, and if we run into trouble, it'll be nice to have a tour guide along who knows the streets."

Travis pondered for several seconds.
"Good idea," he said.

September 25, 1320 hours, Internal Security
Headquarters, Havana, Cuba

Colonel Raimundo was so livid he was almost ill. His
office staff was keeping a low profile.

Raimundo's close encounter of the third kind with the
wavy, death-spewing specter in the dark doorway on
Avenida de las Floras, which had very nearly blown his
ass off, had been the most humiliating, degrading experience of his life. Worse, it had terrified him, and terror
was something he was accustomed to causing, not
suffering.

Raimundo had staggered into the street when he
heard the shooting fade away and be replaced by scores
of arriving sirens. Only when approaching policemen
cautiously came near, and he observed the incredulous
looks of their faces, did it dawn on him what they were
looking at. Colonel Rafio Raimundo, the feared chief of
Internal Security, had had his pants shot off, but evidently not before he wet them.

In spite of a searing headache from beneath his forehead bandage and burning pain from the light flesh
wound on his upper left arm, Raimundo slammed his
hand onto his desk, and swept the ringing phone onto the
floor in a rage. He could just hear the stories that would
travel like electricity through the Internal Security Cell,
the notoriously gossipy police community, and even the
goddamned army! Already, on the hood of one of the
police cars, Raimundo had seen a finger-drawing in the
dust depicting his caricature standing in a puddle
with his pants around his knees, tears pouring from his
eyes. He had flown into a rage upon seeing it and ordered that no effort be spared to bring the impudent wag
who drew this obscenity before him! *Now!* He would *kill*
the dog! Raimundo's minions scurried about looking
busy, but, as the cartoonist was an instant folk hero, no
culprit was produced.

Even now, hours later, Raimundo's blood pressure would probably have alarmed his doctor, but he'd finally realized that he was only complicating the spectacle his image had deteriorated to with his fury. With great will, he had suppressed it. There would come a reckoning. Oh yes. Raimundo would find those American sons of *whores*! He would find them, their invisibility gadgets be damned! And when he did . . . oh . . . when he did.

In the meantime Raimundo had held high-level phone conferences with everyone of power in the military, including Castro himself, telling them he was convinced that an American terror squad was afoot in Cuba and must be located at all costs. The murders of his brave men must be avenged, Raimundo had cried, though he was about as loyal to his people as a lawyer. This terror squad might even be a recon probe for an invasion, Raimundo had shrieked, red faced. He carefully omitted any tales about American killers in invisible suits, as he knew such claims would quickly get him written off as a UFO abductee or another lunatic who'd just seen Che Guevara.

The invasion remark was taken seriously by the Great One, who was as paranoid as might be expected of a man whom someone within or without had been trying to kill for forty years. Castro ordered the military to a state of maximum alert and launched an island-wide search for suspicious or undocumented Americans. He doubted any invasion was imminent, but he did not doubt that the Americans might put a high-tech goon squad down in sugarland to kill *him*. It wouldn't be the first time they'd tried. Besides, there was the not-incidental collateral matter of eleven dead Internal Security officers and four charred blocks of Old Havana.

The search had centered on Havana, as roadblocks had gone up almost immediately after the terrible gun battle with the "drug gang." Besides, why would either the Swords of Allah or the Americans need to be anywhere else? What, in fact, were either of them even doing in Havana?

Raimundo didn't know, he admitted to himself, kicking his chair back and standing, fists on his hips, but he was *goddamned* sure going to find out.

September 25, 1438 hours,
Port of Cienfuegos, Cuba

Hunter and Jen sat on one side of the flower-decor-
ated, umbrella-shaded sidewalk café table, Sarah and
Yuri on the other. They appeared to be just two more
tourist couples, or maybe Russian workers at the nuclear
power plant. Across the busy street, sitting on an old,
moss-speckled stone wall near the harbor's edge, sat a
very large amiable *negro* in a flowery Hawaiian shirt,
probably one of the hundreds of itinerant Jamaican laborers brought in to help with the sugarcane harvest.
Yuri Nobakov's personal car, a battered old Volvo
sedan, sat by the small, palm-shaded park down the
block. Behind Jack's perch on the seawall, the vast Port
of Cienfuegos—geographically almost a huge inland lake
attached by a narrow umbilical cord of the channel to
the great, ice-blue, Carribean Sea beyond. The expansive
harbor spread for several square miles, encompassing
rows of piers sprouting forests of loading cranes.

And ships, Hunter Blake thought, squinting out over
the bright water. A million *ships!* "This is going to take
a lot longer than we thought," Hunter muttered. He
sipped at a tall glass of lemonade.

"Tell me about it," Jen said.

"A suggestion, if I may?" Yuri said.

"Go for it."

"I suggest we split into two . . . teams. One works the
edge of the harbor, one rents a boat and surveys from the
sea. We will cover more ships this way, and we can log even
those vessels which are anchored out in the holding waters."

After a moment, Jen asked, "Who goes where?"

Yuri replied, "I would suggest that Sarah and I rent
the boat, as I have documentation to do so, and I know
the harbor. You and Captain Blake might survey from the
land. Captain DuBois should go with you, as we are
unlikely to need his services on the water."

"I'm game if you are, Jen," Hunter said amiably.
"Your call."

The rented outboard pitched and bounced on the
choppy waters of the bay, but Sarah felt wonderful,

buoyant, and hopeful for the first time since the threat
of the Juragua destruction was made known to her. The
day was fabulously beautiful, the vibrant, teeming harbor
was exciting . . . and Yuri. Yuri was . . . disturbing.
Sarah lowered the binoculars, wrote *Caribbean Maru* /
Yokusuka on the border of a newspaper next to the
previous entries—*Atlantic Trader* / Stockholm, and
Global Wind—Lykes Line / Panama.

"It's so beautiful, Yuri!" Sarah shouted over the high
buzz of the outboard motor.

Yuri turned from looking ahead to smile sadly at
Sarah. "Some parts of Cuba are," he said. "But inland,
away from the port commerce and the money flow it
generates, you have peasants who are living on rationed
food. They recently had scheduled power blackouts to
conserve electricity. Cuba had no internal energy source
to generate electricity before the Juragua nuclear facility.
That is why it is so important to them."

Yuri slowed the boat, let the wake overrun it slowly,
then cut the engine. The sudden relative silence, punctuated lightly by the slap of waves against the Fiberglas
hull, was rich. Yuri rose from the cockpit and walked,
wobbling, feet wide apart against the rock of the small
craft, to the rear of the boat and the broad seat in front
of the motor. He sat next to, but not too near, Sarah.

"Give me the glasses, Sarah. I will scan the ships and
you may write them down. If we are challenged by the
harbor police or the navy, let the newspaper slide over-
board. The ink in that pen is water soluble."

Sarah handed Yuri the binoculars. "Yuri, how . . .
how long have you worked for the CIA?"

"*Gravenar* / Rotterdam," Yuri said. "When Annatava
died in 1994, I was filled with . . . a rage. I needed to
take an . . . action, some . . . how you say, *affirmative*
action! I had to do something to fight back against the
greater terrible forces that led to her death. When I was
appointed to return to Juragua as the chief of Russian
medicine on site, I knew I had my opportunity. *Queen
Victoria* / Sydney. It was simple, really. They—the
CIA—have a number on the internet. In a few weeks
one of their people contacted me. I . . . I don't destroy
communism, Sarah, but now at least I fight it in my small

way. It helps me feel partially vindicated for Annatava. *Commerce Trader* / Southampton."

Yuri twisted to scan past Sarah. In so doing he brushed against her breasts. "Oh, sorry! It was unintentional, I assure—"

"I won't be filing a sexual harassment lawsuit, Yuri," Sarah said, smiling.

"You have a . . . how you say it? Radiant! Yes radiant, you have a radiant smile, Sarah. You are a beautiful woman."

"My uncle is a dentist."

Yuri laughed, raising the binoculars. "*Rogas Hannova* / Lisbon," he said.

With no preamble, Yuri suddenly let the glasses drop to his lap. He looped an arm about Sarah's shoulders, framed her chin with his other hand, and kissed her long and fervently. Sarah was briefly surprised, but found his kiss more than a little galvanizing. She let her arms reach about Yuri's neck and made his sudden courage worth his while.

In a moment they parted, both breathing heavily.

"Wow," Sarah said, softly.

Yuri looked beyond Sarah, smiling with his lips but not his eyes. "Cuban navy patrol boat," he whispered, then he kissed her again.

Sarah got the message as she heard the deep, bubbly grumble of a larger boat behind her.

Now over Yuri's shoulder, the big, gray gunboat hove into view, coasting close. On its bridge, Sarah could see two men, both officers from their uniforms, eyeing them through binoculars. The boat drifted closer.

Sarah suddenly pushed Yuri away, and stood, furious, tugging her blouse into place. She slapped Yuri hard across the face and shouted, *"Bruto! Bestia!"*

Yuri palmed his stinging face and tried to get both his eyes to see the same thing again.

The two Cuban naval officers laughed. One slapped the other on his shoulder and pointed at Sarah and Yuri. They laughed again, and one shouted a command. The engines of the big patrol boat surged, its stern squatted, and it roared away, leaving Sarah and Yuri rocking in its wake.

As the boat faded away, Sarah drew her peasant skirt up her thighs, kicked off her sandals and placed her smooth, white thighs about Yuri's and sat on his lap. He looked up at her, entranced by her smile, now ever more lovely upon its return. Sarah placed her arms about Yuri's neck and began to kiss him lightly on the reddened cheek she'd slapped.

"Bruto," Sarah whispered softly, kissing his cheek again and again. *"Bestia,"* she said with her lips upon his ear.

They kissed like only lovers under threat can do, hard, long, like tomorrow may not dawn. Sarah drew Yuri down atop her on the AstroTurf floor of the rocking little boat. Her blouse was dampened against her back by the water puddles, but Sarah did not notice, nor would she have cared if she had.

The sun was low and cast long hard shadows on the rental boat dock, but Jen saw it right away, as perhaps only a woman can read the glowing face of another woman. And Yuri fairly radiated nervous self-consciousness. Yep. They did it. I knew it. I knew it.

"Get some?" Hunter asked.

Yuri blanched. Sarah clutched and said, "Um . . . excuse me?"

"Did you get any? Ship names! Did you get any ship names?"

"Twenty-seven large oceangoers! And one Cuban navy gunboat. But Yuri saved us." Sarah gazed up at Yuri.

I'll bet, Jen thought, wryly.

"We got thirty-eight." Hunter seemed to be feeling the strain. The nearing extermination by radiation poisoning of up to twenty million people has that sort of effect on you, he reflected. "It's not all the big ones at the docks, but it's all we could get close to. Let's just hope Sam can—uh-oh."

A sober uh-oh was not what anyone in the quartet wanted to hear at that place and time. They turned to see a bizarrely painted red and purple, blue-smoke-spewing '76 Cadillac stretch limo draw to the curb. Four large, dirty-appearing Cuban men got out. One, very dark-skinned, tall and rail-thin, had a shark's smile on his face and his eyes lingered on Jen's tits a lot longer than was tactful. The other three men ranged in size from short and weasel-like to tall and about 230 pounds. The middle-sized man had a shaved and tattooed skull. They didn't look like employees of the Cuban tourism bureau.

"Lenin's bloody ghost," Yuri whispered. "Dock gangs. Like your . . . like your *mafioso!*"

"Wonderful," Hunter said, studying the men for weapons.

A dickhead is a dickhead all over the world, Jen thought. I can spot one anywhere. Now what do you smug fucks want? A smug fuck, I'll bet. Along with our money.

The big one, at least, has a gun, Sarah thought. He's too fat for that shirt to conceal the knobby bulge at his waist. Houston, we have a problem.

"Heeeey!" The dark man said, amiably. *"Americanos!"*

The other three men took up positions to the sides but never where they might hit each other if they had to shoot. Not a good sign, Hunter thought.

Without waiting for an answer, Dark Man eyed Jenny from tits to ass and back, and smiled his approval. "Heeey, you loook reeel fine, little girl! Ju know what I mean?"

Great, Jen thought, I'm a hit on the Cuban dock thug ten-scale.

Jen evinced a nervous fear and clutched Hunter by the arm. "Darling!" she said, weakly, "I'm frightened!" Hunter choked back a grin.

"Andre, honey!" Sarah said in a Southern drawl that would've done Scarlett O'Hara proud. She stood closer to Yuri and took his hand. "Why, who arrrre these . . . men?"

Now the short weasel spoke. "We just' wan' offer you a ride home, little puss," he said, smirking and exposing yellow teeth blackened at their edges.

Hunter figured The Weasel for the leader. "Um, no thanks, we, uh, we have our own car. Look, guys," Hunter said, smiling weakly and holding his hands to his sides, palms out. "We don't have much money, but how about you take it and just leave us be?"

"Ju calling me a thief, *señor*?" The Weasel said meanly, stepping closer. "Hanh? Ju saying we *banditos,* man?"

"I'm just saying we'll be happy to make a donation to the Cuban orphan's fund. I know you men will see to it the money gets there."

"Oh. You funny. He's funny, isn' he," The Weasel said, sneering. He produced a Russian Makarov pistol from his pants pocket and stuck Hunter stoutly in the stomach with it. "Thees funny, you Americano fuck? Hanh? Thees funny?"

"Scotteeeee!" Jen bleated, "he's got a . . . a gun!"

"Oh mah gawd!" Sarah cried, clutching Yuri. "Andre! Do somethin'!"

Yuri was keeping a low profile. He was out of his element again, and he knew it.

Hunter looked around. What few Cubans were still about were averting their eyes, or closing the doors to their shops. The dock gangs were dreaded almost as much as the Internal Security Force.

"Who are you?" Jen croaked, leaning on Hunter. "What do you intend to . . . oh my *god*!"

"Get een the car, *puta*!" Dark Man demanded, and he fired a command in Spanish to Fat Giant and the Tattooed Skull, who moved forward.

"Hey man," Hunter said. "Look, I don't want any trouble, man. Just . . . just take them . . . if you have to, but let me . . . let me go, okay?"

"Whaaaat?" Jen wailed, gaping in indignant shock.

"Go on, and take her, man!" Hunter pleaded. "Just don't hurt me! Okay?"

"Scotteeeee!" Jen cried. The Weasel grabbed her by the arm and yanked her toward the car.

"Ju a smart boy!" The Weasel said, poking Hunter again with the Makarov. "Get de fuck outa here, man!" Hunter began to back away slowly.

"Scotteeeeee!" Jen screamed as The Weasel jammed her into the back seat of the car. Dark Man and Fat Giant took Sarah by her arms and snatched her from Yuri, who held on to her and was yanked with her. He stared hotly into Dark Man's eyes breathing hard.

Hunter jumped forward and broke Yuri's grip, pulling

him back. "Let 'em go, Andre!" Hunter said. "Let 'em go or these guys will hurt us, man!"

Sarah was jerked hard and had to leap to keep her feet. "Andre! Help me, Andre!" she shouted, crying. Fat Giant crammed her into the rear-facing cabin seat across from Jen, who was between Dark Man and The Weasel, and he clambered in next to her, rocking the big car. Tattooed Skull jumped behind the wheel and lit up the gaudily painted old limo.

"Come heeere, *puta*!" The Weasel said in the back seat next to Jen, grinning his yellow-toothed smirk, reaching for Jen.

Out on the sidewalk, Yuri whispered tightly to Hunter. "Can they handle this?"

"Is a duck watertight?" Hunter answered, watching the car.

Predictably, Jen struck first. She extended both her thumbs rigidly and snapped both her arms up with a whipping action that drove her thumbs into one eye each of The Weasel and Dark Man. Both men flinched, clutched their faces, and howled. In the next instant, she crossed her arms and wrenched both her elbows hard into the Adam's apple of first Dark Man, then Weasel. Again both men jerked as though they'd been shocked, but now they clutched their throats and croaked like choking frogs.

As soon as Sarah had seen the rage boil over in Jen's eyes, she turned to Fat Giant, smiled sweetly, and two-hand palm-slapped him viciously over both ears at once, giving him a sensation like having cherry bombs go off in both aural canals. Instantly, Sarah seized two fistfuls of the man's longish, greasy hair and, with her upper forehead, head-butted Fat Giant's face six violent times, making mush of his nose and lips.

Jen, in the meantime, whipped up her skirt, beneath which were duct-taped a grenade to one thigh, and her 9mm Baretta to the other. She ripped the grenade loose and balled it in her hand.

"Oh shit," Hunter said, watching from ten feet away, his hand under his shirt on his SIG.

"*Puta* this, asshole!" Jen hissed. She smashed the baseball-sized steel grenade into The Weasel's face, shattering teeth and splitting lips.

Dark Man groped desperately at his belt for his own gun, though he still held his gasping throat with the other hand. He goggled his one remaining functional eye toward Jen. Sarah drove her fist into Dark Man's crotch from across the car, an Ishinru thrust of the two fore-knuckles delivered with the speed of a sprung foot-hold trap and all the weight of her upper torso. The fingers of both his hands straightened rigidly on contact, and he dropped the Makarov. He gagged unintelligibly and slid onto the floor.

Sarah picked up the Makarov, sprung its magazine onto the floor, racked the slide to eject the chambered round, and pistol-whipped Fat Giant about the head with a vengeance. His eyes became so bloodied as to be unrecognizable.

When the fun began, Tattooed Skull, in the driver's seat, thought for a second that the girls were struggling goofily in the way frightened *putas* always did when the *hombres* went to work on them. He actually grinned, until a glance in the mirror told him he wasn't in Kansas anymore. He clawed at the driver's door to open it.

Hunter lit on his butt on the hood, slid across and landed on his feet. He kneed the door shut on Tattooed Skull's left hand, eliciting a yowl of pain. Hunter reached through the open driver's window with his right hand, grabbed Tattooed Skull by the back of his head, and drew it out of the window. With his left hand Hunter reached inside to the armrest, felt for the left-front switch and buzzed the window glass up, garroting Tattooed Skull rather neatly and not unlike a dull guillotine, Hunter thought. He held the switch down until the window motor blew a fuse. Tattooed Skull pulled at the glass, making choked-chicken noises. He kicked the dashboard spastically and whipped about within.

From across the road, atop the old stone sea wall, Captain Jack DuBois positively cried with laughter.

"Ain' that some shit, man?" Jack said, walking away, wiping his eyes, still laughing. "Even our pussies ain't pussies!"

Wide-eyed locals peered carefully from their shops in amazement at the big negro standing in the street, pounding on a lamp post, weeping with laughter.

Chapter Eight

Rafio Raimundo snatched the phone up. "Yes!"

"Colonel Raimundo?"

"Yes! What do you want?"

"Colonel Raimundo, I am Investigator Juan Juarez, with the Cienfuegos Provincial Police?"

"Yes? Speak, man!"

"*Sí.* I am in receipt of the departmental fax which indicates that you seek information regarding certain *Americano* terrorists?"

Cienguegos Province? Where the mysterious dissolving plastic was found in the cane field? Raimundo sat up, snatched a pen, and drew a notepad near. "Yes?"

"Colonel, I cannot be certain it has anything to do with your request, but we have had a strange incident here which I suspect is connected."

"Yes, yes. Go ahead."

"Down by the harbor, Colonel, we are investigating the savage beating of a small gang of notorious dock toughs."

Raimundo sighed and rolled his eyes. "Investigator! What on earth does this have to do with—"

"Perhaps nothing, my Colonel. It is just that my men tell me the witnesses—those who can be made to talk, at least—tell a strange story. The . . . victims, will say nothing, as usual. One in fact may die."

"Yes?"

"It seems that the victims, four of the meanest cutthroats in all the dock gangs, who were armed, were beaten *loco* inside their own car by two women they apparently attempted to abduct!"

Raimundo didn't make the connection, but he knew an odd coincidence when he heard one. "Women?" he asked, stunned.

"*Sí*, Colonel! Two *Americano* women, apparently with two men."

"American men?" Raimundo stared tensely out the window of his lavishly furnished office.

"One was, Colonel. The other, according to the witness closest to the incident, had a heavy . . . Russian accent."

"Start the helicopter!" Raimundo shouted, banging the phone into its cradle. "Get that pig, General Torejos, on the phone, *muy pronto*!"

September 25, 1921 hours, Nobakov villa, Cienfuegos, Cuba

Sam wiped sweat from his brow and resumed the frantic keyboarding with which he was devising a data-delineation program to filter out the staggering maritime commerce data flooding in by satellite from NSA. General Krauss clearly had pulled out all the stops and Sam was worried. Krauss may even be shooting over too much data.

Tension had escalated throughout the team, including Yuri, since their return from the docks. Everyone knew the unforseen encounter with the Cuban gang had the potential to draw very unneeded attention and thus increase the risk of interference by the authorities. Moreover, the chilling scenario that would follow a failure to stop the assault on Juragua was growing ever more real and terrifying. The Swords of Allah strike was alleged to be tonight, but so little else was known. Exactly when? Where? In what manner?

Sam hit enter and watched the names of ships scroll up the screen.

Jen had changed out of and washed her bloodstained civvies. Travis had the whole team in the sweat-smelly, down-powered LOC suits, in case they were somehow tracked to Yuri's villa.

At her laptop, Jen suddenly frowned. "Travis!"

From downstairs, where he, Stan, and Jack readied the special weapons pods, Travis answered on the BSH intrasquad net.

"No need to shout, Jen," he said, smiling.

"Yeah, well check this out and you'll shout yourself. General Krauss says they just intercepted an aviation band transmission that they confirmed by sat-recon; our boy Colonel Raimundo's helicopter just took off from IntSec headquarters in Havana, and it's headed straight this way. Worse, the monitoring station at Guantanamo Bay says there's increased Cuban army radio traffic involving the Seventh Mobile Strike Infantry Brigade, which is Castro's answer to our Delta Force. NSA doesn't know more yet, but it's clear that Fidel's bad-boy soldiers are being mobilized on the hurry-up for some reason. I don't like the smell of this, boss."

"Shit," Travis swore softly. "Sam?"

"I'm trying!" Sam replied with more force than was called for. "I prioritized ships arriving from the Middle East in the last twenty-four hours, first. Nothing in their manifests that even sounds like a big missile. Now I'm sorting through the rest, but if you go back only a week, you get one-hundred-forty-seven ships larger than thirty thousand tons with destination port of Cienfuegos. There are sixty-eight that haven't left yet, but have you ever seen the shipping manifest for a large, seagoing freight vessel? Hundreds of pages, some of them! Tens of thousands of items. There's no way to know for sure if the ship we want is even a freighter, how long ago it arrived, or even if it has arrived yet. I just don't—"

"I know you're doing the best that can be done, Sam," Travis said gently. "Just let me know right away if you turn up anything."

It was a tense hour later that Sam startled everyone with a sharp, deafening shout on the BSH.

"Hey! Hey, hey, hey! Boss!"

"Comin' Sam." Travis bolted up the stairs.

Jen and Stan joined Travis at Sam's workstation on

the bedroom desk. Hunter and Sarah were on guard. Jack was still battle-checking the weapons.

"Loot at this!" Sam said excitedly, pointing at the screen. "Check it out!"

"What?" Jen said, slightly irked. "So this . . . Panamanian registered *Global Arctic Star* out of Murmansk, arrived Port of Cienfuegos yesterday—carries 'munitions.' So what? I'm sure tons of munitions a month are shipped to the Cuban army, from Russia and god knows where else."

"I see it," Stan said.

"See *what*?" Jen demanded curtly.

"Look under 'type of vessel.' " Stan pointed with a chunky finger to a narrow column to the right of the cluttered screenful of shipping data.

"Pretty smart for a Polack," Sam said.

" 'Type of vessel code: BT-Ag,' " Jen read. "Ah!"

"I wrote my scan program to cross vessel type with manifested cargo," Sam explained to the rest of the team. "It was a long shot, but we're twenty points behind late in the fourth quarter. It paid off! *BT-Ag!* Bulk Tanker—Agricultural! It's a *sugar* freighter! What are 'munitions' doing on a sugar ship?"

"Maybe it's back-hauling freight?" Hunter said.

"No," Stan said. "The little smart-ass is right. Sugar is blown onto modern bulk tankers with compressed air through pipes into huge sealed and dehumidified bulk holds. It's off loaded the same way. The ships aren't set up to carry anything but powdered ag products. You can't back-haul anything but sugar without totally and expensively flushing the holds on each end, unless what you back-hauled was sugar, and *nobody* is hauling sugar *to* Cuba. My money's on the Weenie on this."

Travis sniffed and let out a long breath. "Do we know where this *Global Arctic Star* is in the harbor?"

"Yeah," Jen said looking at a crumpled, blood-stained sheet of typing paper. "I remember the name; it's one of those big ships Hunter and I logged. It's at . . . pier forty-two, berth D as in delta."

"Beautiful!" Travis said. "Sam, have—"

"Way ahead of you, boss man," Sam said. "The harbor docking scheme can be had on the internet through scores of maritime data sites. I'll have NSA draw down the tightest sat-photo data available from any source on pier forty-two, berth D, and—"

"Bet your ass!" Stan said. "If they've modified that ship to load, transport, launch, and guide a cruise missile, it'll have to show at least minor signs of reconstruction on deck. Probably some funky antennas you'd never in hell find on a bulk sugar tub, too."

Sam's fingers fluttered like decorative ribbon-fringe blowing in the wind.

September 25, 1932 hours, Port of Cienfuegos, Cuba

The noisy, windy, French-built Aerospatiale Dauphin helicopter, painted Cuban army tan, landed on the side street bordering the Port of Cienfuegos. Flashing police cars blocked the street. Dust, trash, and jet fumes roiled.

Colonel Rafio Raimundo, bent low, scrambled from beneath the whirring main rotor, gripping his cloth fatigue hat. He wore boots and army utility clothing now, and carried a folding-stock AK-74 rifle with banana magazine. Two of his similarly dressed aides scurried in his wake, one carrying a cell phone. A sweating man in a suit walked briskly up to Raimundo and saluted.

"Investigator Juan Juarez, at your service, Colonel!"

"Have you collected the witnesses as I radioed?" Raimundo demanded, without greeting.

"Exactly as you instructed, Colonel!" Juarez shouted as they straightened and drew away from the helicopter toward the garishly painted old Cadillac limousine. A dozen policemen stood about. Scores of bystanders peered curiously from a distance.

Even Raimundo was surprised at the blood spattered all over the rear interior of the car, and in rank smelling, congealing pools in the foot wells. Fat Giant, Dark Man, Tattooed Skull, and The Weasel had long since been transported to a hospital.

"What did this . . . alleged American woman . . . hit these people with?" he asked in awe.

"There was no weapon, Colonel! The incident occurred within the closed automobile, sir, but witnesses say it appeared she used her fist."

"Her *fist*?" Raimundo gawked at the dreadful cabin of the car.

"Sí! No weapon was observed, sir. Also, Colonel, we have been informed that the most seriously injured victim is in surgery."

Raimundo dismissed this news with a flip of his hand.

"How did they escape?"

"In an old brown Volvo, Colonel! No one obtained a license number; they say mud had been smeared on the identification plate. I have run the motor vehicle records, of course, but there are over eighty Volvos more than five years old registered in Ceinfuegos Province alone."

"Where are these witnesses, Investigator? Perhaps my men and I can persuade them to be more forthcoming."

"This way, Colonel!" Juarez led Raimundo toward a small sidewalk café, before which stood four policemen around a half-dozen seated and very worried-looking citizens of Cienfuegos.

"Colonel!" One of Raimundo's aides called urgently from several steps behind. Raimundo turned to see the aide waving the cell phone.

"Colonel Raimundo! A call for you, sir! From the headquarters operator!"

"Ah!" Raimundo whirled and strode for the café. "Tell her not *now*! Tell her to—"

"But I already have, Colonel!" the aide answered, distressed. "She says you will definitely want to take this call yourself! Immediately, sir!"

September 25, 2029 hours,
Nobakov villa, Cienfuegos, Cuba

"Sat-data photos coming in, boss!" Sam called. Jack and Jen were on guard. The rest of the team, and Yuri, quickly gathered behind Sam and his flat computer screen.

Even though it had meant suspiciously ordering a target-

track priority shift and redirected orbit on three premium military surveillance satellites, at a cost of millions
in surveillance dollars to other "customers," Brigadier
General Krauss had not even hesitated at Sam's request
slightly over an hour ago and made sure it happened.

Sam's screen flickered, changed colors several times,
turned dark, then bright again. An orange rectangle
flashed TRANSMISSION COMPLETE. Sam clicked keys. A
vertical column of numbers appeared. Sam trac-balled
the cursor to the digit 1, and thumbed the enter button.

A remarkably high-resolution, satellite-surveillance
color photograph materialized on the screen. It was
twenty square miles of greater Cienfuegos Harbor and
showed scores of ships docked and many more at anchor
awaiting their call to the loading facilities. A tiny yellow
reticle rested over one ship.

"Direct overhead," Stan said. The sides of the ship
could not be seen. "Can't be sure it's the right ship without being able to read the name."

"As ol' Icarus there would say, 'Oh ye of little faith,' "
Sam said, echoing Hunter's line aboard the C-130.
"Stand by."

Sam thumb-clicked the trac-ball mouse built into the
keyboard and rolled the ball with his fingers. As he did,
the scale of the photograph magnified progressively until
one ship filled the entire screen with uniform pixel re-
duction and perfect clarity, as though the picture had
been taken from the top of the ship's own radio mast.

"Still no name," Travis said.

"Stand by, infidels!" Sam said dramatically. With the
trac-ball he magnified the picture yet again until individual deck planks and rivets were distinguishable.

"Amazing," Sarah whispered in awe. "Look at the
resolution and clarity."

"Welcome to state-of-the-art satellite photography,"
Sam said. "Think about that next time you're fucking in
the great out of doors. There we go! Am I cool or
what?"

Everyone peered sharply at the screen. Sam had trac-
balled the reticle to one of two very large, orange,
roofed capsules hung on davits at either side of the ship's
bridge superstructure.

"Bingo! Life boats! And if all you nonbelievers will just read the black stenciling on the roof, you—"

" 'Motor Vessel *Global Arctic Star*'!" Everyone spoke together. Sam held up his hand. Three others slapped it in sequence.

"Okay, we found the *Star*," Stan said.

"What do you mean, *we*, white man?" Sam cried.

"Now let's find the evidence we need to hit it," Stan finished. "Scan the rest of the deck, Sam, slowly."

"Ask and ye shall receive, oh Hairy One."

Sam rolled the trac-ball, and the yellow reticle moved quickly to the bow, then slowly toward the stern.

"Stop!" Stan said. "No. Forget it. Ordinary fire-access door. Keep going."

Sam moved the reticle.

"Hold. Recent welding burns on the paint there . . . but . . . no, it's just where they welded a hose rack to that bulkhead. Go on."

Foot by agonizingly slow foot, they examined the rest of the deck and bridge overhead all the way to the stern.

Lieutenant Commander Stan Powczuk, U.S. Navy SEAL officer and the TALON Force's nautical expert wiped his lips with his wrist. "I don't see shit so far. Just a modern but completely ordinary sugar tanker. Sam, can you give me any angle shots?"

"Let's see what else they've sent." Sam dumped the photo on screen and cursored some of the other numbers. Various other high-resolution shots of the *Global Arctic Star* presented. Stan examined them carefully, but kept asking for yet another.

"That's it, Stan," Sam said.

"Damn!" Stan spat, sweating. He knew how extraordinarily much might swing on his knowledge of ships, and he knew too well the whole team was waiting for him to derive some breakthrough revelation. But he could see nothing peculiar. Nothing! It was even a relatively new ship, instead of an oft repaired tramp, which made scanning for reconstruction irregularities easier, but still Stan could detect nothing to indicate accommodations for transporting, launching, and guiding a cruise missile. No strange hatches, no launch rails, and most telling of all, no odd antennas.

Everyone present, including Yuri Nobakov, watched tensely. All were feeling the time running out, but all knew to shut up at times like this and let the designated expert do his thing. Travis would ask for team input in due time.

"Back up, Sam," Stan said. "Let's have another look."

Slowly, pausing on each shot, Sam walked the photos back across the screen. The detail was amazing. In one low-angle-oblique shot from the port side, the only side not pressed up to the dock, individual crew members could be seen walking on deck, working, standing at the rails smoking. They were swarthy, bearded, mean-faced men who did not look as though they loved their jobs.

Stan knew that if there was modification of the ship to launch and guide missiles it almost certainly wouldn't be to the sides of the vessel, but he checked anyway. Sam moved the reticle along the side of the *Global Arctic Star* near her stern. A crew member stood smoking and gazing out over the harbor, his eyes squinted. The scan moved past him.

"Whoa! Back up!" Travis commanded, leaning forward. The subtle urgency in the normally tranquil boss's tone got everyone's attention.

Sam jumped. "Where?"

"Back to that guy you just passed."

Sam moved the reticle to square it over the ship's crewman leaning on the port rail, smoking, squinting tightly at the sunlight reflected off the water.

Travis peered closely. "See that big mole or birth mark on that guy's left cheek?"

"Wart?" Hunter said, also peering closely.

"Also, check out the missing two fingers on his right hand. He holds that cigarette with this thumb and ring finger, see?"

"Son of bitch," Stan whispered. "Trav, I think you're right."

"About what?" Sam snapped.

"Sam," Travis said, "call up the file photos of the Swords.

"You got it boss," Sam said typing, "but, man, there aren't many and they're almost all grainy, blown-up, long shots."

"Yeah. Blown-up. That's the key."

All the photographs of the known members of the swords of Allah appeared on the screen. There was one shot of a furtive little man caught striding briskly from a Tehran hotel entrance to a waiting Toyota Land Cruiser. The man was swinging his arms and looking back over his shoulder. The quality of the shot wasn't optimum, but it did clearly show a small black dot on the man's left cheek.

"That one."

"Kiss my hairy ass," Stan whispered.

"You're right, Travis!" Sarah exclaimed.

"Close on the right hand, Sam," Travis said. Sam choked the grainy image tight on the walking man's right hand, which was missing two fingers.

"Now, bring up the guy on the ship and put them side by side.

"I'll be goddamned," Hunter said slowly. "Ibrahim Shanaan, as I live and breathe."

"Brilliant, totally amoral bomb tech for the Swords," Sarah added, staring.

Stan clucked his tongue and stared at the screen. "Good eyes, Trav. Shanaan lost those fingers in eighty-nine when one of his not so brilliant little creations detonated out of turn in Lebanon. Didn't kill the fuck, regrettably."

Travis spoke grimly. "Okay. At least we know where the Swords are. Let's skull us up a fast plan to hit the *Global Arctic Star* right after dark. We're running out of time and options, Eagle Team. We got to hustle and be real lucky. Sam, see if you can find us an interior deck plan for the *Star*."

Stan stood. "All merchant ships registered to dock in the U.S.—and that's almost all of the big, expensive ones—have to have deck plans published in the international Maritime Fire Safety Registry, Sam, so—"

"*www.fsr.mar*! I'm on it!"

Travis and the team members immediately began moving to their equipment, but they didn't get far.

"Hidey ho, down there, children!" Jack called on the BSH from one of the watch stations upstairs. His tone caused everyone to reach for their rifles and look up at the ceiling. "I got the Cienfuegos Province boys coming up the street. One marked car, two cops. They're moving slow and looking right at this place. I don't like it."

Jen's tightened voice now came on the net, also from her watch station on the third floor. "And that's just the good news, people! I got a helicopter coming this way. Looks like an Aerospatiale Dauphin in Cuban military colors. No external armament, but it's coming right for us!"

"Shit!" Sam said immediately. "Travis, I'm getting an emergency threat warning from NSA here—stand by— oh fuck. General Krauss says GITMO just told them elements of the Seventh Mobile Strike Infantry are rolling out of a Cienfuegos base in . . . Christ! *Eight* trucks and a Russian armored personnel car! They're headed this way!"

Chapter Nine

Travis crashed to a second floor window, followed
shortly by Stan and Hunter. Sam frantically stowed the
uplink computer, then snatched his rifle and took up a
window firing position. Sarah scrambled for the med pod
to ready her field-react equipment and drugs. Yuri raced
to her side to help. Each TALON zipped their LOC
suits, plugged in the rifle cloaking, and fastened the chin
straps on their BSH helmets.

All watched the Provincial Policia roll up in front of
the villa.

"The helicopter is moving away to the east," Jen said
over the BSH.

Yuri rushed to the window by Travis. He was sweating
profusely and breathing hard. His eyes snapped from
one thing to another.

"Major!" Yuri said in a tight, low voice. "You must
allow me to speak to them! Perhaps I can settle their
concerns and send them on their way!"

"Yuri!" Sarah said from across the room. "Are you
crazy? If they knew how to find us, then they know
you're with us! You'll do no such thing!"

A quick glance from Travis reminded Sarah who was
calling the plays for the TALON Force. "He's not a
combatant, Travis!" Sarah said softly, over the net, so
Yuri did not hear.

"Please, Major! Remember your mission! It will be
dark in twenty minutes! At least give me the opportunity
to try to delay them until then! Perhaps they only have
questions and I can deflect their interest!"

Jack's deep voice came over the net. "The cops are getting out, Trav. I can grease 'em both from here."

"Hold."

"Major! Travis, please!" Yuri pleaded. "Let me do my part! I can talk to them in their own language. Assure them there is no cause for concern. In the worst event, I can invite them inside to see for themselves, and you can . . . do them. *Think,* Major! You must remain clandestine, to accomplish your mission. Think of the consequences for error!"

"I say we waste 'em," Hunter voted.

"Second the motion," Stan said with an edge. "They're too close and they've got access to a radio. They see us and the whole fucking Cuban world will come down on us."

"No," Travis said, calm as always. "Dr. Nobakov's right. The mission is paramount. There's a good chance Yuri can talk these guys away, and that's best. Leaving dead bodies all over Cuba is going to catch up with us before we get the mission accomplished. We're here for the mission, people; not to shoot Cuban cops for target practice. Go, Yuri. See what you can do. If you can't satisfy 'em, invite 'em for a look-see. Go. Stan, Jack, get down there and take 'em out if Yuri brings them in. Move."

Yuri hurried down the stairs followed briskly by Stan and Jack. Sarah slammed her fist against the carpet and fired a scathing look at Travis. She grabbed her XM-29 and scurried to a window overlooking the brief front yard of the villa and the street beyond. "You're going to get him killed!" Sarah hissed.

"Knock it off, Sarah!" Jen said from upstairs. "We all like Yuri, but Travis commands, and this is no time for debate!"

Sarah peered hotly down at the street to see Yuri walk casually out from the ground floor, waving to the officers who were standing outside their car. He called a greeting in his Russian-accented Spanish. The two Cuban policemen sneered suspiciously and hitched up their gunbelts. The larger lit a cigarette.

Travis sucked up the audio volume on his BSH speakers. "Skinny cop's in charge, people. Says is he Dr. Yure-vitch Nobakov, of the Juragua Nuclear Power Facility."

All saw Yuri nod and extend his hand. It was ignored by the policemen. The thin one resumed with a hostile tone.

"Says he is to come with them," Travis translated. "Says a Colonel—oh shit—Colonel Raimundo wishes to speak with him."

"No!" Sarah said hotly over the BSH. "Travis, we can't let them take him! He'll disappear into a basement cell or an unmarked grave in the marshes, and you *know* it!"

Jack said casually, "Clear field of fire, both targets."

Stan replied tersely, "Same-same."

"Hold."

Below, Yuri waved his hands expansively and laughed.

"Yuri says he can't imagine why any official would want to speak to him, he is only a harmless physician. Skinny cop says turn around, hands on the car."

"Travis, stop them!" Sarah pleaded.

"Skinny cop says Yuri's under arrest and—"

Sarah shouted "No!"

"—Yuri says okay no problem, he'll be glad to go."

Jack spoke softly. "He's leading them away from us. That ballsy little Ivan is gonna draw them off."

"Where's that helicopter?" Travis asked.

"Still holding about a mile east," Jen replied.

"Threat status, Sam," Travis said.

"Sat-recon shows the trucks of the Mobile Strike Brigade have stopped, boss. About two miles from here. Hell, could be a coincidence, right? Maybe they're just on training or something."

Sarah pleaded urgently. "Travis, if we let them take him, we'll never see him alive again! Do something!"

Travis swivelled his gaze to engage Sarah's directly. "Here's the something we're gonna do, people. We're going to sit right here . . . qui-et-ly . . . and let Yuri lead those shitheads out of here. Then, with our cover intact, we'll proceed with the reason we came here, to stop the Swords from radiation-poisoning twenty million Americans and all of Cuba."

Sarah's eyes watered and her face tightened. She

looked down at Yuri, who had placed his hands on the car and was being searched. Still he smiled. The courage, Sarah thought. Yuri is no warrior, but he's sacrificing himself for the mission. Sarah ached from the internal drive to shoot the two police officers, run down, and draw Yuri into her arms.

Jen spoke sharply. "Helicopter's swinging over this way, boss."

"The trucks aren't moving," said Sam. "Ditto the armored car."

Travis continued relaying the dialogue to the team. "Skinny cop says—shit!"

The team watched as the taller and heavier of the two cops circled behind Yuri, then grinned and punched him hard in the kidneys. Yuri arched his back in surprise and pain. The smaller cop then produced a telescoping metal baton and smashed Yuri about the sides of his head.

"Yuri!" Sarah cried, momentarily deafening the team on the BSH net. She would have been heard in the street were it not for the vicious beating being administered to Yuri, who now collapsed to his knees, covering his head. Still, the two policemen kicked and clubbed.

Sarah sprang up and sighted her rifle at the terrible scene below her.

Travis had anticipated this. He slammed into her, knocking her to the floor and pulling away her rifle. She looked up at him, her lips quivering. He stabbed a finger at her for a long moment, his eyes burning into hers, but he said nothing. He tossed Sarah's rifle back to her with force. Sarah caught it and rose to her knees, tears flowing from her eyes. She crawled to the window and watched as the two policemen stuffed Yuri's limp body into the back seat of their cruiser, then departed with a screech of tire rubber.

Sarah sat down hard and wept silently, eyeing Travis. "You bastard," she whispered in misery.

"Guilty as charged, your honor," Travis said softly, watching the police car disappear.

September 25, 2134 hours,
Fifteen hundred feet over Cienfuegos, Cuba

Rafio Raimundo steadied his binoculars against the vibration of the helicopter and studied the villa in the distance. The Provincial Police car, with the Russian, had passed beneath them five minutes ago. Good, he thought, it would be enjoyable to deal with the Russian later. Phase one successful, and not a moment too soon either. The sun was gone. Soon it would be pitch dark, and those American pirates would be hell to take down. But now phase two was unfolding just as he had planned! Raimundo aimed the glasses below, watching the stolen ambulance roll slowly down the palm-bordered residential street.

Fools! Raimundo swore inside. Arrogant Americans think they know it all! They think I don't know by now that they evaded the Havana roadblocks in a stolen ambulance? The *policia* idiots had located the missing medics. Those insidious American bastards! But now, he, Colonel Rafio Raimundo, was on top of the situation, as indeed here they came like he had predicted, from beneath the Russian doctor's villa in a large red ambulance! Now he would have his revenge for his night of shame on Avenida de las Floras.

Raimundo keyed his radio transmit button and fired off clipped Spanish. "IntSec One to Black Machete!"

Another voice in Spanish was heard in his headset, rendered slightly difficult to understand for the engine noise of a Russian-made armored personnel car in the background. "Black Machete, sir, go ahead!"

"They come, Captain! Just as I said. They are in a red Havana Medical Services ambulance truck. Remember! You must annihilate every occupant with over*whelming* fire! If any escape, they . . . will be impossible to contain!" Raimundo was still unwilling to try to make anyone believe his invisible-man story.

Captain Estavo Eduardo, commander of the B Company, 1st Battalion, 7th Mobile Infantry Strike Brigade, Revolutionary Army of the Republic of Cuba, rubbed his hand over his red beret and examined his men's positions for the tenth time. The squad machine guns were set on crossing fields of fire, but with no collateral traverse. The recoilless rifle truck was positioned dead ahead. And if by some stroke of fate the Blessed Virgin herself was riding in that ambulance and one of the American terrorists managed to escape, there were no less than ninety-six crack paratroop riflemen positioned on both sides of the street set to fire at matching oblique angles so as not to crossfire each other. *God* could not escape this trap!

There could be a promotion in this, Eduardo thought, looking up the long road from whence that lunatic Int-Sec Colonel had said the Americans would come. A transfer from this nowhere Cienfuegos command to Brigade Headquarters in Havana, and away from his fat wife's insufferable shrew of a mother!

"Back! Back!" Captain Eduardo commanded in Spanish, and his armored car groaned back out of view, but still remained where the 12.7 millimeter heavy machine gun on its roof could deploy on the target vehicle. This gun, Eduardo thought with excited anticipation, will be mine.

The ambulance sped quickly down the street along which the doomed Yuri Nobakov had been taken only minutes before. It ran with no lights in spite of the fading glow from a sun that had disappeared into the Yucatan. The road joined another residential street and then became a broader boulevard through the more lavish villas of the prosperous. The big red ambulance slowed for a stop sign, then seemed to accelerate wide-open, its diesel engine roaring and its automatic transmission slamming hard between gears.

Captain Estavo Eduardo heard the straining engine first, heard it rev wildly between gears and grunt when the transmission engaged. They're running, Eduardo thought. They're going to try to run my ambush. Come fools. Come to *madre*.

"Preparado!" Eduardo said over his radio. There was a clatter of rifle and machine-gun bolts being racked.

Now Eduardo saw it coming, without lights in the gray dusk. The ambulance was gaining speed fast, recklessly, swerving from side to side. They know! Eduardo swore to himself, startled. Somehow the American bastards know!

"Fire!" Eduardo howled into his radio.

Instantly, from a long steel tube atop a military truck parked in the dark street facing the onrushing ambulance, there was a thunderous *whoom*!, and a long tail of flame shot back from the rear of the tube. A twelve-pound steel and TNT warhead on the end of a former-Soviet recoilless-rifle rocket soared down the street and struck the ambulance over the left headlight pair.

A massive white flare filled the street, followed instantly by an enormous *brow*! Doors and windows blew outward from the ambulance. Wheels flew away in wobbly arcs. Fenders and hood, twisted and torn, flew high into the air and the distorted remainder of the shell erupted in the rich, orange blaze of a diesel fueled conflagration. The fenders and other auto body parts rained down into the street, smoking.

Then the guns opened up, beginning with the heavy staccato thump of Eduardo's own 12.7mm, armored-car-mounted machine gun. The soldiers took this as a signal to spray and pray, and the night outside the roiling blaze positively glittered with muzzle flashes.

The flaming hulk of the ambulance twitched and rocked on its bare axles as enough gunfire was poured into it to sink the Battleship *New Jersey*.

The hellish assault went on for a solid forty seconds, then tapered off as the most ardent gunner realized the silly futility of further ordnance. Hundreds of little orange dots peppered the blazing ambulance body like jewels.

Captain Eduardo watched from the darkness in his open-topped armored car turret, behind a smoking and ticking heavy machine gun. His heart raced. Superb ambush! *God* could not have escaped that assault! He reached for his radio microphone to advise the Internal Security colonel overhead of his magnificent achievement, when he was surprised to feel the heavy armored car rock slightly . . . but the other three crewmen were out by the street, in firing positions with their rifles . . .

Eduardo had a sudden, unsettling premonition for no reason he could explain. His testicles contracted. He

whirled about in the turret. No one. But wait . . . what
was that . . . shimmering, wavy . . . what? Engine heat?
But the vehicle still rocked gently. Eduardo felt a chill.
"Who goes there?" He demanded rather than asked, his
eyes searching the darkness wildly. He reached for his
pistol. "Identify you—accch-gahhgghh!"

Captain Eduardo was dumbfounded, too confused
even to be frightened at first. Something . . . some . . .
thing had seized him about his throat like a huge claw
and was lifting him bodily out of the turret, his booted
feet dangling, kicking spastically! Eduardo was horrified
to smell sweat and feel hot, moist breath on his ear as
he seemed to be suspended in midair above the armored
car, choking, his brain tingling, his ears ringing shrilly.
But not so much that he could not hear the deep, malev-
olent, *Americano* voice so near, so terribly, horribly
near.

"Nice try, little Cube. But no see-gar."

The last sound Captain Estavo Eduardo ever heard
was the wet popping of the vertebrae in his neck.

"IntSec One to Black Machete," Raimundo's voice
sounded on the Cuban army radio net, the whine of a
turbine helicopter engine in the background. "IntSec
One to Black Machete! *Answer* me Captain!"

The radio just hissed a carrier tone.

Eduardo's Strike Infantry troops had orders to remain
silent and in their positions until ordered out, and to
search diligently for anything seen escaping the destroyed ambulance. Odd how Captain Eduardo had said
any*thing,* not any*one.* He'd said that was the very expression the Internal Security colonel had used. Strange.
Nonetheless, the soldiers all stared hard, for their orders
were to shoot anything that moved from the ambulance,
but, what could survive that . . . hell? And why wasn't
the *capitan* answering the radio?

On the north side of the boulevard where half the
Strike Infantry company was positioned, the men peered
into the deepening darkness at the bushes on the opposite side of the road where, they knew, their fellow soldiers were hidden. To their shock, they heard a shout,
and then were suddenly met by a spray of small arms
fire! The muzzle flashes sparked in the darkness! Two

soldiers screamed and four fell! Then there was a second, fast glittering burst of fire, twenty feet away from the first. Two other infantrymen slumped to the ground. Now a grenade exploded in the street!

The men recovered from their shock. Clearly the Americans had somehow escaped and were attacking! To a man, the soldiers began blasting away at the bushes on the south side of the roadway.

The men on the south side were astonished. First, one of their own, somewhere on this side, had bellowed *"Americanos"* in Jamaican-accented Spanish! And then had shot into the company's own men on the north side! Then there was another burst a few feet away and another cry in the same Jamaican-Spanish voice: "There they are! There they are!" Then a grenade blast in the street!

Then *someone* on the north side had shot a withering fire into the men on the south side! Men were screaming and falling like flies. It must be the Americans! They've overrun our *compadres* on the north side!

And thus did a black specter in the black night, named Captain Jacques Henri DuBois, USMC, single-handedly entreat Company B, 1st Battalion, 7th Strike Infantry Brigade, Revolutionary Army of Cuba, to begin annihilating itself.

Initially Colonel Raimundo had been ecstatic. It was clear, even from five hundred meters altitude, that there was no chance in all of fantasy that anyone—invisible tricks or not—had survived that ambush. A direct, close-range hit with a device designed to destroy sixty-ton tanks, followed by a massive overkill of small-arms fire with one heavy machine gun, all topped off by a raging blaze. Raimundo's only regret was that there wouldn't be a piece of the Americans big enough to identify, let alone interrogate.

But then that pretentious peasant of a company commander didn't answer the radio to confirm the bodies. And now, as far as the confounded Raimundo could see from the air and determine from the frantic orders to cease fire being radioed by other infantry officers, the fools were shooting madly at each other!

What in *hell*?

Eusebio Gonzáles was a drunk, but he was no fool. Massive gunfire in Cuba meant that alcoholic old gamblers like himself should make themselves scarce. Maybe it was the army in training, though Gonzáles seriously doubted the army held maneuvers in wealthy residential neighborhoods. Maybe it was another drug war like they'd had in Old Havana last night. Maybe it was the dock gangs fighting again. Maybe it was the fucking American army coming ashore for the Great One, at last! Gonzáles didn't care, because none of it meant good news for a burned-out card sharp. He stopped just long enough to draw a hard slug from his nearly empty fifth of sweet rum, then he resumed his stumbling shuffle away, anywhere away, away from all that mad shooting two or three blocks distant!

Gonzáles neared a bus stop with a large bus parked by it, but, even in his advanced nightly inebriation, he knew the old bus would not operate until morning. The breakdown of the Cuban economy after the collapse of the Soviet Union had crippled all Cuban social services, especially public transportation.

Gonzáles was puzzled to see an old brown Volvo round the curve ahead under a lone street light and proceed toward him. He stopped. This was worrisome. The old car displayed no lights in spite of the darkness, but more, it was all squatted down and the tires were so squashed as to appear underinflated.

But Eusebio Gonzáles's night of epiphany had only begun.

Sensing danger, as a street person does, especially a drunken gambler in a communist nation, Gonzáles lurched into a bus-stop shelter and peered around the side.

Gonzáles gawked bug-eyed at the old brown Volvo as it rolled past him, for there was no one in it! It was weighted down, almost to flattening its tires, but contained only two large, army-colored plastic boxes or something inside the car and one more on the roof, but there was no one behind the wheel!

Gonzáles staggered back against the rear partition of

the bus-stop shelter and gawked. He shook his head furiously, but there it still was! A driverless Volvo full of roundish plastic army boxes stopping right in the street by the parked and deserted bus, not a hundred feet away!

Then Gonzales whimpered and sank to a sitting position.

Before his very eyes, out of . . . the heat waves above the car, six soldiers in fighting clothes appeared out of thin air! All but one sitting on the old car! A sixth, smaller soldier was driving!

Drunk, Gonzales thought, glancing incredulously at the bottle in his hand for a second. I am really, really *drunk. No,* I am completely *fucked up!* I'm hallu-haluci-hal-. Mother of the Savior, I am seeing things!

Eusebio Gonzales cried out as he suddenly felt invisible claws seize him and snatch him to his feet.

"Shut up, you drunk Cube!" a baritone voice said as though there were someone actually near him, but there was nothing but a wavy image of the old bus before him.

Gonzales gasped, then tried with all his might to scream, but all he could generate were hoarse croaks, as immediately before him a huge man . . . monster . . . devil! . . . began to take form out of nothing! It was enormous! And it wore military wear! And, Blessed Virgin, holy mother of Jesus Christ, it *had no face*! And it had spoken . . . Englese!

"Americanos!" Gonzales sputtered in a Godfather rasp. "Invasion! Invasion!"

"Aw man!" the monster said in English, "What the fuck are we going to with this old fart? Man, I don't want to waste some old drunk Cube."

"Americanos y muy bondad!" Gonzales declared emphatically, with a confirming wave of his hand. *"Americanos excellencio! Castro bastardo!"* Gonzales began to cry "Castro!" and then spit on the ground very dramatically.

"Yeah, yeah, I get the message. Hey boss, what do you want me to do with—"

"Let me have him," a female voice said in English as a much smaller soldier with no face stepped into the shelter. Gonzales trembled and gawked as though his evening could get any more bizarre. Then the little woman soldier held up a syringe and squired some fluid from it, and Eusebio Gonzales blew a fuse. He slumped to a heap on the floor of the bus shelter.

Sarah knelt by the old Cuban peasant in the bus stop and took his pulse. "Major ETOH on-board," she said. "He's just passed out drunk. I'll give him this strong sedative. He won't wake up for eight hours minimum. By then it won't matter what he says one way or another."

"Do it," Travis ordered.

The big blue city bus's diesel engine clattered to life and roared, spewing oily black smoke from its stack. Stan crabbed out from under the bus, rose, and stuffed a folding tool device back in his equipment belt.

"Get the pods aboard," Travis said over the BSH. He had ordered LOC suit power-down as they'd arrived on the empty street. Travis knew they needed to conserve the LOC suit batteries for the coming crucial night.

The big bus droned away with Stan at the wheel, his leg sore but functional. Hunter stood watch in the rear, Jen in front with Stan. As they rolled off, Sarah looked back at the sleeping Cuban alcoholic in the bus-stop shelter. She threw the syringe out of the window and closed her field-react box. She slid a window open. The bus—actually the Eagle Team itself, to be more precise—smelled like a football locker room at halftime. Sarah sank to a dark seat and was soon overcome with tears for poor, sweet Yuri. She could well imagine what had become of him, and it broke her apart inside.

Travis ordered BSH face shields lifted, and he smashed heavily into a seat across the aisle from Jack, who stared wearily, straight ahead.

"How'd it go, Jack?" Travis asked, clearly tired.

"Just like you said, man, only better. I drove the ambulance to the bottom of the hill. I set the parking brake, jammed that pipe on the accelerator, popped the parking brake, and let her rip. The Cubes were right where General Krauss's wizards said they were. They shot the livin' shit out of an empty ambulance. Bet that Raimundo dude just loved that."

"And then you hauled balls to the rendevous, like I ordered. Right?"

Pause.

"Mmm, sort of."

"Say what?"

"Well, boss, it didn't seem like a good idea to me to leave that big bunch of mobile and heavily armed Cubanos to come looking for us, you know?"

"So?"

"So I did the ol' chicken-choke on the company C.O., and started the rest of them to shooting at one another, that's all. Then I split."

Travis sighed and stood. " 'That's all.' Jesus Christ, Black Jack. I'm glad I didn't order you to take on a company of Cuban shock troops by yourself." Pause. "Nice work." Travis clapped Jack on the shoulder and walked to the front of the bus.

"You got it, boss man," Jack said, yawning.

Travis joined Jen and Stan. In the distance the harbor lights of the great Port of Cienfuegos were coming into view.

Travis caught Jen's eye. They looked at each other for a minute, then both looked back at the nearing harbor.

Somewhere out there was the *Global Arctic Star,* and the bloody Swords of Allah themselves. Not far away up the coast—much, much too close, Travis brooded—were the deadly Juragua nuclear reactors, with their killing potential hundreds of times that of Fat Man or Little Boy.

As in Hiroshima and Nagasaki.

Chapter Ten

"Jackie, mah man," Sam said over the BSH net, sitting in the floor of the swaying old bus eyeing the laptop readout from his satellite uplink. "I don't know what you did to those guys in the Seventh Strike Infantry, but it must have been sweet. General Krauss says they are burning up the airwaves! He says the First Battalion of the Seventh claims they were attacked by 'overwhelming American forces,' but bravely repelled them!"

"Some ladies say I'm overwhelming," Jack said seriously.

"Oh please!" Jen said, grinning back at Jack.

"How would you know?" Jack's grin nearly lit the bus.

"I don't believe it!" Sam continued. "Get this! General Krauss says the B company XO and this Raimundo clown are having a screaming match over the radio. The army guys admit they can't find a single body part in the ambulance wreck, but they say that's because the Americanos escaped before the hit and somehow counterattacked. Raimundo is calling them incompetent sons of whores—over the open radio!—and the army is threatening to shoot him down! This is great!"

Jack shook his head and chuckled tiredly. "Cubes, man. They're a hot-blooded bunch, ain't they?"

Sam said gravely, "Uh-oh,"

"Aw man, don't be talkin' that uh-oh shit out here!" Jack complained.

"Talk to me, Sam," Travis ordered.

"Sorry. Good news and bad news, guys. The *Global Arctic Star* is not at the pier anymore."

"Shit!" Stan spat from the driver's seat.

"The good news is, it's now lying at anchor in the harbor."

"Damn!" Stan said. "It's gonna be a cast-iron bitch to board that thing quietly away from the fucking dock. Let's hope they leave the goddamned boarding ladder lowered."

"I doubt it," Travis said. "Not with Nassir Al-Husseini in command. The 'Desert Eagle, who never sleeps,' remember? He won't make a mistake like that. Sam, ask Krauss if—"

"If he can confirm whether the Swords are still aboard. Way ahead of you. All they can tell us is they've not seen 'em depart."

"Good enough," Travis sighed. "They wouldn't cross the street to take a piss without Ibrahim Shanaan, their bomb brain, and we know he was aboard less than two hours ago."

September 25, 2221 hours, Cienfuegos Harbor, Cienfuegos, Cuba

The first part of the assault on the *Global Arctic Star* went well.

Sarah was left to hide and guard the bus, the team surmising that it was unlikely to be missed—and thus searched for—until morning. Sarah was the most heavily affected by Yuri's fate, and Travis suspected she would be distracted, unobjective in action, so he gave her the bus job. Her scathing glance at him and her sour "Yes, *sir*! Major, *sir*!" only confirmed his decision to leave Sarah to watch the equipment. Travis hugely revered Sarah, who had performed splendidly on many an op— she'd been a priceless asset—but who knew she'd fall for Yuri Nobakov in the field? The only thing sure about love, Travis considered, was that it can fuck you up.

Jack wanted to annihilate a Cienfuegos Harbor Patrol boat crew and take their boat, on the notion a marked police vessel wouldn't be questioned. Travis vetoed this because they might be missed if they failed to report by radio at a given interval.

Jen suggested stealing one of several yachts moored nearby, as they were unattended. Travis overruled Jen on the grounds that a rich guy's pleasure yacht about the commercial end of the harbor at night would be suspicious.

Hunter suggested nothing, as he knew that flying in by noisy helicopter was not a viable option, even if they could steal a helicopter somewhere and get to the harbor undetected.

Sam kept a low profile, mulling all the ways a nice Chinese-American boy from Queens could get himself killed doing this crazy, fucking commando bullshit. I'm a certified, card-carrying *geek*! Sam fumed to himself, smelling the salty breeze heavy with the stench of seaweed and dead fish, looking out at the glittering lights of the ships at anchor in the great harbor. What the fuck am I doing here? This is what I get for getting caught hacking into the fucking NSA's system for fun! This is what I get for smarting off to a judge who promptly said all right, either you take the NSA up on their offer of employment, or you do three to five in Attica! In a *cell* with some sadistic, homosexual, silverbacked mountain gorilla, no doubt! So here I am! Deep in Cuba, for the love of Buddha's belly, with four goons, a lovesick doctor, and a hot babe who beats thugs to blubber, with a grenade, inside their own car! All right, goddamnit, I'm in lust with her, but what the fuck am I doing here?

Stan said, "Let's heist an outbound garbage tender. Nobody would miss it for nearly a day, nobody would find it of interest, and nobody would find its presence in these waters odd at any hour."

"Bingo," Travis said. And three hapless garbage scow crewmen found themselves trussed mouth, arms, and ankles in duct tape and stowed in their own chain locker. *Americanos! Invasion!*

The team, less Sarah who had left the harbor area in the bus, now motored into Cienfuegos Bay in a small, half-loaded, open-top garbage barge. Everyone had finally gotten all their observations on the nasty smell of their "yacht" out of the way.

Up on the bridge, Stan was giving Sam a fast course in driving Cuban garbage barges.

"I don't know *shit* about boats, Stan!"

"Fine. I'll get Hunter to drive and you can assault the *Star* as point man."

"How did you say this throttle thing works again?"

In half an hour, Stan was swearing again, looking through the gyro-stabilized binoculars, his feet spread against the slow rock of the stinking barge.

"You were right, boss," Stan said. "The boarding ramp is cranked forty feet up from the waterline. Well," Stan handed the glasses to Travis, "I guess it's the hard way, then."

They waited half an hour for the moon to set, then Stan went easily over the side. He wore a black wetsuit as the LOC suits were certified for use in heavy rain but they hadn't been perfected for swimmers yet. More to the point, the manual on the suit said: *Warning! Immersion while wearing the Texas Instruments, Low-visual-signature, combat engagement suit may result in the fatal electrocution of the wearer!* The team watched as Stan stroked away slowly, to minimize any wake, for the *Global Arctic Star,* nearly 700 meters distant. They had been reluctant to approach any closer for fear of arousing the suspicion of a lookout.

In only a few feet, Stan was out of sight in the dark oil-streaked water. Hunter, Jen, Sam, Travis, and Jack dropped their BSH shields and switched on the infrared/ NVG function. Instantly they could see, almost as though it were broad daylight, but everything was a shade of green or white. They avoided looking at ship's lights, which appeared painfully bright in the face-shield viewers.

Stan didn't have gills, but he was the next best thing—a U.S. Navy SEAL. He swam like a beaver, despite many hours of physically demanding labor, little rest, and a painful leg wound. Strapped to his chest was a thin rubber buoyancy vest and a coiled, fifty-foot length of lightweight, knotted, synthetic climber's rope. Down the front of his trousers was a glorified Zip-Lok bag with his silenced H&K .45.

Stan wore special, skintight rubber gloves, which were webbed between the fingers like a duck's foot. There was a forefinger hole to extend a trigger finger through.

On the palm of the gloves was an extremely tacky substance similar to the gunk that pro-football receivers put on their hands to secure incoming touchdown passes.

In twenty-two minutes, Stan approached from upcurrent. The *Global Arctic Star*'s cold steel hull plates rose forty feet from the water, not just up, but outward as well. Porthole lights and red and green marker lights glowed, and water from the heads gushed out of a valve in the hull several meters farther down. The thrum of the *Star*'s diesel generators could be heard deep within the ship.

This far from the shore, the seas were running four to six feet. Stan timed his approach to stroke madly forward at the apogee of a rising wave. He slammed painfully into the meter-wide links of the *Global Arctic Star*'s starboard-forward anchor chain. The succeeding wave stripped him right off it. Now down current, Stan stroked hard to get back up current for another approach. He gritted his teeth hard, for the impact with the anchor chain had ripped something in the leg wound he'd received in Havana. Each kick felt like he was being stabbed in the thigh. "Unh, unh, unh," Stan grunted as he pulled at the heaving water.

The second approach to the chain succeeded but not without further cost to Stan's injured leg. Now it hurt like hell, and Stan had the nasty suspicion it was bleeding again. There were hammerheads in these waters, Stan reflected grimly as he clung to the chain against a rising swell that crashed into him and receded. And barracuda as thick as telephone poles.

The thick chain was coated in a slime combined of a mossy mush of sea flora and fauna interspersed with areas of sharp, grating barnacles. Another wave blasted into Stan. He gasped for breath and shook his head to clear his eyes of water. His leg was singing.

Slowly, Stan wound his way up the slick, yet sharp-in-places, massive chain, which rose at roughly a 30-degree angle to the water.

Thirty feet above the comfortingly noisy waves, the chain occasionally drew taut and relaxed, then twanged tight again, as the ship was shoved by the swells. Stan was hard put to hang on when the slack came out of the huge chain and it suddenly shifted three feet, then relaxed.

Under the overhang of the deck, out of view of any crewman who didn't actually lean over the rail and look in toward the ship's hull, Stan rested for five minutes.

The chain passed through a large hole in the upper bow called a hawsepipe, an elliptical opening bordered by a thick, steel, rounded collar that guided the chain in when the anchor was weighed.

Just as Stan was adequately rested to continue the exhausting climb, he heard a sound that made his mariner's heart clutch.

There was a sudden hiss of steam and several loud clanks from within the chain passage and above deck.

Holy Mary, Stan thought. It's the fucking anchor windlass! The captain's ordered the anchor weighed! Stan fought for control as he visualized having to jump forty feet to the water to avoid being ground through the anchor gear like a watermelon through a tree-shredder.

There came another loud, metallic bang and a hiss of steam, and the big chain lurched as though jerked from above. With a deafening, staccato series of deep, rapid clanks, the colossal chain was sucked through the hawsepipe like a noodle into the mouth of a hungry sumo wrestler.

"Oh shit!" Hunter, Jack, Jen, and Sam said in unison. They had been watching with Travis through their helmet shields as Stan ascended the anchor chain. All had done enough climbing to appreciate what Stan was facing. Also, they need not be mariners to understand what was happening when the big chain drew taut and the upper fifteen feet containing Stan were sucked into the hawsepipe.

"Jump!" Jen said, when she saw the chain start to move.

"Jump, dickhead!" Hunter added.

"Oh no," Sam whispered, as Stan disappeared into the maw of the hawsepipe.

"Aw, fuck, man!" Jack cursed. "Where's that chain go to?"

"I don't know," Travis said with his maddening calm.

"But Stan could've jumped. If he didn't, it was for a reason. Hang tight."

The trick, Stan knew, would be to stay on top of the kicking, thrashing chain as it fed through the hawsepipe tunnel and emerged on deck, where it would cover about thirty feet to the cogs of the windlass and feed below into the *Star*'s chain locker. A daunting task, if you considered not only the high-pressure water jets that scoured the incoming chain to clean off bottom mud, but the possibility of the chain twisting over as it ran, which would, on a larger scale, be roughly like feeding one's fingers beneath the running chain of a motorcycle. Only much messier.

Still, Stan had surmised in an instant's panicky thought as the chain was drawn upward, if he was lucky, he could be pulled right up onto the deck. As soon as he rode the bucking, jerking chain through the mouth of the hawsepipe, however, he deeply regretted what he was now convinced was a dreadful error in judgment.

The noise in the hawsepipe was brain-numbing as the huge steel links clanked and ground through the steel tunnel. And dark as a coal mine. Stan frantically shoved, pulled, and hopped to remain atop the chain. He prayed his fingers or toes would not wedge in the crevices formed by the union of the links and be mashed to jello. Suddenly, the high-pressure water jets seared Stan's skull, back, and legs like a beating with Burmese riot batons. Stan roared with the pain, but couldn't have been heard in the din by anyone a foot away. He felt as though his right foot had been stepped on by a large horse. Now he screamed.

Stan retained enough consciousness to be aware when the chain emerged onto the rear-slanted deck. In the dim deck light, he saw the massive, rotating, lumpy cogs of the ten-foot-wide starboard anchor windlass clawing the chain in only feet ahead of him. He went limp, lacking the strength to pitch himself clear, praying he would fall from the chain in time.

He did feel himself fall. Then he felt himself jerked savagely by the toe of his entangled foot, still caught in the flowing chain.

Sometimes a warrior knows when his time is up. Stan knew.

"I love you, Angelaaaaaaa!" Stan roared, dragged along the wet deck like a rag doll, seeing the huge, rotating windlass cogs eating quarter-ton chain links like popcorn.

But sometimes a warrior can be wrong.

As suddenly as it had begun to move, the chain slammed to an instant halt, and there was a hiss of releasing steam below in the chain locker. Stan was whipped by the sudden deceleration past the bind that held his foot, and his upper body collided hard with the base of the giant anchor windlass.

Holy Mary, mother of God, Stan whispered weeping with a pain that ate his previously and immediately injured leg all the way to his hip. Please! Stan gasped for breath and prayed for the strength to keep from screaming.

A miracle! Stan thought as he lay on his back, heaving. His right leg extended three feet upward to the crushing union between two links of the dripping, quivering anchor chain close above him, where his foot was firmly held. Sweet Mary! Holy Virgin!

They weren't weighing anchor, Stan realized. They were only taking up the slack to reduce the pitching and jerking in the currents! Holy shit! A motherfucking miracle!

Stan's wits slowly fought their way back through the terror and pain that had briefly vanquished them. He rolled his head to see if anyone was observing him but saw no one in his inverted view toward the bridge. Looking back at his seized right foot, Stan tried as hard a jerk as he could muster. The pain was like a white-hot electric rod being skewered up the entire length of his leg and into his hips. He wept. His body jerked spastically.

As he lay on the deck and studied his problem, a solution became clear. Not a "high-tech" solution nor an easy one, to be sure. But a solution.

Stan reached up to the calf of his trapped leg, and unfastened from its hard-plastic scabbard his chisel-pointed, saw-toothed diver's knife, honed shaving sharp.

* * *

"The chain stopped!" Sam cried.

"I don't think they're going anywhere," Jen said, studying the bow of the *Global Arctic Star* through the IFR gyro-binocs. "I think they just took the slack out of their anchor line. Maybe the anchor's dragging on the bottom and they wanted to adjust their position."

"Can you see—"

"Fuck no, I can't see him!"

"Wait!" Hunter said. "Look!"

"I see him, now," Jen said, furiously focusing the binoculars. "He—he did it. He just put the rope over the side! He did it."

"He's hurt, man," Jack grumbled, looking through another pair of glasses. "Man, if Woodchuck looks that bad, he is steady fucked up."

"Let's get wet, people," Travis said.

September 25, 2255 hours, Aboard the *Global Arctic Star*, Port of Cienfuegos, Cuba

Carlo Cruz was a Panamanian galley hand who washed dishes, swabbed the galley, peeled potatoes, and cleaned grease traps fourteen hours a day on the *Global Arctic Star*. He also smoked marijuana on the few breaks he got when he could steal away to some private place on the ship, which, like all ships, had precious few private places for an ordinary seaman.

But at night, forward, behind the big, forward anchor windlasses was tolerable, at least in good weather. Cruz withdrew the wrinkled paper tube, twisted on both ends, from his shirt pocket. He placed it between his lips and fumbled for a match.

Damn, Cruz thought. They must've just adjusted the anchor tension again, for there was slimy water all over the deck and . . . blood? Blood? Cruz stepped around the windlass.

Yes. There. A long smear of . . . yes, blood. Perhaps some sea creature was caught in the chain. A seagull, perhaps, but that's so much blood for a seagull. The smear, it leads over to the starboard rail, then back to that other windlass. But wait. Those are handprints! Those are bloody, human handprints on the rail!

Galley Hand Carlo Cruz went down like a rodeo calf in the roping event. Cruz spat the joint away as he slammed into the hard, steel deck. Terrified, he rolled over to see what had him by the feet.

Cruz couldn't widen his mind enough to encompass what he saw. Some man in black, soaking wet, on his knees, blood all over his arms and face, dragging one leg behind him! He held Cruz's ankle by one hand, and in the other he held . . . a knife!

Cruz howled and kicked frantically, but he was snatched behind the anchor windlass.

Less than a minute later, a limp body wearing a blood-stained galley apron slid over the chain and out the hawsepipe, falling forty feet and splashing hard into the water. It didn't surface.

"Jesus Christ!" Hunter said, treading water in the darkness next to the *Star,* comfortably, even after the long swim. He was grateful for the buoyancy vest that held him up. A huge splash had just erupted right next to him. "What the hell was that?"

"Sssh!" Jen hissed, bobbing in the dark, warm water near Hunter, her soaked hair clinging to her head.

"Dead dude on his way to cater a crab party," Jack said softly, stroking nearby. "But it wasn't ol' Stan. Too skinny, and not ugly enough."

Travis was first up the knotted rope that Stan had secured with bloody hands to a stout, steel lashing ring on the deck above. The TALONs in the water remembered why Travis insisted they all work out at so rigid a discipline. It took arms like a back-hoe scoop and a grip like a leg-hold trap to ascend forty feet of wet rope even carrying no more armament than pistols with suppressors.

Travis's arms were burning when he made the railing. He swung and grappled to get a grip, so he could cross the rail. He was startled by the sudden clamp of a blood-slicked hand tightly about his wrist.

Jen took the rope, when she saw Travis disappear over

the railing. She awkwardly snapped the webbed, sticky-rubber gloves more tightly at her wrists, then hauled herself from the water, hand over hand, up and up, slowing only slightly the last ten feet. She was dragged over the rail.

Hunter was huffing by the time he made the rail.

The disgusting DuBois barely seemed to break a sweat, which was a good thing, as he was too heavy for anyone to have pulled over the rail.

The TALON troopers knelt behind the windlasses. Jack and Jen worked furiously on Stan's bloody, mashed foot. He'd sawn right through the boot sole and toe to free his foot from the chain. Unavoidably, he'd also sawed some of his foot in places.

Travis studied Stan. He smiled. "How you doin', buddy?"

Stan Powczuk was a combat pro, and he knew you didn't endanger your people by pretending bravery. You called it like it was, and you never apologized.

"My whole leg is on fire, Trav," Stan panted. "Toes are mashed bad. Some probably broken. Had to cut the boot away to get my foot outa the anchor chain. I can walk, but not very fast. I'll be able to swim with the vest pumped up. I can shoot. My head's clear. Sit me up on that toolbox in the bow, and at least I can signal Sam. I can do that for you."

"You've done good, Stan. A minute for everybody to get his or her breath," Travis said, "then froggy goes a huntin'. Listen up. We're doing this the old-fashioned way, y'all know, without all the high-tech stuff. We all got grenades and plenty of ammo, but we're going up against some bubba-bubba-bad-to-the-bone folks. So let's stay alert. Everybody stay in eye contact if at all possible. Quiet is the key. First we take the radio room, then the bridge, to shut this tub up. Then we start searching for the Swords and the missiles."

Travis looked at each Eagle Team trooper, then peered around the windlass toward the bridge ladder, well aft. He looked at his watch.

"One hour to midnight. Let's boogie."

Chapter Eleven

Fortunately, on a modern bulk ship, anchored at night in port, most of the relatively small core crew were asleep. The team felt the Swords and the missile support crews would almost certainly be below decks, probably attending to launch preparations. Nassir Al-Husseini would probably have a lookout of his own posted topside in addition to the required lookout the captain would field. Yet both were probably long since bored stiff and inattentive, given the overwhelming unlikelihood of anything to look at besides the occasional passing garbage tender and other small boats every big harbor teemed with. As long as no one ventured within boarding range, what threat could there be?

Wakened suddenly from a deep slumber, the captain was livid. Who dared enter his cabin without knocking? What was—? The captain squinted painfully at the sudden bright lights flipped on. He shaded his eyes. What in the name of Allah? There were dripping wet armed men, and a woman! They were dressed in black and carried guns, and they had taped the mouths and arms of his radioman and his watch officer!

"Why this . . . this is piracy! This is an outrage! You'll all hang! I demand—!"

"Shut the fuck up," the huge, negro pirate warned in English.

Americans! I knew it! I knew this secret political charter would be trouble! I knew it!

Jack and Hunter yanked the small, fat, bearded captain to his feet in his underwear. Jen sprang before him and positioned her diving knife with the edge beneath the captain's broad nose. Jen's eyes burned into the captain's, knowing well the subjugated, indentured-servant status of most third-world Islamic women. Her participation as an aggressor would upset the captain's deeply ingrained sense of religious and social order and unsettle him.

Travis leaned near and fixed the frightened captain's wide eyes.

"English?" Travis said.

"Of . . . of course!" the captain stammered with difficulty, his speech contorted by having to speak with a knife pressed to his upper lip, its edge tingling the root of his nose.

"You're in a hard spot, here, Cap'n," Travis said. "You got two choices: cooperation, or extermination. You know what extermination means?"

The captain nodded his head gingerly, sweat now beading above his bushy one-piece brow.

"You help us out here and I give you my word we won't harm you, your crew, or your ship." Travis leaned closer, his nose almost to the captain's. "But, hoss, you even try to fuck with us, and my lady love here will cut your beak clean off. If you still don't cooperate, we'll burn this ship to the waterline with you and your people in it. Do you believe me, sir?"

The captain nodded with a whimper.

"Am I gonna have to prove to you that we ain't kiddin' here, sir?"

The captain now shook his head slowly, breathing hard through his broad, hair-studded nose. Jen withdrew the knife.

Jack and Hunter bodily lifted the captain and stood him before a framed, wall-mounted, cutaway interior deck plan of the *Global Arctic Star*.

"Where are your passengers, Captain? And how many of them are there?" Travis inquired politely. Jen strode near and placed the tip of the big, gleaming dive knife lightly against the captain's upper lip. He blinked and flinched, but he looked puzzled.

"They . . . they are not aboard, sir!"

Travis shot a glance at Jen, who returned it. "Look, Cap. You'll be going below with us when we go, and at the first sign you've lied to us, I swear you'll die with your left hand in your mouth." For Islamic fundamentalists, the left hand was reserved for wiping one's ass, hence one did not use it to eat with, or to touch another of the faithful.

"They left the ship, I swear it! They went ashore immediately before we left the dock! There are two dead in my freezer! Only one remains! The woman they call Nuhara. She is in her cabin! She will probably die soon! There was some gun battle in Havana last—"

"No shit. Where did they go?"

"I do not know! I am a merchant seaman for eighteen years, sir! I am not a spy . . . or a terrorist! I was instructed by my superiors to bring fourteen people and their cargo to Cuba! They do not tell me more, I swear by Allah!"

"What was the cargo?"

"I do not know! It was packaged!"

"What did it look like?"

"They were ordinary, molded, shipping containers. They are still aboard, empty. I believe they contained only guns and bullets, and explosives."

"What kind of explosives?"

"I do not know! I am not an authority on hazardous cargo! I transport sugar!"

Jen spoke. "Were the boxes big enough to contain missiles?"

The captain stared blankly at Jen, struggling to breathe. "M-missiles?"

"Missiles! Big missiles, not the shoulder-fired kind!"

"No. No! They were all cases the dimensions of . . . perhaps, my desk!" He pointed to a small, metal office desk near the door to the cabin. "They, the passengers carried them aboard! Who can carry a missile?"

Travis wiped his mouth. "Where is this injured woman? Take us to her. Move!"

The woman was in fact dying, in a blood-stained bunk recessed in the wall of a two-berth cabin one deck below, but this did not keep her from trying to lift her AK-47. Jen quickly relieved her of it. She whipped the sheet off the woman, who was shivering and wet from fever despite the heat. She was nude except for bloody bandages wrapped about her abdomen. The small cabin stank putridly. The terrified captain gaped at the pale, weak woman. He sucked air through his nose, his mouth being taped shut.

Travis turned to Jack. "Get the good captain secured in his cabin. Then watch the approaches." Jack escorted the weeping captain away.

"Gut shot," Jen said. She threw the sheet back at the woman, who seized it and covered herself. Jen felt the woman's forehead.

"Fever, big time," Jen said, watching Nuhara. "She'll be in the meat locker, too, in a couple of hours."

Travis came near and sat on the bed. "Listen, Nuhara." The woman flinched just slightly at his use of her name. "We know all you Swords speak English, it's a requirement. You—"

"I have . . . a degree in political science from Duke, you pathetic storm trooper," Nuhara said with strain. "Of course I speak English, but you must know I am a Sword of Allah and I will tell you *nothing!*"

Jen sniffed derisively and opened her watertight bag. She withdrew a syringe. "Look, girlfriend, we both know I can make you beg for death if I want to, but we all know what a brave warrior for the cause you are, so we came prepared. This is piridium norcuron, the third stage successor to sodium pentothal. You people know this shit, you've used it yourselves. One good hit of this stuff and you'll be telling us everything we ask you like we were your best buddies, and you know it. You also know that it'll dumb you down, and you'll be goofy as a bedbug when you go to meet Allah. We both know you don't want that, you want to be pure and clear headed when you pass over." Jen leaned over to look the woman in her eyes and held up the syringe. "Your call, Tootsie. Make it."

The injured Sword stared soberly at Hunter. She looked at Jen, a defeated look coming over her face.

"You are too late, anyway," she said with a long, tired sigh.

"Too late for what?"

"You know what! The great reckoning that your people have so richly deserved for so long! You Americans will die for years from what we do this night! As our people have died for years from your imperialist meddling and your murdering Israeli puppet gangsters!"

Travis said, "We know you're going to hit the Juragua reactors."

"Of course, infidel!" Nuhara reacted with venom. She glanced at the large, round clock on the bulkhead. "In less than two hours we will destroy them! And Americans will drop dead by the millions for fifty years!"

"How will you do it?" Travis asked, fighting to remain calm.

"You will see, soon enough, infidel," Nuhara said.

Jen sprang forward with the syringe, flicking the needle cover from it. Nuhara drew back, watching it.

"You can't stop them," she said.

"How will they do it?"

"They will initiate a meltdown of the core, of course! How else?"

"With what device?"

"Device?"

"What explosive means will they use?"

Nuhara smiled meanly. "You Americans. You arrogant, *decadent* Americans! You think we faithful are some backward, primitive people who only know how to make *bombs*! You think we did not have an advanced civilization thousands of years before America ever existed? Fools! We are patriots, not gangsters! We do not need to use explosives to accomplish everything we are commanded by Allah to do! We will destroy Juragua from within!"

"Bullshit," Hunter said from the cabin door. "You're stalling us with bullshit. A, security's a platinum bitch out there, inside and out! You'll never get in, let alone start a meltdown. And B, even if you did both those things, the steel-lined concrete containment domes would block any escape of radioactive gases into the atmosphere. The domes are huge and very strong for a reason. It would take a hell of a charge to breach them, and you'd have to place it against the dome itself to penetrate it. How? Travis, this bitch is stalling us with crap."

Travis studied Nuhara. "I think you're right. Let's get out of here, pronto." He stood.

"The VVER-four forty reactor is a pressurized water system!" she said, grinning evilly. Travis saw her glance again at the clock.

"So?"

"So we need only breach the massive water system to flood the dome floor!"

Travis looked at Jen. Jen examined Nuhara, then returned Travis's glance. "Yeah. It's possible. So?"

"Fools!" Nuhara laughed in spite of her weakness and pain. "If you combine the flooding with the meltdown, you have a giant furnace, hotter than the sun, boiling tons of water inside a contained structure! Steam, you imbeciles! Steam! Each reactor will become a pressure cooker that will explode like your Mount St. Helens!"

"Talk to me, Jen," Travis said.

Jen wiped her mouth with her wrist and thought furiously, her brow knitted tightly. "Based on the briefings I had, it's possible, Travis. There are safety systems in place to govern that very thing, and they'd need the help of somebody on the inside who knew what they were doing. But I can't rule it out. Enough water heated by the meltdown could make an enormous amount of steam pressure. Maybe enough to blow the dome."

"Domes, fools! *Domes!* We will blow them both!" Nuhara was getting giddy, as though drunk.

"It's possible!" Jen said. "*If* you could get in, and *if* you had the right insider assistance! Where would you get either? Hunter's right, Trav. She's bluffing!"

"We have it!" Nuhara cried, becoming hoarse, still amused, despite grimacing with her pain.

"I don't think so, woman," Travis said. "I think you're just trying to stall us here so we don't catch up with your demented little club. Let's go people. We're wasting time."

The team moved for the door.

Nuhara began to laugh hysterically. She was losing what sanity she had left, Jen knew. No matter. Her race was run.

"Dr. Yurevitch Zobtoi Nobakov!" Nuhara shouted, with immense satisfaction, and everyone froze. Nuhara coughed and spit up blood.

Hunter's head whipped around, Jen stared, and Travis stepped quickly back into the room.

"Who?" Travis said.

Nuhara spat blood. "Do not pretend you do not know who he is! Who do you think warned us you were going to hit the safe house in Havana? He got off a cell-phone call only seconds before you bastards arrived! Who do you think put the Cuban Internal Security police and the army on you? Fools!"

"Liar!" Jen shouted. "He was beaten and arrested by the cops! We saw it!"

"It was staged, you idiots!" Nuhara was enjoying herself, even as she knew death was close enough to touch. "Can you possibly be this stupid? Dr. Nobakov—how you Americans say—cut a deal! With that infidel who commands the security police! Even at this moment, Dr. Nobakov is preparing to escort the remaining nine Swords of Allah right through the senior employee's entrance on his pass, as 'medical technicians'!" Nuhara again coughed deeply and recovered. "He is the senior medical officer! He has been with them for years! He can go anywhere in the plant he wishes, unquestioned, and he will take his 'technicians' with him! It is he who will gain access to the safety systems! It is he who will help us trigger the meltdown! And it is he who will lead us to the water valves!" Nuhara doubled over in an agonizing fit of coughing.

"I don't know about the rest of it," Hunter said, squinting tightly at Travis, "but why would Nobakov betray us? His whole shtick is he hates the risk of out-of-control nuclear power! Why would he blow up—"

"Because of that very belief!" Nuhara answered, now breathing in gasps. "Dr. Nobakov now believes . . . that the only way to halt the spread of deadly nuclear technology is to . . . create a demonstration that will get the world's attention once and for all. What better way than to . . . hyperirradiate the world's largest user of nuclear power? The nation that invented nuclear weapons! The nation who used them to exterminate a hundred thou-

sand helpless Japanese women and babies! The same
nation that destroyed his beloved Rodina so badly it
couldn't even provide adequate treatment for his . . .
poor traumatized Annatava! America!" Nuhara began
to choke and spit more blood.

"But," Jen said, "all of Cuba will also be—"

"Cuba?" Hunter said tersely from the doorway. "The
same Cuba who raped and stuck a riding crop up his
wife? The same Cuba who made Annatava so sick she
miscarried their baby and later died? Yuri's gonna lose
sleep over *that* Cuba?"

"Oh my . . . god," Jen whispered.

Nuhara regained enough strength to resume her feeble
laughing. "Fools! Fools! It's too late! *You're* too late!"

Travis looked at her, coiled in the corner of her bunk,
blood running down her chin, a demented smirk on her
face. "You may be right," he said easily, "but by god
we're gonna find out. Hunter, go give Stan a wave to
signal Sam alongside. Go."

"Gone." Hunter scrambled down the passageway.

Travis eyed Nuhara, who looked back at him with
hate and amusement.

"You're too late, infidel," she rasped with immense
satisfaction, though her strength was clearly fading fast.

"Give Allah our best," Jen whispered as they left Nuhara to die.

September 25, 2339 hours, Juragua, Cuba

The old bus rocked along the highway to Juragua with
Hunter at the wheel, Jack keeping watch at the rear,
Sam in front. Stan lay across the wall-to-wall rear-most
seat, his foot wrapped thickly in brown combat bandages. Dark stains had already begun to seep through.
Stan had taken simple, extra-strength Tylenol, but had
refused anesthetics. Sarah had removed two toenails and
lanced two more to drain the pressure of the swelling.
That and a bandage were the best she could do for the
moment.

"Hunh!" Stan grunted with pain as the bus rolled over a break in the pavement. "Aaaah . . . Jesussss."

Jen sat by Stan and wiped his brow with a wet towel. She looked over her shoulder at the middle of the dark, groaning bus to where Sarah wept wretchedly in the arms of Major Travis Barrett.

"No, Travis, noooo," Sarah cried, shaking. "Please, noooo . . . oh god, I can't believe it! Not Yuri! Not Yuri."

Travis held Sarah and looked sadly down at her. "It's true, darlin'. I wouldn't have believed it either if it hadn't come independently from a dying Sword with no motive to make it up. I'm sorry."

"Oh god, Travis, I was such a putz!"

"Sssh. No need for—"

"He said he was going down that alley in Old Havana to relieve himself! I believed him! When did he tip off Raimundo?"

"Who knows? We all started getting slack on watching him near the end. Hell, I began to trust him myself. If he had a cell phone stashed somewhere, he had a few times when we let him out of sight, when he could've used it."

Sarah clutched herself tightly to Travis, as her crying renewed, out of control. "Oh Travis, I'm so sorry for all those things I said to you! You were right! I was such a stupid, lovesick idiot! You were right about Yuri!"

"Not that right, darlin'. He had us all fooled. I don't trust anyone but you guys, but even I never thought Nobakov was this far off the charts. Don't beat yourself up over this, Sarah. It could've happened to any of us. And this team can't spare one of its most valuable players. Especially with Stan down for the mission. Let's speak no more of Yuri unless we catch up with him, Sarah. It's history. How's Stan?"

Sarah wiped her face and fell instantly back into role. She would weep for Yuri Nobakov, but not this night.

"The first three toes of his right foot are probably broken. It'll all heal in time, but right now, dipping the wound in a harbor full of sewage and petrochemicals and god knows what else has it seriously infected, I'm sure. He's lost some blood, and he has a slight fever.

This tropical environment is awful for this sort of thing. Every bacteria known to medicine thrives down here. I've pumped him full of antibiotics, but he's going to need a hospital within twelve hours or we could be looking at sepsis, a potentially deadly infection in the blood stream. We all know Stan, Travis. He will try to walk into hell with us, but he will probably pass out from the pain if he does."

September 25, 2358 hours,
Policia Headquarters, Cienfuegos, Cuba

"I most certainly did *not* get an entire company of Strike Infantry troops massacred!" An apoplectic Colonel Raimundo shouted into the telephone to General Torejos in Havana. "Those trigger-mad idiots shot *themselves* up, firing blindly in the dark! And *yes,* I need more troops!

"Because, as I have said, General, I have new information as to where the Americans are going to be!

"I believe they are trying to destroy the nuclear power plant at Juragua, General!

"Because we discovered the Russian physician's car abandoned near a bus stop. One of the Cienfuegos policemen present drives a bus as a supplementary job, and he said a city bus is always parked there at night, but we saw none. We put out a province-wide alert for it, and it has just been found only a mile from the Juragua facility. In it, under a seat, was a bloody bandage.

"A *brown* combat dressing, General! How many Cienfuegos citizen bus riders would have discarded a combat dressing? And it was fresh! Still wet!

"Because you remember how the Americans complained when we resumed construction at Juragua. All that propaganda about seismic faults and faulty welds and substandard construction and defective design and inadequate safety measures. They all but invaded us to keep that plant from going on line! They have complained about it ever since! Why else would American soldiers infiltrate Cuba and be traced to the Juragua Nuclear Electric Production Plant?

"And what about the Russian doctor who aided them until he betrayed them to us to save himself? He is the Russian chief of nuclear medicine at Juragua!

"*No,* we haven't found him yet! Two Cienfuegos Province officers I sent to arrest him got carried away with making it look real and beat him up. They thought he was unconscious in the back seat and the imbeciles started talking about what I had in mind for him. He somehow reached over the seat, took a gun from one officer, shot them both, and escaped.

"I *will* find him! And soon. But first, General, you must assign me another company—no! two companies—of the Seventh Strike immediately. There is no time to lose. The Americans may be at the plant even as we speak!

"Excellent! Remember, tell the commanders to bring all the infrared surveillance equipment they possess. Yes, yes. No, we won't fail this time. I know where they are, I have overwhelming force, but most critically, General, I now know the secret to their secret weapon! I assure you, we will not fail!"

Chapter Twelve

The Juragua Nuclear Electric Production Plant looked to the unaccustomed eye like some futuristic installation on Mars. There was the requisite concrete spill wall, six feet high, which extended around the angular perimeter of the greater grounds, easily a square mile. Atop the wall ran another six feet of chain-link fence topped with the outward leaning three strands of razor wire.

Within the wall ran a gravel perimeter road, inboard of which were several boxy, gray, two-story, prefab buildings that housed offices, garages, workshops, storage, and myriad other support functions. A railroad track emerged from the wall beneath heavy concrete gates. The track extended hundreds of meters inward to the reactor complex itself, terminating under two massive, overhead traveling cranes.

At the epicenter of the plant the two enormous, steel-lined, concrete containment domes towered eight stories into the night, as though hiding a terrible secret from the world. Thin, railed ladders ascended the curved sides of the domes to large, cylindrical ventilation filter/valves at the peaks. Sprawling, thick, blocklike buildings were built into and against the bases of the domes. A low hum, combined of ventilator fans, air conditioners, pumps, and other machinery, covered the scene in a constant white noise.

The offices, billeting, food, and parking facilities were brightly illuminated by floodlights, but, except for blinking red aircraft warning lights atop the filter/valve cylinders and some small street lamps along walkways, the ominous containment domes were dark shadows against the night sky.

They left Stan with the equipment pods, hidden deep in the tropical forest some distance from the abandoned bus. They LOC suited him, including his BSH, propped him up between the roots of a huge tree and against the trunk, and left him with his XM-29, his suppressed .45, several magazines for the guns, grenades, and his suit bladders full of medicated hydration fluid.

Sam set Stan's BSH so he could see everything happening at the plant through his overbrow, holographic display fed by the camera in Sam's BSH.

Sarah reminded Stan that he could vocally summon anesthetics from the suit if needed.

"No dope," Stan had insisted. "I can handle the pain, and I don't wanna be doped."

Travis, Jen, Hunter, Jack, Sarah, and Sam all studied the nuclear plant a half-mile distant from them through the magnification and night-vision capacities of their BSH face shields.

What they all saw were guard bunkers at all four gates around the complex, all within rows of huge, heavy concrete planters designed to prevent a ram-through in a tank, let alone a truck. Incoming vehicles had to make a long traverse parallel to the wall between a row of the giant planters, make a U-turn at the end, and traverse back through another row of planters to the actual gate through the wall. AK-74-armed guards in dark blue jumpsuits stood at booths by the planter entrances and others manned towers to either side of the gates. Each tower sprouted a squad machine gun. Eating, sleeping, and lounging facilities for the guard force were housed in yet more one-story prefabs outside the wall. A few Russian- and French-made military vehicles were parked outside the main gate.

As Eagle Team, including, at least visually, Stan, surveyed the distant sprawling complex from their vantage at the edge of a wood line, they observed the onset of bad news.

Additional floodlights began to come on all over the facility. The electrical clacks and hums were audible in seconds to the team. Shortly, they could hear the brash, mulelike honking of warning klaxons sounding throughout the complex. At the gates, the guards unslung their rifles. Additional guards hurried from the outbuildings, shrugging into their uniforms as they trotted, to take stations by the gates. The tower guards illuminated big, swivel-mounted, sodium-vapor search lamps and began sweeping the approaches to the plant with bluish, bleached light beams. The harsh *Awwnnnnk! Awwnnnnk! Awwnnnnk!* of the warning klaxon carried on the slight, warm wind.

"Damn," Travis said softly over the BSH net. "So much for the element of surprise. Somebody's onto us."

"Nobakov?" Hunter asked.

"I doubt it. He set us up with Raimundo. He thinks we're dead meat. Or Raimundo's prisoners at best."

"I think Raimundo's onto us," Jen said.

"How?" Sam asked.

"Who knows?" Jack grumbled. "That asshole has been just one short step behind us this whole op. Sure would like to see him through a scoped sight."

Sarah put in, "I think Jen's right. Raimundo has somehow figured out we're here. I don't know how, but we know he's relentless and dedicated. If he's Castro's chief henchman, like they say, then he's bound to have virtually unlimited assets and resources."

"We're gonna have to hustle, then," Travis said. "If they think we're coming, it's only a matter of time before they show up with the army and put patrols out looking for us."

"Travis, how do we even know the Swords and Yuri are in there yet?"

"We don't, but—"

"We're going to," Hunter interrupted. "Just as soon as Honeybee is fired up and humming."

Hunter was toiling over a round, saucer-shaped device about the size of a softball. It was gray on the bottom, cammo-colored on top, and looked like a big doughnut with little plastic stalks extending from it like spider legs. Sam dropped down next to Hunter with the flat-folding laptop monitor.

Hunter set the Honeybee on the ground five feet away

and retreated to a fist-sized black box with a tiny antenna. He opened two fold-out wings on it, each topped with glass, touch-activated TV screens. He lay his hands upon the screens, each finger and thumb over a dimly lighted square, and pressed lightly with his fingers. The Honeybee began to emit a high buzz like an electric shaver. Blades of grass near it lay back from it.

"Counterrotating rotors!" Hunter said, like a kid at Christmas with a new toy. "This thing is almost as slick as the BSHs."

"Cool," Sam said over the net.

"Blastoff," Hunter said, keying the finger pad. The Honeybee leaped into the air to a stationary hover, rocking slightly in its own turbulence. "I crashed eight of these things trying to learn the control touch." Honeybee tilted toward the plant and zipped away like a fleeing bird. "Off we goooo," Hunter sang softly, "into the wild blue yon— Sam, you got contact?"

Sam unfolded the flat monitor, which was already aglow. "Contact, Icarus." Sam slid the laptop before Hunter. The remainder of the team gathered behind it.

Hunter was still visually watching Honeybee go, but now he quickly switched to the laptop monitor. The picture on the monitor flickered briefly, then solidified to a clear, green-and-white NVG picture. Superimposed upon the bottom of the picture were red numbers depicting airspeed, altitude, range to obstacle, range to ceiling, battery status, and on-board camera mode. In the upper corners were a small compass/heading rose at one side and a tiny altitude indicator at the other. The screen displayed four views at once separated like split-screen TV, forward, left, right and rear, all of which traversed up and down 90 degrees. With a press of a monitor key, Sam could blow up one view to dominate the screen and minimize the others.

"Accent forward," Hunter said, both hands on the screens.

Sam clicked a key and the forward-looking view magnified to dominate the screen. In it, the huge Juragua facility could be seen in the distance, quickly coming closer. In less than a full minute, Honeybee shot over the wall between guard towers. Hunter touched it to a hover.

"Balance," Hunter said. Sam caused all four screens to equalize. As far as could be seen on the screens, no one within range seemed to be aware of Honeybee.

"All that machinery noise is covering the slight prop buzz," Hunter said, smiling.

Jen sniffed. "I bet you tested this thing on nude beaches all over Southern California," she said dryly.

"Heyyyy," Hunter said, never taking his eyes from the screen. "Now there's an idea. Give me the plans, Sam."

Sam played with the BSH field controller in his belly pack. On Hunter's BSH readout, computer enhanced, 3-D diagrams of the VVER-440 export reactor began to scroll furiously.

Looking up at his own holographic BSH readout, Sam raced through the diagrams until he found the one he sought. "In-wall, exterior grounds," he said.

Hunter could now glance up and see a virtual reality display of the facility's exterior. With tiny finger adjustments of the touch pad he flew the Honeybee about the grounds and buildings. Guards and other personnel could be seen hurrying about below, but no one the team recognized. Hunter worked the outbuildings first, then worked his way in toward the domes.

A column of workers passed by beneath the zipping Honeybee.

"Seize!" Hunter said.

"Seized," Sam said instantly. A red X appeared in the bottom of the screen. As Hunter turned Honeybee, the red X moved around the edge of the screen to the top. The running column of workers reappeared in the forward screen.

"Forward prime, pan down, follow 'em Sam."

"I got 'em," Sam answered squinting at the screen. The view filled the screen and followed the running workers, all wearing white lab coats. "Closer, Hunter."

"Closer you want, closer you get."

Travis leaned close and squinted. "Only eight."

"Maybe they left somebody to guard escape vehicles," Jen said.

"Closer Hunter," Travis said.

The Honeybee descended and circled away, then back in. The running, lab-coat clad figures were nearly to a door into one of the structures abutting the west dome. The screen image of the workers jiggled as it corrected for movement of the Honeybee. Hunter steadied the device. Sam focused on the lead person, only thirty feet from the door now.

"Ah. God," Sarah said. "Yuri."

"Get him, Hunter!" Travis said urgently, "before he gets in the building. Take him out and the Swords are lost."

"That thing has a weapon?" Sarah asked, her eyes watering.

"The oldest kind," Hunter said, as he guided the Honeybee to full speed and hard after a running Dr. Yuri Nobakov. "Kamikazi."

The laptop screen image now seemed like a jerky video on fast forward. The running people displayed in green and white were only ten feet from the building. The picture bobbed up and down as Hunter pushed the little machine to its maximum speed of 140 miles per hour and it became hard to control. Now the image of Yuri Nobakov was recognizable to all, even from behind and to the side. First his whole running body from head to foot, then his upper torso. Now his face, as Yuri turned his head to see what that furious buzz growing nearer could be. Then a microsecond widening of the eyes in realization.

"Yuri," Sarah whispered.

There was one last extremely close image directly on Yuri's startled face as the screen went instantly dark, then blank.

September 26, 0036 hours, Interior, Juragua Nuclear Electrical Production Plant, Juragua, Cuba

Yuri Nobakov had known that ogre, Raimundo, could not be trusted, of course. He also knew that Raimundo had not made the connection with him. The Cuban Security Chief had not remembered the poor Russian beauty who pleaded with him those years earlier, after he and his men had raped her, but before he thought it amusing to gouge her inside with his bloody riding crop! Was she not but one of hundreds Raimundo and his men had brutalized? Even as he had talked to Raimundo by phone, in hushed tones from the bathroom of his villa, Raimundo standing on the street in Cienfuegos by the bloody dock-gang limo, Yuri had known the man's promises were treacherous lies. Yuri had sealed the cell phone in a plastic bag then hid it back beneath the toilet tank cover, before exiting the bathroom, back to his American baby-sitters.

So he was not terribly surprised when the two Cienfuegos police officers worked him over, and he had dropped, pretending unconsciousness. Then, in the car, when they laughed about what the dreaded Colonel Raimundo was going to do to him at Cienfuegos police headquarters, Yuri had not been shocked either. As both cops laughed, it had not been hard to reach over the seat, pull the driver's gun, shoot the passenger and then the driver. He had pushed the bodies into a drain culvert, then driven away in their car.

With a University of Havana passenger van stolen by the Swords, Yuri and the Swords had driven from the docks to Juragua.

Yuri knew well what he had to do, and he had long since become convinced of the righteousness of his cause. He must make the world see. He must make the world pull its head from the sand and face the terrible threat of nuclear energy. For decades antinuclear activists had trumpeted the potential of nuclear power to end human civilization, instead of power it. Even after Three Mile Island, the apocalyptic Chernobyl disaster, which was still killing Russians and Europeans, and the near-meltdown in Japan, no one would listen! The power politicians and the nuclear industries were incestuous bastards, reaping profits and power, and pretending away the ominous threat posed by every nuclear reactor in the world, and there were hundreds of them! All manufacturing poisonous radioactive wastes by the hundreds of tons, which no one knew what to do with. The waste rods and water remained deadly for thousands of years in some cases!

But no more. Now they would listen. Now the whole world would have to recognize the terrible killing potential of nuclear energy, and act, at last. They would see. Nuclear power wasn't the genie in the magic bottle offering cheap, clean, unlimited energy to power commerce, health, and recreation, it was a horde of demons to make hell look like America's Disney World. Now they would see.

Sure. So many would die. And that was regrettable. But they would die anyway, if this nuclear madness were not resolved! And many millions more! Perhaps even the entire human species! Perhaps all life on earth!

Entering the outer gate had been the easy task Yuri had known it would be. Supply truck drivers, visitors, and others came in and out daily. He passed off the seven Swords in the stolen passenger van with him as associates from the University of Havana, a ruse made easier by the University logo stencils on the doors and the false identification badges Yuri had purchased.

They'd had a brief start when the lead-lined box containing the Swords' guns had gone through X-ray. Radiation detectors, Yuri had said with a smile. They must be protected from X-ray if they are to accomplish their functions for the reactor workers!

Yuri was the Russian chief of nuclear medicine for the entire facility, had been known and trusted by even the Cubans since the late '80s when he'd first come to the site as one of many Russian, on-site nuclear-medicine physicians. For three years now he had enjoyed the highest security clearance attainable at Juragua. Tonight it had served him well, until the klaxons sounded while they were on foot, inside the wall but still outside the reactor compound, which had its own separate security in the form of an elderly, fat guard who rechecked the badges of everyone entering, regardless. Even when the Great One had visited the plant on its opening last year, the guard had taken great pride in insisting on seeing the entry badge of El Presidente himself! How many chuckles that had produced.

But when the klaxons sounded, the floods came on,

and people began to rush about, Yuri knew it was a
security threat lockdown alert, not the wailing sirens of
a nuclear systems emergency. He had no idea what had
triggered the alert, but he knew he and his dreadful but
necessary companions must hurry.

The old guard had self-righteously shaken his head in
his little booth at the fence to the reactor compound and
had shaken his finger, even in the face of the renowned
Dr. Nobakov. Even El Presidente had to show the correct badge. While the Russian doctor and his associates
waited tensely, the old guard perused the IDs presented
him, peering through bifocals. Dr. Nobakov's identification was in order, of course, but there was something
odd about the badges of the others. A different kind of
plastic, peeling here. Wait. But this is . . . he looked up
suspiciously and reached for his telephone.

Nassir Al-Husseini had pulled his silenced pistol from
beneath his lab coat and shot the guard dead without
hesitation. The old man had toppled over backward in
his chair, with a shocked expression. Yuri barely noticed.
He was committed now. Nothing else mattered.

As they ran for the doors to the west reactor building,
Yuri sensed something wrong. Then he was sure. That
buzzing. That high-pitched little howl didn't belong.
What was that?

Yuri turned his head while running and had just
enough time to realize that there was only one party on
earth who could have put a tiny flying surveillance machine inside Juragua Nuclear Electric Production Plant
on this night.

It felt like being hit by a baseball bat.

Sarah held her hand to her mouth and stared at the
blank monitor screen "Is . . . Yuri . . . is he . . ."

"No way to be sure, Sarah," Hunter said gently as he
passed her. "I hit him. I don't know how . . . well."

Travis peered through the infrared binoculars. "Eagle
Team," he said. Everyone stopped to look at him. "You
know we still have to go in. We can't be sure we got
Yuri Nobakov, for one thing. For another we aren't sure
the Swords can't bring this off on their own."

Silence.

"He's right," Sarah said. "There's too much at stake. We have to be certain even if it means . . . even if it means we . . . don't come out."

More silence, broken at last by the baritone of Big Jack. "Travis, can we just walk through that gate powered up?"

"I doubt it, Jack. Too much light down there since they went on alert. Too close quarters. Too many folks runnin' around to bump into us. We can walk right up to the gate, but as good as these LOC suits are in the dark, with all those flood lights somebody's gonna see a shadow, or the end of a muzzle, or the bottom of a boot."

"If we're just detected going in," Jen said, "they'll lock those reactors down so tight Castro couldn't get in. Let alone out."

Each member of the team now glanced at each other as they suddenly all heard chuckling on their BSHs. It was Stan from half a mile away.

"People," Stan said in everyone's headsets, tightly, as though he were hurting, but enjoying himself no less, "we must be livin' right! We are truly blessed!"

"Stan, are you all right?" Sarah asked, frowning.

"My leg feels like a barracuda just bit down on it, but otherwise I'm just wonderful. You're gonna be too, soon, 'cause the answer to your problems is coming your way!" Stan enjoyed another painful laugh.

"Stan, what—"

Hunter cocked his head, like a quizzical puppy. He grinned. "I hear it too, Stan! It's a—"

"Train!" Stan crowed from his tree. "It's a big-ass freight train, headed right into the plant!"

"Let's move," was all Travis said, and he was hard down the slope toward the train tracks with the rest of TALON Force Eagle Team right behind him.

Chapter Thirteen

Yuri Nobakov was knocked right off his feet. Ibrahim Shanaan, hard on his heels, tripped over Yuri and also fell. The Swords quickly pulled Shanaan to his feet. Nassir Al-Husseini knelt by Yuri and examined him. The entire left side of the Russian's scalp was split open and bleeding badly, but he was alive.

"Hai! Hai!" Ibrahim Shanaan exclaimed. Nassir looked up to see everyone leap back from something they saw on the ground. Nassir now saw it too.

It was a small round object with little antennas and small propellers within a circle, but it had suddenly begun to sizzle and smoke, causing Ibrahim's sudden alarm.

Nassir leaped to examine the object but it was involved in some sort of self-immolation process and was too hot to touch.

In seconds there was nothing where the device had lain but a scorched spot in the grass.

"The Americans!" Nassir hissed, looking about. The other Swords suddenly crouched and looked anxiously around, holding up their arms, as though they might be the next ones to get coldcocked in the head by a motorized boomerang.

"We must hurry!" Nassir said. "The Americans are *here*!"

And indeed they were.

They rode in atop two railroad boxcars, face shields

down, LOC suits on full power, squatting on their heels, the muzzles of their XM-29s covered with the integrated gloved hands of their suits.

Two massive concrete doors swung outward on huge steel casters rolling on a steel plate.

Armed security guards inspected each car·as it rolled through the perimeter. They examined the interiors with flashlights, the bottoms with boom mirrors, and the roofs with their own eyes. They saw only the heat waves rising from the cars. Odd, this late at night, but then, the cars were steel and Cuba was a hot country.

As the last car of the train entered the complex, there was a loud, electric hum, and the giant concrete track doors swung shut, forming a slight outward angle designed to stop a ramming from the outside by train.

Several hundred meters later the train stopped by warehouses beneath the giant traveling cranes. There was a smell of diesel and creosoted rail ties, and the loud diesel roar of the large locomotive eight cars ahead spooled down to idle.

Moving in the shadows to maximize the effectiveness of the LOC suits, the TALON Force hurried to the pair of doors through which Yuri and the Swords were attempting to enter when the Honeybee monitor screen went blank. Pairs of armed guards still roamed about, but some of the urgency that ensued after the security-threat alert had sounded had subsided for lack of finding anything alarming.

On the sidewalk where the Honeybee had struck they found blood.

"Scalp wounds bleed like hell," Sarah whispered softly over the BSH. "I . . . don't see any brain matter or skull fragments, so I don't know if he's dead."

Hunter looked down through his face shield at the burned spot on the grass. "Honeybee self-destructed right on cue," he said.

They'd almost walked right past two guards who had taken alert stations just inside the double-glass door employees entrance to the west reactor building, but the light within was intense. Banks of overhead fluorescent fixtures bathed the tiled hallway and reflected off the polished stone floor. Numerous workers hurried along two halls moving away from the doors at right angles.

Jack was walking as silently as a 250-pound man can when one guard glanced in his direction, looked back down at the papers he was reading, then snapped his glance back up.

Jack froze.

The guard rose slowly from the console behind which he sat, staring at where Jack stood, staring as though very confused. His partner noticed his puzzled gaze and looked but thought he saw nothing.

The first guard walked round the end of the console and slowly across the hall to where Jack stood. The XM-29s were cloaked and the muzzles were held down. If Jack stood perfectly still and nothing behind the LOC suit moved or radically changed colors or patterns there might be a chance. Moving caused the LOC suit to race to match the pass-through patterns behind on four axes per fiber-pixel. In a stationary environment, the suit was almost flawless.

The guard was clearly baffled. He was sure he'd seen something, but what? But he *had* seen something. Could it be the wall?

Jack knew that if he remained motionless the guard would actually walk into him. If he moved, he would create enough of a visual anomaly to alert the guard that something very strange was happening at the door to a nuclear reactor building.

Very strange, the guard thought. Too strange. Already, Dr. Nobakov had been helped through the door, bleeding! But his associates from the University of Havana, Arabs by the sound of them, had said he was not seriously hurt, he had just fallen in the confusion of the alert. The alert. That was the thing. The alert message stated there had been information from an outside source that unknown persons might attempt to breach security, presumably to damage the facility. Now this. This wavy—

The guard thudded into something soft on its surface, softer than the tile of the walls, to be sure, and closer than the wall! He leaped back and reached for his gun.

As the guard drew his weapon, the now hugely confused second guard was astonished to see his *compadre's* head snap back and hear the impact of a solidly landed punch! His partner collapsed on the floor, his gun skittering across the tiles and bouncing off the wall like a hockey puck!

The second guard did not have a clue what was happening, but he knew he needed help. And a lot of it, fast. Gazing wildly about for something that made sense, the second guard raised his knee and stomped the red emergency alert button on the floor behind the console.

Now deafening electric bells clamored throughout the building.

The first guard breathed but didn't move.

Eagle Team raced down the hall, carefully dodging the few workers moving along it. Several workers stopped, puzzled at the sounds of movement near them and the smells of sweat and the sounds of breathing.

"Through these doors to the next hall and right!" Sam said on the BSH, snapping fast glances at the interior floor plan for the VVER-440 reactor building projected from his overbrow readout.

When the dual fire doors crashed back against the walls, apparently by themselves, the trio of Cuban security men in blue jumpsuits and gun belts running the opposite direction were bowled ass over teakettle as though they'd just walked in front of the Dallas Cowboys front four when the ball was snapped. One skidded on his back down the slick stone, scrambled to his feet only to be knocked ten feet onto his back again by . . . *what*!?

A sign over a doorway read R-1 CONTROL ROOM. The team dived through it. It led down a short hall to another.

"Combo door!" Travis said on the BSH. "Jack, watch our backs!"

The hall was tempered glass from the waist up as was the near wall of the control room to reactor one. Through the glass, Travis could see the bodies of technicians laying on the floor and three Swords of Allah at the bank of monitors at the far wall frantically spinning dials and pulling levers.

Sam scurried quickly past Travis, slapped what appeared to be a wad of clay with a small wire in it against a six-button combination fire-door lock.

Sam backpedaled ten feet. "Clear!" he shouted over the deafening alarm bells.

The team flattened themselves against the wall and turned their heads away. There was a sharp *bang*! Some of the nearby glass shattered and bowed outward, held together by the wire screen laminated between the layers. The heavy door swung open slowly in a cloud of smoke, a blackened hole where the lock had been.

Travis and Jen were through the door instantly, in the control room, a high, brilliantly lighted cavern composed of three walls of switches, gauges, readouts, monitors, levers, more monitors, and broad rows of computer consoles. One Cuban control tech was on his knees holding his head. Two others did not move.

"Get close!" Travis said, "Don't tear up the equipment!"

The three Swords at the console spun about when the door was blown in, snatched their folding-stock AKs from the counter, and gaped, wondering what had happened. One was still staring when his rifle was snatched from his hand and he was clubbed in the head with it. When he hit the floor, he was shot cleanly through the base of the skull with his own gun.

The other two Swords began to fire wildly, but were cut down almost instantly.

"Report!"

"Olsen okay!"

"Blake okay!"

"Wong okay, boss!"

Sarah, moving to examine the technician on his knees said, "Greene is fine, Travis."

Jack, over the gunfire and jangling alarm bells in the background, shouted, "Wonderful, just fucking wonderful! The cavalry is arriving out here!"

"Go help Jack out, Sam."

"Oh, hot damn. I'm gone, boss." Sam scampered out the corridor.

Jen slid in by Sarah and the injured technician on her knee. Sarah had powered-down so the man could see her. He was gawking in wide-eyed terror already. When

Jen materialized before his eyes he gasped like a beached grouper.

"This guy's dead," Hunter said from the other side of the room by a downed technician.

"How is he?" Jen asked Sarah as they looked at the astonished technician.

"He's frightened, obviously. He's been beaten, with possibly a mild concussion, but he's coming around fast."

Travis came over, powered down, and fired fast Spanish at the technician: "Do you understand me?"

The man nodded, still gaping wide-eyed.

"We are not here to hurt you. Do you know how to tell if the reactor is secure? Quick! Speak up!"

"Sí!" the man cried, looking at the wall of controls and indicators. He attempted to get to his feet and was yanked up by Travis and Jen. *"Sí!"* he repeated in Spanish. "These *terrorista,* they entered with Dr. Nobakov! Then they started shooting! They hit me. I pretended to be *muerto! Madre de Dios!* They have been trying to destabilize the core! But these people, foreigners, they do not know what they are doing! Thank God!"

The technician swept his eyes over a confusion of gauges, dials, and digital readings. He pushed a lever, flipped two switches, pulled the lever back. "Dr. Nobakov tried to tell them how to destabilize the core, retract the control rods! He spoke of flooding the core pit! That could . . . that would—you cannot imagine! The whole containment dome might—"

"Can you get this reactor under control?" Jen demanded.

"Sí! It is already under control. They . . . these fools, they tried to retract the rods but they did not know what to do. They did not understand Dr. Nobakov's instructions!"

"So we're all right here?" Travis asked.

"Yes . . . yes . . . see the temperatures are receding, the rods are dropping. What is happening, *señor*? Who . . . who in God's name *are* you?"

"Where'd Nobakov go?" Travis demanded.

"I do not know, *señor*! But they spoke of reactor two!"

"I'll bet. Pull out team, we're outta here. Move!"

As the four members of the team ran back down the

corridor, they could hear exchanges of gunfire, the slower, hollow pops of AK-74s answered by the high, fast ratcheting of Jack's and Sam's XM-29s. Everyone powered back up and disappeared as they ran. When they dropped their shields back into place they could see each other clearly.

In the hall, Jack and Sam had overturned two metal office desks and were firing from behind them. Down the hall four bodies lay near dropped weapons.

"Security people coming from everywhere, boss!" Jack said, his voice clear over the BSH despite the gunfire and insanely rattling bell system.

"Chunk 'em," Travis said, diving to the floor by Jack, followed by Sarah.

All six TALONs switched their XM-29s to the grenade setting, leaned out or popped up, and fired.

Six 20mm grenade rounds sailed down the hall, careening off the walls, and detonated, sounding like six licks of a large stick on a garbage can lid. Shrapnel went about like a cloud of Bay of Pigs mosquitoes.

All firing instantly stopped.

Jack switched to rifle and fired a three-burst into the big jangling bell high on the wall. It flew off and bounced clanging down the hall.

In the relative silence, all members of the team froze.

There arose a hellish wail of unbroken siren tone, the nuclear systems emergency warning.

Something was very wrong at reactor two.

Stan knew they had to be Raimundo's people. Who else would be searching the woods near a stolen city bus?

He breathed heavily, leaning against the trunk of a tree, the two huge roots of which cradled him at either side. Through the night-vision capacity of his BSH face shield, he watched a two-man patrol, waving flashlights, smashing around in the sandy scrub like a herd of water buffalo, smokin' cigs and yappin'. Farther in the darkness, Stan could hear other patrols moving about, searching, calling. Well, that was good news. These bozos were conscripts, not pros.

Stan tensed as he watched one stop, aim his flashlight

at the ground, and call his partner. Both looked up the slope where Stan sat, though he knew that even with the suit powered down they couldn't begin to see him motionless. Still, the two soldiers conversed nervously in Spanish, threw their cigarettes to the ground, raised their rifles, and began walking cautiously closer.

Colonel Raimundo was exhausted. Goddamn that fat, son-of-a-troop-whore, General Torejos! He had promised Raimundo two companies of Strike Infantry; instead he had sent one almost useless *platoon* of regulars! Conscripts! Peasants! These cane hackers weren't fit to guard prisoners!

Look at them, bashing about in the dark like a bunch of soccer players looking for a lost ball! Raimundo swore. He would have that bastard Torejos fed to the dogs as soon as he spoke to *El Presidente*!

"Lieutenant!" Raimundo snapped.

"Yes sir, my colonel!" A skinny, acne-pocked boy of maybe twenty-five scrambled before him and saluted.

"Do not salute me in the field, you peon!" Raimundo hissed tightly. "You will mark me for a sniper!"

"Yes sir!" the terrified lieutenant said and saluted again out of reflex.

Raimundo rolled his eyes heavenward and sighed. "Spread your people down that way, Lieutenant! We are searching for American terrorists, not having a picnic! Move them."

"B-b-but, sir!" the lieutenant sputtered. "Juan and Ruiz, the Alvarez brothers, they have not returned! They do not answer to our calls! We last saw them up there!"

Raimundo narrowed his eyes and gazed up the slope, but he could see nothing beyond the nearby truck's headlight and a few flitting flashlight beams farther away. "Indeed?" he said. He snapped open a molded-plastic case and removed a brand-new pair of Russian-made night-vision optics.

It would be a bad day tomorrow for poor Mrs. Alvarez, Stan thought, leaning on a forked stick improvised as a crutch and looking down at the two dead Cuban boys. Both their name tapes read ALVAREZ, and they were clearly brothers. *Why couldn't you little shits just have walked on by?* Stan thought. *No, you had to come nosin' around like a pair of fucking heroes, sticking a flashlight right in my eyes. Pweet. Pweet. No more Alvarez boys.*

Fuck, I hate shootin' kids. What I hate worse though, is sooner or later these dorks will be missed and the other dorks will come looking for them. Judging from the voices and the sounds of at least three trucks, there must be about thirty of 'em. Jesus, Mary, and Joseph, my leg hurts!

The team must be inside the containment domes. All I hear on the BSH is static. Radio won't penetrate steel-lined concrete that thick. Stan hobbled back to his tree. *Got to get good cover. Get as many of these pricks as I can. Hold 'em off 'til the team gets back.*

If the team gets back.

Inside the Juragua Nuclear Plant Compound

For fire, blast, and contamination reasons, the two reactors within their respective domes were a hundred meters apart and had no connecting access. The TALONs raced across open ground for the reactor two complex among scores of running workers and armed guards in dark blue jumpsuits. In the relative darkness at the edges of the floodlighted zones, the LOC suits functioned flawlessly. A system-wide siren wailed the coming of hell on Earth.

A crowd of civilians and guards were milling about the main entrance to the reactor-two building, so the team moved along the wall until they reached a service entrance with securely locked steel doors. Sam blew the doors with semtex, and the team rushed in through the smoke. The long, tiled tunnel led to a warehouselike supply room, which opened through double doors on a hallway full of scurrying, worried-looking workers carrying clipboards, fire extinguishers, and radiation detectors.

Then they heard shooting and shouting coming from

far down the hall to the right. They couldn't know the Swords of Allah were battling plant security for the reactor-two control room, but they understood not to bring clipboards to a gunfight. The workers in view gasped and turned briefly, then hurried away in the other direction. If any of them noticed the slight visual signatures of six passing TALONs in powered-up LOC suits, no one saw enough to question.

The team rounded an intersection twenty meters from the entry to the control room to reactor-two. The hall was a pandemonium of gunfire, smoke, shouting, blue-suited guards who were shooting down the control-room corridor at the remaining Swords. Alarm bells and sirens permeated the din.

"Do we *have* to kill so many civilians!?" Sarah yelled on the BSH.

Travis was maddeningly calm as always. "We've got to get to the control room. The only way in is blocked by a gunfight between the Swords and the plant guards, both of whom will kill us if they can. What do you suggest?"

"Aaah!" Sarah yelled, switching her XM-29 to grenade. "I hate this!" She plooked a 20mm grenade shot down the hall. It was followed instantly by five others. The team jerked back behind the edge of the intersecting hall.

The grenades detonated in rapid succession, and the shooting stopped. The TALONs ran down the hall toward a cloud of smoke above seven heaped blue-suited guards.

Jack looked down the corridor toward the control room. "Yes Virginia," he said softly on the BSH net, "there is a Santa Claus."

Walking slowly along the control room corridor toward the team, carrying smoking AK-47s, were four of the remaining Swords of Allah, led by none other than the mad bomber himself, Ibrahim Shanaan. They looked fiercely right at an old enemy and, in the smoke-shrouded LOC suits, they saw them not. The last thing the three men and one woman did see were the sparking muzzle blasts of six XM-29s.

The TALONs kicked the AKs away from the

sprawled Swords in the corridor, but it was an unneeded precaution for these four Swords of Allah would never again blow up ships, trains, buses, buildings, and aircraft.

Or nuclear plants.

The team spilled through the open door of the control room to find Nassir Al-Husseini holding his AK and looking about wildly. One Sword lay dead on the floor near the apparent Cuban civilian. To the right, holding his pistol to the head of a Cuban engineer, stood Dr. Yuri Nobakov, blood running viciously down the side of his head and neck and staining his shirt. The frantic engineer was pressing buttons at Yuri's shouted commands.

"Jack," Travis said on the BSH, "you and Sam watch our asses."

Jack and Sam hurried back down the corridor, leaping the dead Swords.

"Shanaan!" Nassir shouted hoarsely, dividing his gaze between the smoky corridor down which he had dispatched four comrades to hold off the Cuban guard force, and Yuri with his captive. Suddenly his vision fixed on the entry door, for he could not explain the odd distortions in the smoke-filled air.

Travis powered down his suit and materialized before a shocked Al-Husseini. Sarah, Hunter, and Jen also powered down and appeared.

"Just wanted you to see who finally got you, patriot," Travis said.

Nassir Al-Husseini went to join Allah honorably. There was a fast flicker of revelation in his eyes that culminated in a desperate attempt to swing the AK-47 in time, but Major Travis Barrett was fresh out of courtesies. He blew Nassir Al-Husseini, for fourteen years the leader of the world's most deadly terrorist cell, hard back against the console behind him. The AK-47 skittered across the floor. Al-Husseini slid down the face of the console and folded over like a Raggedy Ann doll, bleeding from fourteen rounds of 4.55mm, XM-29 slugs. He was already lifeless.

Yuri had yanked the engineer around before him as cover. He still held the pistol to the engineer's head.

The engineer recovered from his shock and began yelling frantically in Spanish and pointing at the wall of the digital readouts glowing behind him. A bank of red warning lights pulsed brightly.

"He's saying Yuri made him pull the control rods!" Hunter yelled, maneuvering around a desk, closer to Yuri and his captive. "He says the rods absorb the neutrons and stop the chain reaction! Al-Husseini made the other Cuban shut down the primary cooling system and both chilled-water backups, before killing them! He says the core temperature is rising dangerously. The rods must all be dropped immediately or a meltdown will ensue!"

"Silencio!" Yuri Nobakov shouted, clearly near the end of his wits. *"Siiiiilennnncioooo!"* He gasped for breath. "Do not move! Do not move! This man is the only person here who knows how to stop the meltdown! If you come any closer, I'll kill him!"

"Everybody hold," Travis said.

"It's over, Yuri!" Sarah called over the din. "We've stabilized reactor-one! They're shutting it down! You can't make this work, Yuri! Give it up!"

"I can! I can make it work!" Yuri bellowed in his heavily Russian-accented English, heaving, crouching to conceal himself behind the terrified engineer. "Soon the core will overheat beyond a temperature that the rods and cooling systems can control! Meltdown! The core will burn hotter than the sun! It will burn a pit through the floor of the structure, down into the earth! Nothing can stop it! Then I will flood the reactor pit with hundreds of tons of water, which will instantly become superheated steam! It will rupture the dome! Rising heat and smoke will carry the radiation contamination high into the northerly jet stream and on to America! Even with only one reactor the deaths will number in the hundreds of thousands in less than a week! Then the world will see! The world will see at last! They will end nuclear power forever!"

"He's mad," Hunter said on the BSH.

"He's nuttier than Mr. Peanut!" Sam said, nervously, from out in the hall. "Do them both and let's get outta here before the whole fucking Cuban army shows up!"

"We need this engineer," Travis said, watching the wide-eyed man and Yuri. "He may be the only guy left who knows how to stop the acceleration before it goes into meltdown. Ball's in your court, Sarah. Talk to Yuri."

"Yuri, please!" Sarah called over the alarms. "This is not the way!"

"It is the only way!" Yuri shouted. "It is the only way the fools will take notice! Thousands will die, but in the end, millions will survive!"

The Cuban engineer in Yuri's grasp cried out in Spanish, his voice cracking with fear.

Travis translated. "He says there's no time. The reaction will accelerate beyond critical any second. The rods must be dropped. The cooling systems must be reactivated, now."

"Tell us how to—" Hunter began.

"Silencio!" Yuri snarled, and he smacked the engineer in the side of the face with his pistol. The sweating engineer began to cry and mumble like a frightened child.

"Yuri, listen to me!" Sarah yelled. "Think of Annatava, Yuri! Annatava! She would not want this, Yuri! You know she would not want this!"

"Silence!" Yuri said, now beginning to weep himself. Jen shouted, "We are out of time!"

Sam nervously added, "Man, let's fucking *gooo*!"

"Quiet. Talk, Sarah. Talk," said Travis.

Sarah made her impassioned plea. "It's true Yuri! You know it! If Annatava were here she would tell you, do not *do* this terrible thing! Would you have her death be the cause for the murder of millions? Would Annatava want that, Yuri? Is that how you will have her remembered throughout history? Forever? Think, Yuri!"

Yuri stared at Sarah, and they could all see his face presage the collapse of his resolve. Dr. Yuri Nobakov had come face to face with an immutable truth. Annatava would be horrified at his actions. She would certainly tell him, no, no, Yuri, not this, not this!

Yuri slowly broke down, weeping, his gun arm dropping, his grip on the engineer's neck releasing. The engineer staggered free. Yuri sank to a sitting position weeping wretchedly.

Sarah hurried to his side and took the pistol from his

weak grasp. He leaned into her, clung to her, and began to sob uncontrollably.

Hunter, Jen, and Travis rushed to the engineer and helped him to the control console where he feverishly pressed buttons and drew levers. He staggered across the room and struck two large, red-lighted squares. Quickly he swerved back to his seat and stared at his instruments and digital displays. He pounded the counter with his fist. Bam. Bam. Bam. Then he raised his fist and froze it in the air before his face.

Now the engineer began to both cry and laugh at the same time, like a Cuban Homer Simpson. He stood, hugged Jen like she was his wife, and cried and laughed and mumbled in Spanish.

Jen patted him on the back and turned her head toward Travis. Her own eyes were watered. "The core temperature is receding, Trav. The rods are in, the chain reaction is arresting, the cooling systems are back on line. No meltdown, guys. We've done it. We've done it."

As if to confirm Jen's words the nuclear systems emergency warning siren now began to wail down and fade.

"Swell!" Sam said on the BSH from his position guarding the hall. "Now can we please get the fuck outta here!?"

"Soon," Travis said, watching Sarah kneeling by Yuri, who still heaved with racking sobs.

"I am sorry, Sarah," Yuri wept. "I did not mean to hurt you! I only wanted the madness to stop. I thought . . . I thought that if there was a convincing demonstration . . ."

Sarah held Yuri. "I know. I know."

"It was so easy to put out the word of who I was and what I wanted to do. The Swords contacted me within a month. In two weeks we made plans. When my contact at CIA told me American force was being sent to find Swords and stop them, I knew I had to help you . . . until I could maneuver you into trap! But how could I know of you, Sarah? How could I know you would come?" Yuri sobbed and clung to Sarah.

Sarah patted Yuri lovingly. "I know, Yuri. I know."

"I can—" Travis began.

"No," Sarah said, instantly.

"Or me, Sarah," Hunter said. "I'll—"

"No." Sarah sat Yuri back against the console and patted his face, smiling. "We all know who it has to be."

Dr. Sarah Greene, tears running down her cheeks, raised her rifle and fired a three-burst into the head of Dr. Yuri Nobakov.

Chapter Fourteen

"Damn!" Sam swore as they ran out of the reactor-two complex, powered up again. Guards were arriving by the truckload, bailing out with rifles and—

"Dogs!" Sam exclaimed.

Hunter surveyed the grounds with Travis. "Man, they're putting this whole place in lockdown, Trav. Those gates will be swarming with people."

"Yep." Travis scanned about furiously.

"We might make it out one of the gates, boss," Jack allowed. "It'll be nasty though. There're a lot of Cubes manning those gates. They got barricades in place. They got heavy weapons, dogs, maybe even infrared."

"Yep." Travis's eyes now homed in one direction.

Sam was audibly tense. "We'll never shoot our way through a concentration like that without the toy boxes! No gas, no NLG, no rockets, and I don't have enough semtex left to celebrate the Chinese New Year."

"Yep."

Hunter wiped his face with a sweep of a gloved hand beneath the drop-shield of his BSH. "And we can't call in air or the navy, because then the whole world will find out what happened here."

"Yep."

"Fuck!" Sam said, looking back toward the reactor-one complex. "Here those guys come with their dogs! And there's some officer scanning around with binoculars and at night that can only mean—"

"He's got infrared!" Hunter said, watching the tall officer by a truck on the perimeter road. "He can see us, even powered up!"

"Yep."

"I can cap him from here, Trav," Jack said.

"Nope."

"Nope!?" Sam exclaimed.

"No. We shoot that officer, we might as well send up a flare. Right now they've got no goddamn idea where we are. They don't even know for sure if we're still on the inside. We bust that son of a bitch and they'll know we're still inside and roughly where we are."

"Man," Jack said looking about. He paused briefly to study Sarah, who knelt nearby, silently weeping. "We could sure do with a real bright idea right about now, folks. Anybody?"

Silence.

Travis spoke. "We're leaving. This place is too noisy to suit me."

"Leaving?" Sam piped hopefully.

Jen hissed, "How?"

"Same way we came in."

Hunter eyed the distant locomotive. "The train? Trav, they're not letting anything out of this place 'til they sweep it! That train won't budge for hours!"

Travis's voice was cold and determined. "Oh yeah. It's going to budge. It's leaving the station, right now."

Jack shook his head. "I like the idea, boss. But you saw those walls when we came in. They're made specifically to stop trains."

"From coming in," Travis said levelly. "We ain't coming in."

Sam was about two heartbeats short of an aneurism. "What!?"

"He's right!" Jen exclaimed. "The doors are angled outward to bear the stress of an *inbound* train ramming. They never planned for anyone to ram their way *out* of a nuclear plant! It could work!"

"There's a quarter-mile of runnin' room," Travis mumbled, almost to himself. "That thing will probably get up to about thirty or so in that space. Not very fast, but those cars haven't been offloaded yet and they're

heavy. It could derail the whole train, but there ought
to be enough mass to breach the wall first."

"I like it!" said Jack, who greeted the prospect with
genuine enthusiasm. "No troops or guards over there,
because they don't think anybody'll try to go through
the train gate wall."

"Just one problem," Travis grumbled sourly.

Silence.

Travis popped the balloon. "The train crew's in lockdown. Anybody got any idea how to drive a train?"

Stan joined in, via the BSH net, from half a mile outside the perimeter. "Travis! Is it running?"

"What, Stan?" Travis frowned.

Stan asked again, "The locomotive. Is it still running?"

Pause.

"Yeah. It is. I can see heat blowing from the exhaust vents."

"That's what I figured!" Stan said, his excitement
showing through the strain of his pain. "My uncle Mo
always said railroaders never turn them big diesels off
unless they're not gonna use 'em for days 'cause they're
such a bitch to start up again!"

"Your uncle *who*?" Sam said.

"My uncle Mogedowizc Laslo Powczuk, Chopsticks.
Uncle Mo! He was an engineer for the Norfolk and
Western and used to take me with him on runs when I
was a kid. Get it?"

"Uh-oh," Sam said soberly, eyeing the train with
doubt.

Raimundo tensed and raised a hand. The Cuban lieutenant frantically waved shut-up-and-be-still motions to
his men.

Raimundo cocked his head and listened to the sounds
carrying on the sea breeze. Yes. Now he was sure of it.
Someone talking. From over there.

Raimundo raised his night-vision, infrared-capable optics.

English, Raimundo thought, moving forward quietly
with the troops. The voice. It speaks English. Something
about . . . trains?

*   *   *

Travis determined that they were still downwind of the deploying dogs and handlers. With the LOC suits powered up, the team made the train on a dead run without detection. Travis and Hunter climbed into the cab of the huge, greasy, oil and soot covered, yellow-and-green, Soviet-made locomotive. It radiated heat and trembled with life from the thrumming of its two huge diesel engines aft of the cab.

Sarah stood at the nose, under the huge headlight, staring at the commotion in the compound, but seeing only the exploded head of a sweet man she had once loved, if only for a brief moment.

Jen, Jack, and Sam took positions along the steel-grate catwalk that ran along both of the great steel monster's sides.

Travis read the Cyrillic-alphabet letters of the placards in the train's cab. Some had been written over in Spanish with felt pen. "It's a Russian rig, Stan."

"Figures," Stan answered on the BSH net. "Well, they all work the same way . . . probably. Hell, half of everything the fucking Ivans build is a pirated U.S. patent."

"Hey!" Jack called over the BSH. "Those guys with the dogs, they must've happened on a scent 'cause they're coming this way in a hurry!"

"Where are you, boss?" Stan asked quickly.

"Cab. Right side," Travis said. "Buncha levers and switches and gauges. Something looks like a fireplug, right in the middle of the floor. One big steel pedal on the left."

"Okay, Casey Jones, you're standing in the engineman's station. That fireplug thing is the automatic brake valve, but we won't sweat that right now. Look for a well-worn rocker switch, probably on the upper left."

"There's four of 'em.

"Well, flip 'em. One of 'em's got to be the generator field breaker."

The first switch Travis threw resulted in a loud electric snap and hum. "I got it. I think."

"We'll find out soon enough. Should be a directional lever on your left, a fist sized handle on it."

"Yep. Arrows point forward and reverse."

"Select reverse."

"Those fuckin' dogs are comin' right for us!" Jack said.

Travis clicked the direction selector to the arrow pointing rearward. "Reverse."

"All right, squeeze the brake handle grip on top of that fireplug and shove it forward."

Travis did as instructed and the entire train blew a deafening blast of escaping compressed air. It rocked slightly, as though freed.

Jack's voice flashed over the comm net again. "That got their attention! They're bustin' ass in this direction, big time!

"Big air hiss, Stan."

"Right! Stand on that pedal from now on. You step off it and it'll kill the engines and dump the brakes."

Travis stepped on the thick, steel pedal. Through the windshield he could see running guards with leashed dogs. A leader was radioing as he ran, calling for help, no doubt.

"Big lever on the left, Travis, is the throttle. You have to click it forward, release it, click forward, release it, and so forth, you can't shove it all the way open in one throw. If you lay on too much power you'll probably get some kind of warning light saying you're about to break traction. Open the throttle one click at a time. Give it as much as she'll take without spinning. If it spins the train will just sit there."

Travis clicked the forearm-sized lever forward. It ratcheted forward one half-inch click at a time. The engine noise rose accordingly and the locomotive lurched rearward. Couplings banged all down the train as the play bore out. Through the windshield, Travis saw guards running toward the railroad from all over the compound, all with weapons. "Get some cover out there!" he said.

"Is it moving?" Stan called.

"Yep." Travis shoved the throttle forward two more clicks, but a buzzer sounded and a light blinked, and the train seemed to brake slightly. Travis backed the throttle, one click. The wheels bit again and the train moved, agonizingly slowly. He opened the throttle one more notch, heard the engine roar increase, and felt the train surge rearward.

Jack scrambled into the left side of the broad cab near Hunter. Jen clanked down the walkway and in by Travis. "Sam," Travis called. "You and Sarah get to the rear of the locomotive and take cover between it and the next car!"

In a side mirror, Travis saw Sam scurrying down the gangway to the rear of the locomotive, which was actually forward in their direction of movement.

"Where's Sarah?" Hunter said just as the windshield glass on both sides was starred with bullet holes. The mean clank of bullets bouncing off steel echoed in the train cab.

"Aaaah!" Jen yelled, deafening everyone on the BSH. She dropped her weapon, fell against Travis and sat down hard on the floor. She gripped her left arm with her right. Blood oozed between her fingers. She felt the fibers of the LOC suit begin to curl and contract under her hand.

Travis opened the throttle two more notches and felt the train vibrate and gain speed. "How bad, Jen?"

"Arm. Can't tell more. Numb."

Travis knocked out the plastic laminated shattered glass with his rifle and saw XM-29 grenade rounds arcing out from the nose of the train beneath his view and landing among the running and shooting guards. White puffs of smoke appeared and guards fell by the fours and fives. Sarah had remained exposed on the nose to lay down covering fire. "Sarah!" Travis ordered. "Get back here under cover! Now!"

More incoming shots pinged and ricocheted off the steel of the locomotive, but Sarah kept firing. Hunter, Jack, and Sam were blazing away in return. Sarah must've run out of grenade rounds as she was now firing full-auto sweeps of rifle rounds. Travis could see the return fire was taking a toll. Many blue uniforms lay in the gravel; many more were scrambling for cover, some dragging their thrashing dogs by the leashes. Travis opened the throttle to the eighth and last notch. A loud, straining, mixed sound of diesel groan and electrical hum filled the air.

Occasional rounds of small-arms fire still pinged off the train, but the volume of fire was hugely diminished as the train began to outrun its foot pursuers. "Jack, slide me that toolbox! Sarah, answer up!"

"I'm here, Travis. I'm okay." Sarah sounded disappointed.

"Yeah, well Jen's not! Get in here, doctor. Now. Move!"

Sarah quickly ran in and knelt by Jen. She pulled a small wire from her belt pack and plugged it into Jen's LOC suit belt.

Travis took the toolbox Jack handed him and placed it on the deadman's pedal to keep it down. He swung out onto the steel-mesh gangway and looked past the train of eight cars, but the track curled right and he couldn't see the end. He clambered past Sarah and Jen in the cab floor, between Hunter and Jack, and out onto the opposite gangway. In their direction of movement Jack could see the lights atop the perimeter wall growing quickly nearer, but the rate was hard to judge. There were few visual references by which to calculate a rate of closure. It was impossible to tell if the train was moving fast enough to breach the heavy perimeter track gates.

One thing was certain. The train was still gathering speed, fast.

Looking back toward the nose of the train at the reactor complex growing ever more distant, Travis saw vehicles moving, bouncing, pursuing. Their lights were off to make them harder targets, but he could see them passing through pools of floodlight.

"Sam, you better get back here with us," Travis said, calm again. "We're gonna hit that wall with all the speed this old tub will bring. The farther aft we are the better. Move." Through his face shield he saw Sam strolling confidently along the catwalk, one hand hovering above the handrail as the big locomotive rocked and roared. He might as well have been riding the Number 7 elevated train from Flushing to Manhattan.

When everyone was inside the cramped cab, Travis asked Sarah about Jen.

"Serious ricochet slug hit to the upper left arm. Probably broken. Bullet still in her. Her cardiopulmonary rates are acceptable. Blood loss under control per LOC suit. She'll be able to walk, maybe run for a limited time. But this arm is out of service for weeks."

"I'm all right Travis," Jen said, tightly. "I can run."

"Ohhhh shit!" Sam said, leaning out the cab door, looking in the direction of movement. "The wallllllll!"

"Everybody down!" Travis ordered. "On the floor against the bulkhead! Move!" Travis wedged himself into the engineman's station hoping to be able to keep the deadman pedal held down during the collision with the wall.

When the first car hit moving rearward, the darkness sparkled with huge electrical flashes, and metal-upon-concrete sparks. Concrete chunks and pieces of metal rocketed into the air, spraying outward in a fountain. The first car crumpled like an accordian, and its sides blew out—crates, boxes, and barrels vomiting forth—and it compressed against the heavy concrete gates. In less than a second the second car smashed against the wall with similar results.

In the locomotive cab the impact wasn't as bad as Travis thought it would be. The eight cars acted as shock absorbers.

At the wall the first three cars derailed and the fourth plowed through them to hit the wall, the dead cars scraping down both sides in a cascade of spark and screeching, tortured metal. The fourth car was an open-topped carrier full of steel reinforcement rods with far more mass than the previous three cars. When it hit the gates they shattered and blew out ninety degrees. The train smashed through, rocking and screeching, lit now by fires from the first three devastated cars.

In the cab the TALONs could feel a sudden release as the train broke through and began to regain lost speed. Travis sprang to one catwalk, Jack to the other.

"We're through!" they shouted, and they cheered like college kids witnessing a winning touchdown.

"Next stop, Forty-Second Street!" Sam yelled, waving his rifle in the air.

"Nice work, coach," Travis drawled dryly to Stan. "Now how do we stop this damn thing?"

                    *   *   *

Raimundo could see him through the infrared night
optics. There. A stocky, hairy man in a camouflage uniform, leaning against a huge tree trunk, his elbow on a
metal canister. There were some sort of odd-shaped suit-
cases nearby. He spoke, but he held no radio. He must
have some kind of communication in that odd helmet.
Silently, Raimundo signaled the Cuban lieutenant. Thirty-
eight armed soldiers moved to their briefed positions.

The team left the now-stopped train—what was left of
it—and ran up the slope through the scrub toward Stan's
position. Jack and Hunter tried to help Jen, but she
pushed them away, picked up her rifle with her good
arm, and moved off ahead of them. That was the good
news. The bad news was all the LOC suits were now
showing low-power alerts. Travis ordered the suits powered down. The team was now naked-eye visible.

Stan himself had relented at last and dosed himself
with a shot of Demerol to ease the throbbing that had
come to feel like he was being slugged with a tire-iron
along the length of his right leg. He hated the dulling-
down the drug would cause, but the alternative was passing out from the pain. Sleepy now, Stan thought. Tired.

The team entered the clearing, Jen white-faced but
managing. Sam hurried to the pods and began packing
them furiously. Sarah and Travis went immediately to
Stan. Sarah plugged into Stan's suit to run his vitals.

Stan had warned the team of his observations earlier
in the night, and of the two men he'd shot. He had
expected the others to come looking, but they had not,
Stan reported.

Sam was pitching ammunition "cakes" to the team,
forty-round clusters of XM-29 rounds glued together
without benefit of traditional metal magazines, combustible hulled bullets that left nothing behind when fired.
He reached for the shoebox-sized Battlefield Motion
Sensor in a pod to move it, so as to reach more ammunition, when he noted to his shock that it was registering
multiple, mobile, organic targets within 700 meters! It
was set to ignore targets within ten meters, so it could
not have been triggered by the arrival of the team.

"Luuuucy," Sam whispered on the BSH, and the team froze. "We got companyyyyyyy!"

"You will *not move*!" a voice commanded in heavily Spanish-accented English from out in the darkness, "or you will all be killed instantly! You will not move! Fifty soldiers are looking at you this very moment over their gun sights!"

"Raimundo!" Sarah whispered.

"Do not try your invisible suit tricks!" Raimundo warned sternly. "We have the infrared devices! We will fire immediately if you move or begin to fade from view!"

"Hold," Travis said softly, peering into the darkness. With the suits powered down and the face shields up, the TALONs could see no better than Raimundo's men, worse than Raimundo himself, who wore the NVG optics.

"I warn you again!" Raimundo shouted. "I will take great pleasure in presenting you live in Havana to those cackling asses who doubted my warnings, but I may present you dead just as well! Drop your weapons! *Now!*"

"Who da fuck izzat?" Stan slurred groggily.

"Drop your weapons!" Raimundo all but screamed.

"Set 'em down, people," Travis said. "Everybody stay cool." Travis bent at the knees and set his XM-29 on the leaves at his feet. "We've come too far to fuck it up now."

The team placed their rifles at their feet.

"Get away from your weapons!" Raimundo ordered.

Travis stepped slowly back. The team followed.

Raimundo shouted a command and scores of flashlights stabbed out of the darkness. The team squinted and shaded their eyes with their hands.

Colonel Raimundo emerged from the darkness wearing a self-satisfied smirk and headband-mounted NVGs. He carried a folded-stock AK-74 and a large flashlight, which he played in the TALONs' faces. More than two dozen uniformed Cuban soldiers with AKs came out of the darkness, nervously pointing their rifles.

Not a sight to warm one's heart, Sam thought, his heart pounding like a pile driver.

"Whaz goin' on?" Stan mumbled. His eyes were narrowed, his mouth hung open, and he drooled.

"Americans!" Raimundo crowed triumphantly, gleefully, spearing the flashlight at the eyes of each TALON. "How I will enjoy parading you before that bastard Torejos and the others in Havana who have called me delusional!"

"Fffuuck you, chicken dick," Stan said, drunkenly.

Raimundo snapped the flashlight at Stan. His expression of volatile anger dissolved into a sneer as he noted that the seated American was bleary-eyed, slack-jawed, and drooling like a moron. Drunk. Or perhaps drugged. Harmless. When he sobered up, there would be special dues for him to pay.

"See!" Raimundo said loudly in Spanish to the soldiers who seemed to just keep coming from out of the dark brush, who now stood in a broad, heavily armed semicircle before the team. "Behold the mighty Americans! With all their trickery and money and arrogant superiority, see them now!" Raimundo walked closer, standing by Stan's outstretched feet. "Like this one." Raimundo kicked Stan's heavily bandaged foot.

"Haaach!" Stan stiffened, his face contorted. "Haaaaaggh! Christ!" Stan pitched back against the tree and collapsed from the pain, one arm flopped across the camo-green canister at his elbow.

Jen went for him like a mother leopard, injured arm and all, but Travis and Jack grabbed her and jerked her back, thrashing.

"You sick prick!" Jen raged in English, still struggling. "I'll tear your fucking eyes out!"

Raimundo flinched with genuine concern at first, then quickly resumed his contemptuous sneer when he saw the American men had this Amazon wildcat under control. He stepped toward her.

"Aaah, yes." Raimundo still spoke Spanish. "The *puta* who kills. Perhaps I can find a . . . special use for you at my villa in Havana." Raimundo looked over his shoulder at the troops and hunched his hips forward and backward, in a way that evoked loud, knowing cackles from some of the men.

Jen jumped forward against Jack's grip and spoke in

perfect Spanish. "I would crawl naked on my hands and knees to suck your pitiful little noodle, shit-for-brains! Just long enough to chew it off at the root and spit the meat in your face! *Try* me!"

Raimundo and every man behind him knew the difference between a threat and a blood oath. In his innermost mind, every man pictured Jen fulfilling her pledge and not a soul thought it was erotic. No one laughed now, and the smirk faded quickly from Raimundo's expressions.

"No," Raimundo said coldly, in English, after an uncomfortable pause. He stepped before Jen, who was still held by her good arm by Jack. Her injured arm was encased in an inflatable splint and swung from a makeshift sling. "I think . . . I think . . . you are too . . . *demente* . . . *loco.* I think we take you to a special place we keep just for tough cases like you. Where we make even the toughest curse his mother for giving him birth, before we are done."

"Curse *this,* asshole!" Jen snarled. She jumped, using Jack's grip on her good arm as a fulcrum, and whipped one booted foot through the air to impact Raimundo's face so hard his head snapped to the side. He grunted, staggered rearward three steps, dropped his rifle, and fell on his back.

"Oh shit," Sam whispered.

Raimundo leaped to his feet like a man possessed, wiping blood from his mouth and flattened nose, burning with pain, purple with fury. "Damn your *soul!*" he sputtered, choking with rage. And he went for his rifle in the leaves at his feet.

"NLG!" Stan shouted in clear, well-annunciated speech, and he twisted a broad, black plastic knob atop the basketball-sized cannister at his elbow full to the stop. Travis and Hunter sprang forward, kicked the rifle from Raimundo's grip, seized him, and pulled him back with them.

As they did, a loud electric hum, like a powerful transformer, filled the air.

Stan rolled to his left and elbow-crawled behind the tree.

It had taken the young Cuban lieutenant a second to recover from the shock of seeing the American soldier-

woman knock Colonel Raimundo, dreaded commandante of the feared Internal Security Cell, flat on his ass.
The lieutenant had then tensed, raised his weapon, and
sucked breath to shout orders when a wave of nausea
engulfed him like something hot and foul smelling! His
eyes clenched as though full of sand, his ears rang shrilly,
and his brain tingled with dizziness. His abdominal muscles cramped tightly at once, he doubled over and vom-
ited violently. Involuntarily, he dropped his rifle and
staggered spastically, hunched over, to keep his feet. In
the brief pause between the first wave of uncontrollable
vomiting and the next, the lieutenant forced his eyes
open. Though they watered heavily he was horrified to
see every member of his command bent, gagging, or laying in a tightly clenched fetal ball on the ground. It was
more than he could comprehend. He toppled forward
onto the leaves and hit with a grunt. Then his stomach
contorted still again like a hot pitchfork had been thrust
into it. The spasms were so severe and came so often he
could never expand his chest enough to get a full breath!

Rafio Raimundo's heart thundered. Things had suddenly taken a very wicked turn. In an instant, in his rage
at the woman, the Americans had disarmed him and
pulled him into them. The *demente* woman had somehow
broken loose from her comrade and had attacked him
again, beating him bloody and stunned in the few seconds it took the men to drag her off him. Gasping on
his hands and knees, he was aware that his lips were
split, his nose ran blood, and his testicles screamed in
agony. He felt sick. Then he was snatched to his feet by
the big negro.

Raimundo couldn't believe his eyes. The entire army
platoon lay writhing on the ground. Flashlights gleamed
in the leaves. Not a single man stood.

Raimundo turned his head to see the savage, *loco*
woman jerking to free herself from the two comrades
who held her. She was still trying to kill him! She cried
with fury and glared at him with the hottest eyes he had
ever seen. The tall American stepped suddenly before
her, put a hand on her chest and a finger in her face
and commanded: "That's enough, Lieutenant!" To Rai-

mundo's quantum relief, she stood still, heaving for breath, but her scalding eyes never left him.

Stan's sudden shout of the three letters, NLG, was not the mystery for the team it was for the Cubans. The small, self-contained transmitter produced a powerful ultra low-frequency radio wave that severely disagreed with the human nervous system. It was largely directional, meaning that if one was not on the delivery end of the radio emission, one suffered only a temporary ringing of the ears and a slight, involuntary fluttering of the eyelids. Down-range, however, was a different story, hence each TALON, including Stan, had been quick to get on the good side of the nasty little device, and drag Colonel Raimundo with them.

Raimundo was weak with relief now. The Americans were ignoring him, busy stowing their equipment in those plastic cases. He could not believe his eyes! They were departing! They were leaving. They deployed that strange, canlike device upon the troops again, causing a new round of exhausted dry heaving and gasping, then they moved away into the darkness toward the sea, carrying their cases and assisting the one who had leaned upon the tree, the one Raimundo had so foolishly allowed to dupe him into thinking he was drunk! They had gone. They had left him! Alive!

But alive for what? Raimundo's reactive euphoria caved in fast. He had once again failed to stop the Americans, this time before a platoon of witnesses. The Great One was not noted for his tolerance and understanding. Raimundo felt ill as the truth sunk in. He was not redeemed, he was condemned. Castro would put him in the very dungeons where Raimundo had sent hundreds to die slowly. What they would do to him there defied description.

Shaking visibly, Raimundo retrieved an AK-74 dropped by one of the wretchedly sick soldiers still writhing on the ground.

The team was close enough to the surf to hear the breakers crashing. Still, they heard the single shot carry on the wind.

Jack spat on the sand as he helped Stan hobble toward

the beach, and he eyed a grinning Hunter sourly. "I owe you twenty, birdman. Pay you when we get stateside."

"Told you," Hunter said. "That bastard knew what Castro would do to him."

Where the sea met the land the team looked up to see the six men rise, dripping, out of the surf, dimly visible in the cloudy quarter moon. They were cloaked in black rubber wet suits and bulky dive masks with night-vision optics built into them. They stared from glass faces, holding black, automatic rifles trained on the TALONs.

One of the men splashed ashore through the scurrying, bubbly, white surf, still holding his rifle toward his them, approaching them from an angle so as to remain clear of any field of fire from his men. He walked over the wet sand to where Hunter and Sarah helped Lieutenant Commander Stanislaus Michael Powczuk to stand. The black-clad figure studied Stan's face for a moment from behind black glass.

The big, black alien suddenly stuck a hand in the air with a thumb up. One of the men standing in the surf behind him spoke and instantly a large, black rubber, inflatable outboard hummed out of the darkness and beached.

The big man before Stan lowered his weapon and whipped off his dive mask to reveal a lean black man's face with a gleaming smile. He saluted smartly, then extended his hand. "Commander Powczuk, Lieutenant Lon Caleb, United States Navy SEALs Team Four, sir. What took you so long?"

Epilogue

September 30, 1453 hours, Coast of Oahu, Hawaii

It is possibly the most beautiful stretch of beach on Oahu, in the great American state of Hawaii, bathed in the sun, swept by a warm, fresh, salty breeze. Clear blue waters washed against the shore and powerful breakers cascaded farther out in rows of sugary white surf. The sand was white and powdery and soft and warm, and it felt good upon sore feet thrust within.

Five large, expensive, glass-and-cedar beach homes sat on thick piles above the dunes. It was fine beach, not unlike the south coast of Cuba, but as far away from Cuba as one could get and still be in the United States.

Yet not a single tourist was in sight, despite the fabulous weather. The signs and chain fence warned them off two miles away, and any who ventured beyond would be quickly approached by civilian-dressed men in an unmarked Humvee who would politely say this was restricted U.S. government property, and the visitors were cordially invited to leave. If anyone was inclined to dispute this request they would probably look at the racked rifles in the vehicle, and the two large if plainclothed U.S. Marines in opaque sunglasses. Thereupon, they would smile, turn around, and walk briskly away.

Down the beach, Hunter, Sam, and Jack played vigorous beach volleyball with five statuesque, tanned, laughing young women in string bikinis that have positively not caused a worldwide fabric shortage. Next to the volleyball net was a colorful portable cabana containing a bar, behind which stood a smiling bartender in a white coat who prepared a bowl of nacho chips with the scalding hot sauce the big, black Marine captain loved so much.

Not far away, Stan lounged under a large beach umbrella, his bandages removed to allow the sun and sea to work their healing wonders on his purple, swollen, and sutured right toes. Angela Powczuk popped fresh strawberries into his mouth and rubbed his hairy shoulders with lotion. Occasionally, she would bend to kiss his forehead, or cheek, or the tip of his nose. Stan was content, though he knew that one longing glance at the bikinied girls playing volleyball would suddenly become hazardous to his improving good health.

Farther up the beach, beneath another spreading, fringed umbrella, a tall, lean, Texan lay on a propped-up, double-wide, cushioned chaise lounge smoking a Cuban cigar. Laying next to him was a tall blonde wearing her own fetching bikini. She had one tanned, muscular leg folded across his lap, and an arm—in an autograph-scribbled cast—draped over him. She rested her head contentedly upon his chest. She drowsed, half asleep in the warm breeze.

A passing gull cawed and hovered into the wind briefly before moving down the beach toward the ball-playing humans and their food.

Travis kissed Jen on the top of her head and held her taut waist snugly to him. He looked down at the nearby breaking surf.

Betty Sue, his daughter, clearly metamorphosing into a charming young woman before his loving eyes, surfed the easy waves. And his happy boy, Randall, splashed about, grinning up at his father, wearing that worn, soaked, old green beret three sizes too large for him.

On the sand next to Travis was a newspaper folded back on a page-two story:

Cuba Denies Nuclear Plant Unsafe

Havana Cuba, AP—Cuban officials today vehemently denied U.S. charges that security measures at the recently activated Juragua Nuclear Electric Production Plant are inadequate. Authorities insist that any foolish attempt to breach security at the Juragua facility would be "quickly and easily foiled" by state-of-the-art plant security, augmented by the "great army of the Cuban people."

Cuban officials issued a press release Monday, saying there has never been and will never be a terrorist takeover of any Cuban institution, especially the Juragua nuclear facility. The release further assures that the Juragua facility is completely safe, and that U.S. security objections are mere political meddling.

When pressed by reporters, Cuban officials admitted that a runaway train crashed through the perimeter all around the nuclear plant one week ago, but say that as it was outbound, it thus presented no hazard to safety. At no time were the two reactors disturbed.

Unnamed sources in Cuba report that immediately following the runaway train accident, massive shakeups in Cuban Internal Security, and in the Cuban Nuclear Commission, resulted in numerous firings and transfers of personnel. Some accounts even allege certain high-ranking security officials have mysteriously disappeared. Cuban officials deny the reports, accusing the U.S. of trying to discredit the Cuban nuclear industry as part of its decades-long vendetta against the peace-loving Cuban people.

Travis gently shook Jen. She squinted up at his face to see him gazing up the beach. She turned, uncurled from his lap and sat up.

They hadn't seen much of Sarah this last week. She had kept to her cabin. Dined alone. Refused all invitations. Sarah had been sitting Shiva, the ritual Jewish period of mourning.

Now, though, Sarah walked down the white sand from the dunes in her bathing suit, sunglasses masking her eyes. She carried a towel.

A cheer went up from the volleyball area. Sarah looked to see the men and their playmates waving to her. She stared at them for a moment, then smiled very lightly and raised her hand to them.

Sarah walked to Travis and Jen. She leaned against Travis's hairy chest, hugging him and beginning to weep softly. Jen sandwiched Sarah between Travis and herself.

Together they held Sarah as she cried for the late Dr. Yuri Nobakov.